THE GOBLIN CROWN

THE
GOBLIN
CROWN

BILLY SMITH AND THE GOBLINS

Book I

ROBERT HEWITT WOLFE

TURNER

Turner Publishing Company
Nashville, Tennessee
New York, New York
www.turnerpublishing.com

The Goblin Crown: Billy Smith and the Goblins, Book 1

Cover artwork: Tom Fowler
Cover design: Maddie Cothren
Book design: Glen Edelstein
Interior artwork: Brandon Henderson
Map originally drawn by Robert Hewitt Wolfe

Library of Congress Cataloging-in-Publication Data

Names: Wolfe, Robert Hewitt.
Title: The Goblin Crown / Robert Hewitt Wolfe.
Description: Nashville, Tennessee : Turner Publishing Company, [2016] | Series: Billy Smith and the goblins ; book 1 | Summary: Socially awkward Billy, beautiful Lexi, and star quarterback Kurt mysteriously enter an underworld of goblins, animal hybrids, and powerful magic, where one may be destined to become Goblin King.
Identifiers: LCCN 2016007633 | ISBN 9781681626123 (pbk.)
Subjects: | CYAC: Fantasy. | Goblins--Fiction. | Kings, queens, rulers, etc.--Fiction. | Fate and fatalism--Fiction.
Classification: LCC PZ7.1.W627 Gob 2016 | DDC [Fic]--dc23
LC record available at https://lccn.loc.gov/2016007633

Printed in the United States of America

15 16 17 18 19 20 10 9 8 7 6 5 4 3 2 1

For Celeste

"Fair is foul, and foul is fair:
Hover through the fog and filthy air."
—AN ENGLISHMAN
FROM SOME PLAY ABOUT SCOTLAND

C⊘NTENTS

CONTENTS

CONTENTS

THE GOBLIN CROWN

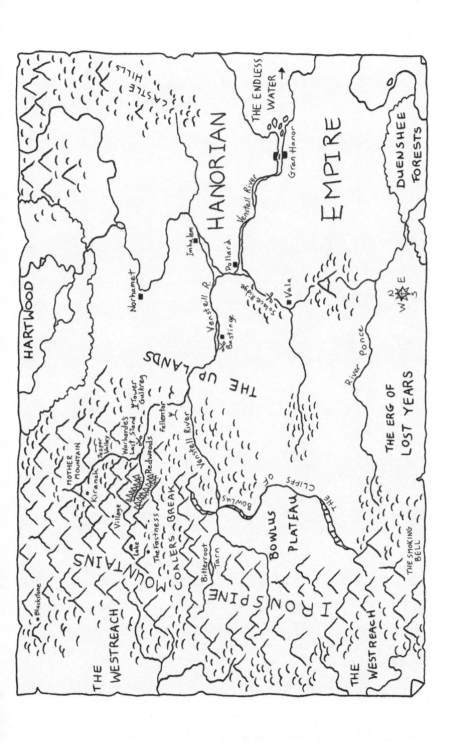

PROLOGUE
A Story from the Inside

S un and Fire," the goblin swore as he shoved his way out from under a dead body. "What a bleedy, terrible day."

For the past few hours, the goblin, who went by the unlikely name of Hop, had considered lying beneath this particular corpse to be a wise, if uncomfortable, tactic. But the battle he'd been avoiding had finally ground to its fatal conclusion, and the victors were busying themselves with the traditional murdering of the wounded and looting of the dead. It was time for Hop to move on.

Hop surveyed the carnage. The goblin army was in flight, the Dark Lady's command post on Solace Ridge swarmed with their enemies, and Hop could see a suspiciously feminine head impaled on a pike where her banner once flew. So she was dead, most likely. This didn't come as much of a surprise to Hop. He'd heard enough stories on his grandpa's knee to know that anyone who went by a name like "The Dark Lady" or "The Emperor of Night" or "The Invincible Overlord" usually didn't end up on top. Inevitably, some intrepid farm boy or brave orphan or innocent milkmaid would find the Sword of Fate or the Ring of Truth or the Milk Bucket of Happily-Ever-After or whatnot and then that was that.

As a lad, Hop had loved those stories. Now, though, Hop had experienced a story from the inside. From the inside, stories were a lot uglier than they seemed from the outside. It was as if the storytellers were up in the clouds somewhere, looking down. From up high, everything might look simple and tidy, but down here where Hop was, there was mud, there was blood, and most of all, there were corpses.

Corpses as far as the eyes could see.

That's what you got when you took two enemy armies and jammed them between a river and a ridgeline. Add a few dozen half-mad wizards lobbing around fire and ice and other assorted nastiness, and the end result wasn't a glorious battle. It was a slaughter. To the soldiers on both sides, human and goblin alike, it didn't particularly matter what happened up on the ridge between the fanatical, black-robed prophetess and the intrepid farmer's son (or innocent milkmaid; Hop had been too far away to tell for certain). Down in the valley, the armies fought and soldiers died.

So Hop didn't care much who'd won or who'd lost. To him, watching the human victors parade the Dark Lady's severed head around the field was just one final bloody act in a bloody, muddy day. The only things Hop cared about at the moment were, in order: getting away from the corpse-strewn battlefield, patching up the arrow wound in his leg, stealing something to eat, and finding a safe place to sleep.

"*Bosh*, time to go." Hop tossed aside his helmet, shield, and spear. He didn't want the extra weight to slow him down.

Because there was one more thing that Hop knew from being *inside* a story. When you were inside a story, it didn't end once Righteous Young Hero destroyed the Evil Tyrant. Stories might have Happily-Ever-Afters, but life just had Afters. And in the wake of the Battle of Solace Ridge, the After was full of dead friends, lost limbs, bitterness, and anger.

Hop spied a cluster of human generals standing around the Righteous Young Hero. Generals reminded Hop of ravens. Throw a battle and sooner or later a general or three would show up to peck out the occasional eye and claim credit. Right now, the victorious generals were gazing down at the dead, seeing their soldiers and sons and brothers lying in the red mud. Even from a distance, Hop got the impression they weren't ready for this particular story to end just yet.

What they were ready for was revenge. And once that started, Hop planned on being in a land far, far away.

As far away as he could get.

CHAPTER ONE
The Weird-Looking Kid Sitting on the Sidewalk

B illy Smith stepped off the city bus and prepared to meet his doom.

The sandstone walls of Francis Drake College Preparatory loomed ahead, obscured by a light fog. Fall had come early. Billy zipped up his hooded sweatshirt and adjusted his brand new, first-day-of-high-school backpack as other students streamed past him, headed for Drake's impressive front doors. But no matter how hard he tried, Billy couldn't make himself follow them inside. Drake Prep was the most prestigious private school in the city, and deep in his heart, Billy knew he didn't belong.

That was Billy's problem. He didn't belong anywhere.

He hadn't belonged in Vermont, where he was born. People were nice enough there. But even when Billy was little, he could tell they didn't know what to make of him.

With his mixed features, he was a bit of a mystery to people. It was okay when he was with his father. At least when people saw William Tyler Smith Junior with William Tyler Smith Senior, they seemed to get it. *Black kid*, they'd think after the initial confusion. "Oh, what a handsome boy," they'd lie. But one thing was clear. He wasn't one of them.

When he was with his mother, it was worse. Despite their matching reddish hair and freckles, Billy and his mother didn't look much alike. Her skin was pale, her eyes the same blue green as her surgical scrubs. Billy was several shades darker. When he was with his mother, people didn't stare at *him* in confusion. They stared at *her*. *How'd she end up with him?* they'd wonder to themselves. "What a handsome boy," they'd lie. "You taking care of him for a friend?"

Billy's mother was an ER nurse; his father built hospitals. His mother could work anywhere, but once William Senior was done with a project, their family had to move on. In his fourteen years, Billy had lived in Vermont, Virginia, Kansas, Georgia, and now California. Not once had Billy felt like people accepted him for who he was. In Virginia, they hadn't liked his strong New England accent. In rural Kansas, his skin had been too dark. In urban Atlanta, he wasn't dark enough.

Billy's parents had said California would be different. And maybe it should've been. There were all kinds of people in San Francisco. But by now, Billy was so used to being an outsider, it had become a reflex. He didn't even try to make friends anymore.

Plus . . . there was his father. When they'd gotten to the city, it had seemed like just another stop. But a few days later, William Senior had another of his "upset stomachs." A few days after that, he'd finally gone to see a doctor. Now

William Senior wasn't just building hospitals. Between the surgeries, the chemo, and the radiation treatments, he was practically living in one.

So fitting in at Drake Prep was the last thing on Billy's mind. It was just one more place he had to get through on the way to . . .

To where? That was Billy's other problem. He wasn't very good at goals. He'd spent his whole life avoiding undue attention, trying not to embarrass his parents, and trying not to get hurt. He'd been so busy dodging and disappearing that he'd never had time for much else. He'd never had a girlfriend, never thought about what he wanted to do with his life, never done much of anything except play video games.

Billy stared at the walls of Drake Prep, emblazoned with an elaborate crest and the school's motto: "Educating Exceptional Young Men and Women." He didn't feel exceptional. Freakish, awkward, disappointing, but definitely not exceptional. Billy wished he were someplace else. Anywhere but here, standing in the fog, certain his high school career was going to disappoint his ailing father, waste his parents' tuition money, and leave his family miserable and poor. In that instant, as Billy yearned fervently for an entirely new life, for a split second . . .

The world changed.

The fog grew denser, like walls closing in around him. The smooth sidewalk felt cracked and uneven beneath his feet. The morning breeze died away, and Billy smelled dirt and rotten vegetation and a whiff of sulfur. The light dimmed, and everything went cold and still.

Claustrophobia seized Billy. He sensed a looming, oppressive weight just above his head. Blinded by the encroaching darkness and overwhelmed by a panicky, desperate fear, Billy wanted to shout, to scream, to run in terror. But his instincts told him he couldn't. He had to be quiet.

Or something might hear him.

"Keep moving." That was the refrain Hop heard over and over as he shuffled along with the column of goblin refugees. "Forward with you, do *nai* look back."

The goblins came from all over the Ironspine Mountains. From the Bowlus Plateau and Blackstone and Coaler's Break. From Bitterroot Tarn and Hartwood and the Smoking Bell. From the gentle foothills of the Uplands to the crags and precipices of Mother Mountain herself. They brought their children, their elders. They came with everything they owned, dragged on sledges or packed on the backs of their animal companions. They traveled by moonlight, through ancient tunnels or old growth forests, but always in shadow or night or darkness, out of the glare of the blazing sun.

Fear drove them from their homes. Fear of fire and blinding light and death. But it was another feeling that guided their path, a small, fragile emotion that slept deep in the goblins' great underground city, Kiranok, in a long abandoned hall lined with black marble and obsidian. In that hall, flanked by ten ancient stone statues, sat a throne, meticulously kept free from the dust and spiderwebs that choked the rest of the vast room. Above that throne, on a simple stone shelf, lay an intricately wrought iron circlet mounted with a single uncut ruby the size and shape of a man's eye. Dark now. But ten times in goblin history it had burst forth with light. It had glowed. And each time the Eye of the Goblin Crown had glowed red, a savior had come, a Goblin King to lead them through their darkest days.

So it wasn't fear alone that brought the goblin refugees to Kiranok, the City of Stone. They also came out of hope. Hope in a promise. Hope in a savior. Hope in a miracle.

Hop shuffled along at the back of the column of refugees, alone, bereft of clan and kin. He'd survived the disaster at Solace Ridge, even managed to reach his land far, far away. Sadly, it'd turned out to be not far enough, and the vengeance and the fire had reached him after all. So even though Hop had done his best to escape from the inside of this particular story, here he was, slouching toward Kiranok and yet another chapter.

Hop looked around at his fellow refugees, poor and afraid, clinging to their desperate, fragile faith. And for their sake, somewhere deep inside himself, Hop found a small, simple, unlikely hope to call his own.

"*Ahka*. I hope this story will *nai* end with so much blood."

Lexi Aquino wasn't good at minding her own business. She was insatiably curious, bursting with energy, and a continual annoyance to her parents. Sometimes it seemed like her mother was one of those old-fashioned dolls that could only repeat a few sentences when you pulled the string on her back: "Calm down, Lexi." "Sit still, Lexi." "Lexi, for once, try to be quiet."

So while most of the students streaming into Drake stepped carefully around the weird-looking kid sitting on the sidewalk, Lexi couldn't help herself.

"You okay?"

The boy looked up, confused. He had curly reddish-brown hair, light brown skin, and a smattering of freckles across his nose. Not Filipino like Lexi. Or Mexican. Or black or white or anything in particular. Some kind of mutt. But that was okay. Lexi liked mutts.

"Yeah. I just got dizzy, I guess." The boy stood up, still a little shaky.

Lexi noticed the boy wore bright purple canvas sneakers. It was a bold choice. Maybe he wasn't as hopeless as he first looked.

"Nice shoes," Lexi said. She probably should have stopped there, but she couldn't help but add, "Thought you were going to puke. You having a panic attack or something?"

"What? No. I mean, I wasn't panicking or anything. I just . . ."

"Yeah, right." That was Lexi's other problem. Once she got an idea in her head, it stuck. "Why are you so stubborn, Lexi?" was another of her mom's favorite phrases. Lexi looked back at the doors of her new school. "Scary-looking place, huh? But my cousins went here, and they say it's not as terrible as it looks. They try to intimidate you, but the teachers are smart and they want to help."

"Like I said, I'm good."

"Whatever, Freckles." Lexi went inside. *Some people,* Lexi thought, *just can't be helped.*

Billy watched her go, the short, fast-talking, hyperactive girl in the cute skirt and the ever-so-slightly-too-tight red sweater. He wasn't used to attention from pretty girls, especially not ones with such perfect skin and lively brown eyes. He was sure he'd made an idiot of himself, trying to pretend nothing was wrong, acting like his weird dizzy spell was no big deal.

But the truth was that for a moment, he'd been lost in his vision of darkness and cold and pulsing red light.

Only the voice of this well-meaning, if annoying, girl had snapped him out of it.

He owed her, and he hoped one day he could thank her properly. Not that she'd ever want to talk to him again.

The bell rang. Time to face his fate. Billy shouldered his backpack and marched like a condemned man into the hallowed halls of Francis Drake College Preparatory.

Four hours later, Billy's head was swimming. English first period meant Shakespeare's *Julius Caesar* and a bunch of sonnets to read. Second period was geography. Memorize the name and capital of every country on Earth. Algebra came third. Billy's father might be some kind of math genius, but numbers made Billy's head hurt.

Fourth period turned out to be Latin. Latin? Seriously? A language nobody had spoken in two thousand years? Billy vaguely remembered a question on the admission form asking him what language he wanted to study. He'd checked "no preference." Now it turned out that everyone who'd checked "no preference" got Latin. Why couldn't there have been a box for "anything *but* Latin"? He was supposed to learn all the forms of the Latin verb for "to be" by tomorrow. The teacher, a gray-haired man with a tendency to shout rather than speak, had made the entire class chant it over and over. Billy struggled to recall the strange words. *Sum, es, est, sumes* . . . Was it *summus*? *Sumus*?

Billy probably would've gotten it eventually if he hadn't been so distracted. Because unfortunately, she'd been in Latin too. Lexi Aquino. That was the name she'd answered to when the teacher had barked out his roll call. Lexi Aquino, the small, intrusive, brown-eyed girl with her too-tight sweater and an internal motor set on overdrive.

Billy had spent most of class sneaking glances at those eyes when he was supposed to be conjugating or declining or whatever it was you did with Latin nouns.

Then Lexi had noticed him glancing. And he'd noticed her noticing. Which was okay, but Mister Shouts-a-Lot had noticed too.

"Mister Smith, how would you say 'You have beautiful eyes' to Miss Aquino in Latin?" Shouts-a-Lot said, much quieter than usual. Dangerously quiet.

Billy managed to squeak out an "I don't know."

"Then pay attention!" This time it was a roar. The entire class had laughed, causing Billy's ears to blush a deep red. His ears always got beet red when he felt embarrassed. The worst part was that even Lexi had laughed a little.

Better not to think about it. Billy could feel blood rushing to his ears. *Breathe, just breathe.*

At least it was finally lunch. Billy could get his head together. And in the afternoon, things should get a little easier. He had computers, then gym, then public speaking.

As Billy joined the line for the cafeteria lunch counter, he realized he was starving. Billy hadn't wanted to get detention for being late on his first day, so he'd only had a little cereal for breakfast. The pasta and steamed broccoli in the warming trays didn't look especially appetizing, but at least it was food.

Then, as Billy shuffled toward the front of the line, disaster struck.

She got in line behind him. Lexi Aquino. Luckily, she was busy chatting with her friends and hadn't seen him. Yet. Then Billy realized she was telling the story of what happened in Latin class. In excruciating detail.

It was Billy's worst fear. New in town, first day in school, and already people were talking about him like he was some kind of freak. He'd blown another chance to fit in. Billy couldn't help himself. He had to get away. He spun around and rushed out of the line—

Only to slam right into someone walking toward a table with a full tray. Billy and his unintentional target tumbled to the floor in a cascade of flailing limbs and spilled spaghetti. Tomato sauce spattered everywhere. Billy recovered, tried to stand, slipped on the spilled sauce, and splatted back to the floor again. The cafeteria erupted with laughter.

"Oh God. It's him." It was Lexi's voice, a mix of embarrassment, amusement, and, worst of all, pity.

Then a shadow loomed over Billy—a shadow wearing a letterman's jacket stained with marinara and speckled with spaghetti.

Billy looked up at his victim, a tall, square-jawed blond jock, buff and no doubt far more popular than Billy. Perfect.

"You're dead, kid," the jock said.

Which is when it happened. Again. Just as it had outside the school, Billy's world went dark, cold, and still. The smooth linoleum floor became rough and rocky. Billy felt water dripping on his face. And he could hear a distant shouting and the beating of a single monstrous drum.

Hop quickly realized that he wouldn't be leaving the goblin capital anytime soon. The news trickling into Kiranok wasn't good. Living up to Hop's worst expectations, the victorious human generals had gathered their surviving troops, mixed in countless new recruits, and forged them into an instrument of vengeance. Now their new "Army of Light" was advancing on Mother Mountain like a giant wave, churning up the foothills with death and ruin.

So while Hop had reached the relative safety of Kiranok, now there was no place else to go. He would have to settle in for the long haul. Fortunately, for him anyway, since the disaster at Solace Ridge, most soldiers from the mountains were either too old to lift a spear, too young to carry a shield, or too dead to do much of anything. Which meant that, given his level of experience, coupled with the advantage of being neither infirm nor deceased, it was easy enough for Hop to secure a position as a sergeant in the City Guard. The job came with three meals a day, a place to sleep, and a shiny, copper-inscribed breastplate that Hop figured he could sell if things really went bad.

The only downside was that Hop had to work. Most days that meant protecting the granaries and supervising the bread distribution (always a good opportunity to skim a little off the top for himself). Today, though, work meant standing guard in Kiranok's Hall of Kings as thousands of pilgrims crowded inside to file reverently past the Goblin Crown.

Hop found duty in the Hall of Kings infinitely annoying. There was no place to sit, and he had to look alert and professional at all times. That meant no slouching, no leaning, and absolutely no napping, which in turn meant sore feet, an aching back, and a generally cranky disposition. Still, as he watched the devout bow and pray in front of the Crown, its ruby Eye still dark, Hop felt a funny thing happen to him.

Hop was not, by nature, an optimist. In addition to the still-healing arrow wound in his leg, his nose was twisted from one too many bad breaks, most of his left ear was missing, and he carried more nicks and scars that you could count, all testaments, in his mind, to the inherent unfairness of life. Still, watching all those hopeful faces made Hop, for the briefest of moments, wonder if the prophecy might actually come true, if the Heir to the Crown really would return to save his people in their darkest hour.

To Hop's relief, the feeling went away as quickly as it came. He straightened up and prodded a lagging devotee with the butt of his spear. "Move yourself."

A goblin would have to be a complete idiot to feel optimistic in a time like this.

"It's my fault," Lexi said, stepping between the jock and the boy from Latin class. Billy, that was his name. Billy Smith. Lexi could tell he was having another one of his dizzy spells. *Poor kid. There must be something really wrong with him.*

"No, it wasn't. It was my fault," Billy said as he struggled to his feet.

Lexi didn't understand. Why wouldn't Billy let her help him? No way this stupid bully was gonna hit a girl. If only Billy would play along, Lexi was certain she could fix this mess. "Don't listen to him. I tripped and pushed him. He must have fallen into you. He didn't mean it."

But Billy didn't seem to get it. "She didn't push me. She wasn't even close to me. I did it."

Which is when Lexi realized that Billy understood exactly what she was trying to do. He just didn't want her help. Because she was a girl? Because she was so tiny? Lexi wasn't sure which. Both possibilities made her mad.

"I'm sorry," Billy said before Lexi could intercede again. "I'll pay to get your jacket cleaned."

"You're gonna pay, all right," the jock replied.

"Nice. You learn that thug-talk watching TV?" Lexi said. "Because I'm thinking you haven't read many books."

Lexi regretted her interjection almost as soon as she finished it. *That's the problem with being hyperactive*, Lexi thought. *Sometimes my mouth outruns my brain.*

The jock stepped closer to Lexi, looming over her, almost a foot taller than she was and twice as heavy. He glared down. "See you after school, shrubs." With that, Letterman Jacket stalked away, shaking off spaghetti with every step.

Lexi looked at Billy. She'd stuck herself in the middle of things, as usual. Now she was going to share in the jock's wrath. And all for nothing.

"You shouldn't have done that," Billy said. "I could have handled it myself."

"Boys are so stupid." Now it was Lexi's turn to storm off. Why did she bother?

The rest of Billy's first day of high school was a blur. He kept going over all the mistakes he'd made: daydreaming in Latin, allowing himself to get flustered in the cafeteria, the spaghetti disaster. He'd since found out that the jock he'd pasta-ized was Kurt Novac, the star quarterback of the Drake Wildcats, a terror both on and off the field. In a few quick, colossal missteps, Billy had made himself look like a fool, alienated the only girl who'd talked to him all day, and ticked off the most popular jock in the entire school.

And that wasn't the only thing bothering Billy. There was no denying it. When he was lying there on the floor and looking up at Kurt, something had happened to him. For an instant, *he'd been somewhere else.* Somewhere dark and dangerous. The kind of place you could stumble into easily enough, but good luck ever finding a way out.

Before Billy knew it, the last bell had rung. Billy joined

the rush of students spilling out of the school, hoping to disappear in the crowd as he slunk toward the bus stop.

Which is when he saw Kurt standing there by a brand-new black SUV, waiting, along with two of his jock friends. Billy froze in his tracks. They hadn't seen him. Not yet. Maybe he could still escape.

"I say we just get it over with." It was Lexi. Billy turned and saw her standing behind him, carrying a bulging book bag, a determined expression on her face. Billy couldn't help but notice how trying to look tough made Lexi's nose crinkle. To Billy, the crinkling made her look even cuter.

"Are you even listening to me?" Lexi sounded annoyed.

Billy realized he'd been staring again. "Yeah. I . . . uh . . . What if we just went around back?" Billy asked.

"And hide from him and his jockboys for the next nine months?" Lexi shot back. "Not me."

With that, Lexi strode toward Kurt and his two linebacker buddies. Or at least she tried to stride. Lexi was barely five feet tall so she didn't make it very far with each step. Billy followed her, his lanky legs easily making up for her head start. Acting braver than he felt, Billy stepped in front of Lexi just as Kurt spotted them. Billy put on his best defiant expression and managed a "You looking for us?"

Unfortunately, Billy's voice cracked when he said it, making him sound like a dying field mouse.

"Here's the deal," Kurt said, his two hulking henchmen looming at his side. "We could beat the snot out of you two freshies, but we've decided to give you another chance."

Another chance? That was the first good news Billy had heard all day. But then . . .

"What you decided is that you didn't want to get kicked off the football team for fighting," Lexi said, glaring at Kurt.

Why did she have to do that?

"Get in." Kurt opened the door of his black SUV. Its tinted windows made the interior dark and cave-like. Kurt's thuggish friends closed in on Billy and Lexi. Lexi looked defiant, but from past experience Billy knew that while standing up to bullies might sound great in theory, in practice, it usually meant getting beat up, bad. And while Billy was willing to take his lumps, he really didn't like the way Kurt's thuggish friends were ogling Lexi.

"Oh, hell no." Billy pulled Lexi from the SUV and shoved her away. "Run!"

As if Billy had broken some kind of spell, Lexi suddenly seemed to realize that getting into Kurt's SUV with the two big, dumb, leering linebackers was probably not a good idea. She bolted.

"This way!" Lexi shouted.

Taking advantage of the jocks' surprise, Billy sprinted after Lexi as she dashed around the side of the school, passed the faculty parking lot, then vaulted over a guardrail and disappeared.

Running up to the guardrail, Billy saw Lexi jump down into a concrete culvert. "Quick!" She gestured for him to join her. "Before they catch up."

Billy clambered down into the ditch. The culvert ran down toward the ocean, dipping underground as it crossed beneath Drake's football field. A trickle of sluggish water ran down the middle into the tunnel, but most of the concrete was dry.

"They're faster than us. We have to lose them!" Lexi ran toward the dark hole downstream. Billy hesitated. The mouth of the tunnel was pitch black, and the water and darkness reminded Billy all too much of his strange visions.

"There they are!" he heard Kurt yell.

No more time for second thoughts, Billy dashed into

the tunnel, feet splashing in the shallow water. The tunnel swallowed him up. Trying not to think about his strange, claustrophobic visions or the sounds of Kurt's splashing footfalls closing in from behind, Billy plunged ahead, running blind into the darkness.

Then he ran into a wall.

Billy never saw it coming. It was too dark. One second he was running, and the next—*wham!*—a face full of concrete, a sudden pain mixed with the splashing cold of the water as Billy fell back onto his butt in stunned shock.

Blinking back the pain, Billy looked up, barely able to make out a curve in the concrete wall. Now that he wasn't moving, in the dim light he could just barely see that the culvert forked ahead of him; a side tunnel brought another flow of water from uphill, while the main tunnel curved down and to the right. Billy had run headlong into the turning wall, not noticing the split in the darkness.

Splash! Splash! Billy could hear Kurt moving toward him, more cautious but steady. Getting closer.

"Lexi! Which way?" Billy whispered.

But instead of an answer, Billy heard a scream. A girl's scream of pain and terror. Lexi's scream.

It was coming from the smaller, side tunnel. The one that went uphill. "I'm coming!" Throwing off his backpack, Billy plunged into the tunnel, quickly leaving even the faint light of the main passageway behind. Groping through the darkness, Billy called out, "Lexi! Lexi?"

Billy heard a faint groan. Feeling his way forward, Billy soon touched a small crumpled form. Lexi.

"My leg," she moaned.

Billy's hand was resting on her hip. As carefully as he

could in the darkness, he moved his hand down, past her thigh, past her skirt to her bare knee. And then he felt it, near the top of her shin. Something wet. Sticky. And sharp.

Lexi let out a painful hiss as Billy's hand came in contact with a spike of bone sticking out of her skin.

"It's broken," Billy said, trying to keep the fear out of his voice.

"I know that, idiot." But Lexi couldn't maintain her tough front. She moaned in pain. "My foot got caught. I tripped. And . . . ahhh . . . it hurts so much."

"I have to get you out of here."

Lexi didn't answer. Maybe she'd nodded in the darkness. Maybe she was just in too much pain to care. Billy reached under Lexi, trying to lift her. But that's when his own injury kicked in. Suddenly his face felt like it was splitting in two. His head throbbed; his ribs ached. Billy fumbled his grip on Lexi, his every shift intensifying her pain and his own. *What do I do? Please, please*, Billy prayed silently. *I have to get her out of here.*

At that moment, Billy saw real light, a shining cell phone, illuminating the culvert. Unfortunately, it was being carried by the last person Billy wanted to see.

"What are you idiots doing?" It was Kurt. And he sounded furious.

Billy tried to catch his breath, push past the pain, and lift Lexi, anything to get her away from Kurt. To get Lexi to safety

I need to get out. I need to be anyplace but here.

Then, suddenly, as if in answer to Billy's unspoken wish, the world around him shifted, warped, bent. His stomach lurched. His ears popped. And just like that—

Billy was somewhere else.

The Hall of Kings exploded in a frenzy of dancing, singing, and shouting, a riot of pure joy. Even Hop, as cynical as he was, could feel it. All he had to do was look up at the shelf where the Goblin Crown sat, its central ruby pulsing with a sporadic red glow, faint but undeniable.

The Eye had opened. The stories were true. The Goblin King had come.

CHAPTER TWO

An Army of Monsters

Disoriented, Billy tried to get his bearings. The narrow concrete walls of the culvert had vanished. Instead, Billy found himself in a huge, glittering cavern, studded with enormous stalactites and stalagmites and infused with an eerie yellow glow. Bioluminescent fungi covered a vast ceiling, the source of the strange light that filled the chamber.

And Billy wasn't alone. Lexi was sprawled on top of him, moaning in pain, semiconscious. Billy's face ached; he could barely breathe. He looked around, hoping to find an explanation for the unbelievable situation he'd found himself in.

Which is when he saw Kurt. The blond quarterback still had his smartphone out, and the glowing screen flickered fitfully. He shined the light around him, looking deeply freaked out, staring at the cavern with his mouth agape. Then he spotted Billy and Lexi and headed their way. "That you, shrubs?"

"Get away from us," Billy snarled, his pain lending him courage.

"What happened? Is she hurt?" Kurt looked down at Lexi, aiming his light her way.

"Yeah, she's freaking hurt," Billy shot back. "She broke her leg. Thanks to you."

"I never touched her."

"You ran her down. You and two linebackers chasing a girl who barely weighs a hundred pounds."

"We weren't going to hurt her. Or you. Just dump you both down in Fort Funston and make you walk home," Kurt said softly. Seeing Lexi's shattered leg seemed to have blunted Kurt's self-righteous anger. He knelt next to the injured girl. "We have to get her out of here."

"Yeah. Except . . . where are we?"

"Good question." Kurt said, looking around at the shimmering rock formations and strange fungi. "And I got another one. How did we get here?"

Billy couldn't answer that. Though deep inside he knew . . . wherever they were, somehow he was responsible. If they couldn't get Lexi to a hospital, it would be his fault.

"*Drak*," Hop muttered as he fended off frenzied devotees from the Goblin Crown. "Prophecy are *nai* a bad thing, but it only get you so far."

According to the stories, when the Crown opened its Eye, the Goblin King's heir would appear. The Goblin Crown's central ruby had pulsed red. The Eye had definitely opened, but as of yet, no one had located the newest heir. So where was he?

Just then, as if in answer to Hop's thoughts, heavily armed soldiers shoved their way into the Hall of Kings bellowing, "Make way for the King. Make way for the King."

Hop perked up. This should be good. From his position on the throne's elevated dais, he peered over the crowd toward the hall's entrance. Though the heat of the crowd interfered with his redsight, Hop could just make out a large figure at the center of the column of troops, head held high, a monstrous sword slung over his back.

Despite the heat haze, Hop recognized the new arrival instantly. Whatever faint optimism he might've felt vanished like a cavebug scuttling from a torch.

The goblin carrying the sword was General Skargordek Sawtooth, the commander of the Army of the Dark Lady. Sawtooth was a towering figure, charismatic, imposing, and a fierce combatant. He was everything you could want in a general.

He was also, in Hop's opinion, dangerously ambitious and astonishingly incompetent. It had been General Sawtooth who'd turned the Dark Lady's religious movement into a military crusade, who'd pounded the drumbeat of war with the Hanorians, and who'd led the goblin Warhorde to disaster at Solace Ridge. This was their savior?

Hop moved closer. When he heard Sawtooth speak, his despair only deepened: ". . . worst crisis in our history. But a *maja* crisis are a *maja* opportunity. We can rebuild our mighty Warhorde. Confront our foes on the field of battle. March side by side, shoulder to shoulder. To victory!"

To Hop's relief, the crowd's reaction was muted at best, a smattering of foot stomping and a halfhearted chant of "*chom-chom, chom-chom.*" There were even a few boos. Hop double-checked to make sure he wasn't booing along with the others. Thankfully, he'd maintained enough of his common sense not to fall into that trap.

The lukewarm response wasn't enough for Sawtooth's men. They waded into the crowd, bashing the unenthusiastic goblins with their shields and raising their weapons threateningly.

"All hail King Sawtooth!" they shouted. Bit by bit, the crowd joined in, a few with genuine excitement, most managing just enough feigned enthusiasm to avoid a clubbing from the guards. "Sawtooth! Sawtooth! *Chom-chom-chom!* Sawtooth! Sawtooth! *Chom-chom-chom!*"

Hop had heard enough. He'd followed Sawtooth into battle once. Only a fool would make that mistake twice. Taking advantage of the noise and confusion, Hop abandoned his post and retreated from the Hall of Kings.

It turned out Hop wasn't the only one who realized that having Sawtooth as king might not be a particularly good idea. As he slipped away from the crowded chamber, a few dozen others did the same.

"*Ahka*, One-Ear," a wrinkled old crone said to him. "You going to look for the real king? 'Cause if so, I're with you."

Hop looked around at the others who'd fled the hall. They were watching him expectantly. Hop never thought of himself as a leader, but by being the first goblin to walk out of that room, and an armed city guard at that, he'd become one. Whether he wanted to be or not.

"Guess I are," he admitted reluctantly. "Guess I are at that."

General Sawtooth took in the acclaim of the crowd. He knew many of the cheers were forced, but that didn't bother him. Genuine praise or accolades inspired by fear, he'd earned them either way.

Sawtooth figured a *gob* had to fight for what he wanted in life. He'd been fighting since birth. His parents had been dirt poor, already straining to feed a squalling brood of children when he'd come along. Not long after, his over-worked mother had despaired at raising him herself and abandoned him on the steps of a monastery. But he wasn't destined to become a priest. He was too impatient, too aggressive. And most importantly, he'd shown no talent for magic. His prayers went unanswered; even the most basic blessings eluded him. Eventually the priests, like Sawtooth's parents, had given up on him. They'd turned him over to the Templars, the goblin soldiers who guarded their monasteries and temples, enforcing the peace of the sacred grounds.

Once the Templars placed a weapon in his hands, Sawtooth had thrived. Through a combination of intimidation, ambition, and will, he'd risen quickly through the Templars' ranks. He'd fought more battles than he could count, raids and border skirmishes mostly, far to the east in the Uplands. Somehow he'd survived them all.

At the Fastness, the fortified mountain town that served as the headquarters of both the Templars and their faith, he'd met and married a local lass named Cuttingword. Though a bit plain, and as sharp-tongued as her calling-name suggested, Cutty was the best dancer in the Fastness. Sawtooth had found her challenging, but honest, loyal, and intelligent. They'd made a comfortable home for themselves, raised a daughter, and planned to grow old together. After forty years of service, Sawtooth became the commander of the entire Templar Corps. Cutty had beamed proudly as he'd received his crested general's helm.

Then, only months later, the wasting sickness had taken Cutty from him, just before her fiftieth nameday. Thinking of her still hurt.

Not long after his wife's death, Sawtooth met the Dark Lady. When he first came to her, he'd been lost, alone. She'd given him clarity and purpose. She'd told him he was special, fated to help restore his people to greatness. He'd sacrificed everything he had to make her visions a reality. He'd brought war to the Uplands. Soldiers had died; towns had burned. There'd been great victories and one ruinous defeat.

But Sawtooth never gave up. He prided himself on that. Even with his army shattered and the Dark Lady dead, he never surrendered his ultimate goal, the complete obliteration of the enemy and the reclaiming of his people's ancestral lands.

Now, according to prophecy, some outsider was about to walk into the Hall of Kings, put on the Goblin Crown, and rule Sawtooth's people in his place? Stop him from getting his justice and revenge?

No one ordered him around, not anymore. If some stranger thought otherwise, well, he was prepared to fight.

Sawtooth was always prepared to fight.

According to Kurt, Billy was supposed to be "scouting." That meant he was walking up front, with Kurt's glowing cellphone, while Kurt followed a few yards back, Lexi in his arms. Kurt had decided that they'd somehow fallen through a hole in the culvert. Which meant all they had to do was keep heading up and eventually they'd find their way back to the surface.

Billy knew that didn't make sense. There were no caves under San Francisco. Especially not out near Ocean Beach. It was all sand dunes. Plus, Billy had seen the inside of this cavern twice before. First when he'd freaked out at the bus stop, then again in the lunchroom. Both times he'd told himself it was his imagination, but there was no denying it now. Somehow Billy's fervent wishes to escape, from school, from the culvert, from his life, had come true, and he'd brought Lexi and Kurt along for the ride.

Then Billy realized . . . if he really had gotten the three of them here, maybe he could get them back out again. Billy didn't believe in magic and wishes coming true and all that junk. Still, wishes and magic seemed as likely an explanation as any, so it was worth a try. Concentrating intently, Billy wished he, Lexi, and Kurt were back home. Or better yet, in the hospital emergency room where his mom had started working. He pictured the place in his mind. The white curtains, the tile floor. He focused all his mental energy on convincing himself that when he opened his eyes, he, Kurt, and Lexi would all be in the ER, safe and sound. For a moment, he even convinced himself he could smell a faint whiff of antiseptic and hear the hospital's static-filled PA system.

Unfortunately, thinking about the hospital reminded him of his father. He could picture William Senior, thin and weak, waiting for his latest appointment, for the chemicals and radiation that were supposed to cure him but seemed to be killing him by inches. Lately, hospitals were the last place Billy wanted to be.

Billy's fragile vision of the ER slipped, faded . . . and then it was gone.

When he opened his eyes, they were still in the cavern. His fault. Billy felt guilt as heavy as the stone roof above him.

He wanted to give up, but he knew that if he did, Lexi could lose her leg. Or worse. So Billy pushed past the guilt and resumed his search.

The cave system was a maze. Tunnels led in every possible direction. Large corridors would suddenly dead-end without warning, and one tiny hole barely big enough for Billy to slip through led him to an enormous cavern that stretched beyond the limits of his feeble cell phone light. While some of the tunnels and chambers were lit by bioluminescent fungi, many were pitch black, and Kurt's phone was barely enough to light the way. Loose stones constantly turned and crumbled under Billy's feet. Parts of the path were so slick with water and lichen that it was like walking on ice. Billy lost count of the number of times he slipped and fell. So far, he hadn't plunged to his death into one of the cavern's countless deep pits, but he figured it was only a matter of time.

Billy reached a narrow side passageway. It didn't look like much, but it sloped up sharply. Hopefully it would lead out. Billy turned back to Kurt and Lexi.

"Wait here. I'll check it out."

Billy wormed his way through the tunnel, rounded a series of tight turns, and finally emerged into a huge, dark cavern. He stepped forward, trying to find an exit with the light of Kurt's fading cellphone, and—

Billy slipped on the slick stone floor. His feet shot up into the air and he came down hard, banging the back of his head against a jutting rock. The fall jarred Kurt's phone loose. Before a stunned Billy could react, the glowing phone dropped into a jagged crack in the floor. On his hands and knees, Billy scrambled to the hole, arriving just in time to see the phone rattling down into a vast chasm. For several seconds, the phone's light tumbled end over end, then Billy heard a distant impact, the faint sound of breaking glass and cracking metal. Kurt's phone went dark.

Billy immediately realized the precariousness of his situation. His only source of light was gone, the floor was impossibly slick, and there were pits all around him. Billy was alone in the dark. Again.

"Kurt? Lexi!" he shouted back toward the winding tunnel.

Faintly, Billy heard Kurt calling back, "Now what?" Billy had to admit he was glad to hear the quarterback's voice.

"I fell. I lost your phone." Billy tried to enunciate each word, speaking them as loudly and clearly as he could.

"Damn it. Why do you have to be such a dork?" Billy could hear the disdain in Kurt's voice.

"I'm doing my best. It's not easy," Billy replied.

"Stay there. We're coming."

Despite himself, Billy felt relieved. He could definitely use some help. The back of his head had hit the rocks pretty hard, and he thought he could feel blood seeping through the bruise. He was a little dizzy and had a throbbing headache. Plus, he was cold, hungry, and his tailbone hurt from the fall.

"Be careful!" he shouted. "There are holes! And the floor is slippery!"

"Just stay still!" came Kurt's reply.

"Yeah, seriously," Billy said, more to himself than to Kurt. He struggled onto his hands and knees, but he didn't dare move in the darkness. There was nothing to do but wait.

"How did you get through here?" Kurt shouted.

From that Billy knew Kurt had reached the last hairpin turn before the passageway opened into the cavern. It had been hard enough for Billy to slide through. For Kurt it was going to be a major challenge.

"You can make it," Billy replied. "It's not that bad."

"Yeah, but what about her?" Kurt asked, sounding dubious.

Billy imagined Kurt with his imposing height and wide frame working his way through the turn while carrying Lexi. It was like one of those spatial puzzles on the IQ test his mom had made him take. But this time it wasn't multiple choice. And if it were, the answer looked like "none of the above." Unless . . .

"Put her down," Billy said, thinking it through. "Go first. Then pull her behind you. Gently. You don't want to jar her leg."

Kurt didn't respond, so Billy figured he was following his suggestion. Billy hoped it worked. He pictured the tunnel like a part of a video game and Kurt's bulk as a game piece. A twist and a turn and Kurt should just barely fit through. But if he didn't, if the big football player got stuck in the narrow passageway, Billy and Kurt could end up trapped in the cavern forever. And Lexi could die.

Billy tried to stay calm. His father had recently started meditating to help him with the pain from his cancer and the various treatments. Billy worked to center himself, the way his father did, to block out the distractions, to find a sense of inner tranquility. Unfortunately, between the darkness, the treacherous rocks beneath him, the continued danger to Lexi, and his aching head and tailbone, Billy wasn't feeling very meditative.

Then, when it seemed like things couldn't get any worse, Billy heard noises in the darkness. Muted whispers and small metallic clanks and strange shuffling sounds. Billy tried to tell himself it was just water. Or bats. Or distorted echoes from Kurt's struggles. But as the sounds grew louder, Billy spied strange shapes moving through the darkness ahead of him. Apparently the cave wasn't entirely dark after all. Now that Billy's eyes had adjusted, he realized there was just enough light so that every once in a while he could catch a glimpse of motion, a shift in the gloom.

Someone, or something, was coming his way.

Billy should've been overjoyed. The moving shapes had to be people. People meant rescue. For him and Kurt and especially Lexi. But there was something wrong with the way the shadows moved. They lurched and crept. They scurried from one hiding place to the next. They practically skulked, as if they weren't so much searching for him and the other two teens as hunting . . . and Billy was their prey.

Billy wanted to run, but he knew that if he did, he'd probably fall into a chasm and plunge to his death. So instead, he braced himself against the slick floor and tried to keep still, to breathe slowly and quietly. He even tried to keep his heart from beating too loudly.

It didn't help. The shadowy figures moved steadily toward him. Billy could see distinct silhouettes now. There was something odd about them, something misshapen. Their heads seemed too big and their arms too long. They were whispering to each other, gesturing. The group of them spread out. Whoever they were, *they* weren't having any trouble keeping their balance on the slick stones or avoiding the dangerous pitfalls in the darkness.

A chill ran down Billy's spine as one of the ill-formed figures stepped away from the others and made its way toward him. There was something in its hand . . . something long and sharp and pointy. A weapon.

Then the light came on.

Kurt pulled Lexi around the final turn in the tunnel and raised a lit cellphone above his head. "Hey, check it out. She had a phone in her pocket. It even has a flashlight app—"

Kurt fell silent. A shocked, horrified silence. The quarterback backed up, finally managing to sputter a few choked, disconnected words. "What . . . what is that?"

Billy turned slowly from Kurt to look toward the creeping figures. In the light from Lexi's phone, Billy could see them clearly. But he wished he couldn't.

Only a few yards from Billy stood a monster. It was about five feet tall and slightly bowlegged. It had long arms with clever, tapered fingers wrapped around a deadly looking barbed spear. Its head was disproportionately large for its body with short, spiky black hair, and pointed, bat-like ears, one of which appeared to have been bitten halfway off. Its skin was pitch black, and its eyes were huge, yellow, and slitted like a cat's. When it opened its mouth, it flashed a set of canines long enough to rip out a man's throat.

Worse, the monster wasn't alone. There were dozens of similar creatures following behind it. An entire army of nightmares.

Hop had expected to find humans. Or at least *a* human. That had been the entire point of this expedition. After all, the first Goblin King had been human. So were all nine of his successors. It wasn't something Hop and his people were proud of, but the old tales had been very specific. And the statues of the former monarchs that decorated the Hall of Kings all depicted folk who were freakishly tall, short-limbed, small-headed, and unnaturally pale. In other words, typical humans.

What's more, according to the histories, the first King, and each of his successors, had emerged from the "deepest cavern of Mother Mountain." This was the deepest cave that Hop or any of the assorted dreamers, madmen, and fools who had gathered around him could think of. So that was where Hop and his little band of anti-Sawtooth malcontents had started their search.

Despite all that, Hop wasn't a big fan of humans. No one who'd lived through Solace Ridge could be. And while the younger boy and the injured girl looked fairly harmless, the older one with the magical light box looked like he was tensing for a fight.

Sadly, the hostile boy was the only one of the three that looked like king material. He was certainly more promising than the young stripling or the broken girl. And his paler pinkish skin matched the old marble statues better than the others. Light brown speckled marble for the boy, bronze for the girl. Did that mean anything? Hop knew that skin tone meant more to humans than to *goben*, but he was hardly an expert.

The big pale boy shouted something and tried to look menacing. A loud-mouthed buffoon, in Hop's estimation. Still, at least he showed a little spirit. Based on the outlandish clothing the three young humans wore, they certainly weren't Hanorians. The larger boy wore a dark shirt under a bulky jacket with leather sleeves, the smaller boy a hooded cotton tunic of some sort and purple canvas shoes. The girl wore a patterned skirt and a soft-looking red top. All the humans' clothes were woven with such impossible fineness that Hop couldn't make out a single thread. Perhaps their garments had been sewn together by magic? There had to be something to this. It wasn't as if humans were constantly emerging from the caverns of Mother Mountain. Hop summoned up his best trustworthy expression, placed his spear down on the ground, and stepped forward.

The older boy gasped and stepped back. The smaller boy, who was on all fours for some reason, inched away as well. They were both obviously terrified.

Hop tried to sound friendly. "Night and Day, what're wrong with you people?" he said. "Have you never seed a goblin afore?"

CHAPTER THREE
Proper Introductions

Billy hadn't screamed. He was proud of that. The bowlegged creature in front of him might be pitch black, fanged, and pointy-eared, but Billy got the distinct impression it wasn't there to hurt them. The opposite, actually. It looked anxious, worried, and nervous, almost as if it wanted their help.

The two male humans stared at Hop blankly. Hop was confused. They were acting like they hadn't understood a word he'd said. But he'd spoken Hanorian, and every human he'd ever met knew *Hanoryabber*. Hop was secretly proud of his ability to speak human. He'd learned it while working guard duty for an Uplands trade caravan long before the war. The caravan leader had insisted that his guards study the language, the better to prevent misunderstandings between the goblin merchants and the suspicious human townsfolk who traded dyed wool and worked leather for the goblins' copper pots and jewelry. Hop knew his accent was a little thick, but he'd always been able to get his point across.

He tried again. "*Ahka.* Are you stupid? I're talking to you."

If anything, they looked even more confused.

"Are it important to talk to these humans?" came a voice from the crowd who'd followed Hop.

Hop looked back at the cluster of goblins. He couldn't tell which goblin had spoken. "Course it're important," Hop said. "We need to know if the prophecy are real. And to do that, we have to have a proper *yabber, zaj?*"

"Then allow me." A small goblin in a ratty blue robe pushed his way to the front of the crowd. The new arrival had a wispy beard, and his ears stuck out so wide they looked like bat wings. He wore a heavy necklace of runic symbols linked by gold chains. Hop shook his head. *Just what we need. A wizard.*

Hop regarded the little wizard suspiciously. "Do I know you?"

"Atarikit Bluefrost. Folk call me 'Frost.'"

This didn't do much to alleviate Hop's worries. "Frost" was a typical wizard calling-name. The little goblin might as well be nicknamed "Winter" or "Blizzard" or "Ice" or "Midnight," or any other calling-name that evoked something dark or cold. Goblin wizards drew their powers from the unlit mountain depths and the night sky, from glacier winds and freezing waters. This made them subtler and craftier than their fire-wielding human counterparts, but unfortunately, it didn't stop them from being just as crazy. That was the problem with magic. It was immensely powerful, but sooner or later, every *gob* who used it went insane. Magic was bad for the brain.

On the bright side, at least this Frost fellow was young. That meant he probably hadn't been working magic long enough to be completely bonkers.

"You an apprentice?"

"Once. But *nai* more. Me master were killed at Solace Ridge. So now I're on me own, *zaj*."

"You any good?"

"Are I good? Put your eyeballs on this!" With that, Frost focused his energy on the young humans. The cave grew cold. A blue light so dark it was almost black played across Frost's fingertips. The human children backed even farther away, terrified. And then . . .

Billy scrambled back in fear as blue-black light blasted from the hands of a smaller, bat-eared monster. But there was no avoiding the light. It sprayed across the cavern, playing over the temples of all three teens. Billy staggered. His brain felt as if it were full of razor-sharp ice, like the world's worst Slurpee headache. Flashes of blue filled his vision. It was hard to see, and everything hurt.

"Ah!" Billy sputtered. "Brain freeze."

Then the cold faded. Billy's vision returned to normal, and he felt like himself again, though with the nagging thought that something inside his head had been . . . rearranged.

"Can you understand me now?"

The monster with the spear and the mangled ear was talking to them again, and to Billy's amazement, this time he could understand every word. The creature wasn't speaking English. Far from it. It sounded like a dog growling in

German or something. But somehow what it was saying made perfect sense.

"I . . . Yeah. I can understand you." When Billy spoke, it was even stranger. He was thinking in English, but what came out of his mouth was the same *achtung-grrr* gibberish the creature was speaking.

Billy turned to Kurt. "Are you hearing this?"

"Yeah. And it's freaking me out. Even more than I already was."

"Wizards," the one-eared monster said. "They do that to folks."

"Wizards?" Billy said. "You have wizards?"

The smaller monster, the one who seemed to be a wizard, smiled with amusement. "*Ahka*. You do *nai*? Guess we have a lotta *yabber* to do, *zaj*."

"That part I didn't quite get," Billy admitted.

The smaller monster looked slightly embarrassed. "I do *nai* do accents well. May have some translation issues."

"Good enough," the bigger monster said. "We can make it work."

Billy stared at the strange creatures. He wasn't good at much, but one thing he had a lot of practice at was meeting new people. And as bizarre as this situation might be, it felt wrong to let things go any further without proper introductions. "I'm Billy. What . . . I mean, who . . . who are you?"

The one-eared monster smiled again. Billy thought it was trying to look friendly, but it wasn't having much luck, what with all the teeth. "As to what, like I sayed afore, we're goblins of course."

Goblins? Visions of evil, twisted cannibalistic monsters flashed through Billy's head. They were talking with goblins?

The one-eared goblin continued. "As to who, the shortie

what ensorcerated your brains are Frost, the wizard. Me, I're Korgorog Hoprock. Most folks call me 'Hop.'"

"Uh, nice to meet you, Hop," Billy managed. "This is Kurt." Kurt nodded dumbly, overwhelmed. "And that's Lexi."

Lexi let out a little moan. That sealed it for Billy. He might not like the look of Hop and his goblin friends, but Lexi was in trouble. So he didn't have much choice.

"She's hurt," Billy continued. "Can your . . . uh . . . wizard help her? Please?"

General Sawtooth allowed himself a moment of grim satisfaction. His soldiers controlled the major entrances to Kiranok. The City Guard had pledged its loyalty, giving him authority over critical fortifications like the Overwatch and Sunderwall. He'd long ago installed his own loyalists at Deepden, the Bat Cavern, and the Winches, and his personal bodyguards held both Valkazin's Fist and Seventurns. Militarily, his position was unassailable.

Of equal importance, the Elders had thrown him their support. Goblins of influence and authority, the Elders included merchant guild masters, clan matriarchs, gang bosses, moneylenders, and landlords, the demagogues of the mob and the quiet leaders of the wealthy. Together, they made up the informal governing body of the city. With them on his side, no one would dare move against him.

Good planning, Sawtooth thought. *That're the key to victory.*

When he'd served as the Dark Lady's warlord, Sawtooth had worked hard to win over the rich and powerful of Kiranok. A bribe here, a profitable supply contract there, threats, appeals to religious zeal, blackmail, extortion, flattery, and intimidation . . . he'd used every weapon in his arsenal to ensure their loyalty. In a few extreme cases, he'd even taken hostages, "recruiting" the children of influential families into his Warhorde and assigning them to distant outposts where his followers could execute them if their parents ever dared defy him. As the old goblin expression went, the Elders knew Sawtooth was the one grilling their eggs. And the one who'd eat their breakfasts if they didn't fall in line.

Sawtooth sat on the Obsidian Throne, with its intricate carvings of past goblin victories, confident no one in Kiranok would challenge his authority.

Even if the legends were true.

His eyes went to the ten statues that decorated the Hall, one for each of the previous kings. Could another heir be on the way? Sawtooth scoffed at the thought. The legends were *drak*. The Dark Lady had prophesized Sawtooth's greatness. Surely the Goblin Crown had pulsed red as a sign of his ascendance. The general had sacrificed everything for his people. If anyone deserved to rule them, it was him.

And suffering and death to anyone what say different.

Lexi felt like she was on fire. Not just from the pain in her leg. Her entire body roiled with a strange internal heat. Lexi was the sun. Floating through the heavens, aflame.

But how could she be the sun when, all around her, it was dark and cold? Lexi had vague impressions of Staring Kid, what was his name? Billy? And Kurt too, though somehow not the scary Kurt she had already grown used to. No, this Kurt wasn't scary. He was scared. Which didn't make any sense at all.

And the floating? Was she floating? Flying? No. She was being carried. By hands that felt lumpy, pokey, and odd. Socks full of walnuts tipped with rose thorns. Bodies moved around her, shadows in the cold dark. Not people. People didn't move like that. Or sound like that. But the lumpy, sharp hands were careful. They carried her gently. As gently as her own father when she was little and had a fever.

A fever. That made sense. She was sick. She was at home in bed, and the strange shapes, the stony walls, the fire in her brain, they were just dreams. Fever dreams.

Except why would she dream of a frightened Kurt or a set-jawed, determined Billy?

The walnut hands fumbled a little, and Lexi shifted in pain and dreamed she was the sun.

Billy was worried about Lexi. She'd been semiconscious at best since they'd arrived in the cavern; her skin looked pale and clammy. Two large goblins were carrying her up through the caverns, doing their best not to jostle her unnecessarily. Despite their efforts, she frequently moaned in pain or whimpered in her sleep.

Billy had tried to convince Frost to treat Lexi immediately, but Frost explained that after working a complex spell like the one that let them understand and speak *Gobayabber* (the goblins' word for their own language), he needed time to recover. Plus, Frost was no expert on healing spells and wanted to check some texts back at his home. That's where they were bringing her. To a goblin's home. Whatever that might look like.

According to Hop, the mountain they were in was riddled with tunnels, both natural and goblin-carved. Frost's home was located in a goblin city, a place called Kiranok, itself made up of hundreds of interlocking caverns, caves, and mines. There weren't any big mountains within a hundred miles of Billy's new home. And there certainly wasn't a goblin city. As far as Billy could tell, they'd somehow been magically transported to an entirely different world, an alien place where wizards and goblins and things from fairy tales and nightmares were all too real.

Billy thought about his parents. He'd been missing for hours now. His mother and father must be worried sick. Lexi's and Kurt's too. He looked over at the jock, who was trying to get a signal from Lexi's phone. Again.

"I don't think that's gonna work," Billy whispered.

"I know." Kurt hung up. Then he dialed again.

"We'll make it out of here. Somehow." Billy tried to sound confident, but he wasn't having much success. Probably because between Lexi's broken leg, his own aching head and throbbing ribs, and their bizarre situation, he didn't believe it himself.

After a few more twists and turns, Billy, Kurt, and their goblin escorts, including the ones carrying Lexi, emerged into a long, smooth, carved corridor. The corridor was lit dimly by cultivated growths of the same bioluminescent fungi that coated some of the cavern ceilings, only here it had been carefully pruned and tended, presumably by green-thumbed goblins. As a result, it grew in neat rows along the walls, occasionally exploding into elaborate patterns where a more ambitious gardener had chosen to express some creativity.

"Getting there," Hop said, leading them through the carved corridor.

As they marched along, Billy finally got a chance to examine the individual goblins. Though they were just as diverse as humans, the goblins did share certain characteristics. They all had darkish skin, varying in tone from Frost's muddy green to Hop's blue black. They had prominent pointed ears, bulging catlike eyes, and sharp predatory teeth. Their hair tended to be sparse, dark, and coarse, though some of the females sported elaborate hairdos made up of tiny braids woven with beads, gemstones, and bits of fabric. The male goblins mostly had their hair cropped short, like Hop, though one youth sported three carefully maintained parallel Mohawks. Only Frost had any kind of facial hair, and it barely looked worth the effort.

Though the goblins wore practical, dark-colored clothing, they decorated themselves with a surprising amount of jewelry, Frost's thick gold necklace being the most eye-catching example. Both males and females wore bracelets, armbands, earrings, nose-rings, and plain old ring rings, most made of gold and studded with gems and semiprecious stones. Even Hop, who came across as more conservative (or perhaps poorer) than his companions, wore a burnished breastplate inscribed with copper, three gold rings, a large diamond earring (in his less mangled ear), and an intricately worked copper wristband. Good miners, Billy guessed. And good metalworkers too.

Billy watched the goblins lope through the tunnels around him. Hop seemed more or less in charge, but his allies were an unruly bunch. There'd been several arguments over which route they should take and who should do what. Hop kept scouts ahead and behind and made sure the goblins checked every intersection carefully before they moved on, which didn't make Billy feel particularly calm about their situation. Bad enough he was surrounded by freaky monsters from some whacked-out storybook. But freaky monsters worried about someone else presumably even scarier than them? That wasn't a pleasant thought.

The group reached a guarded intersection leading into a

large chamber. Two goblins dressed in copper breastplates identical to Hop's stood alertly at the entrance. Hop signaled everyone to wait, then went to talk to the guards alone. After a moment, he slipped off a gold ring and offered it to the other guards. They looked around to make sure they weren't being watched, then took the ring and wandered off, pretending they'd never seen Hop or his followers.

Hop returned to the group. "Put some cloaks on the humans, *zaj*. We need 'em to look normal."

"We do look normal," Kurt said.

"Not here we don't," Billy reminded him.

Billy took a hooded gray robe from a helpful goblin. Once he had it on and pulled the hood over his head, it was hard to tell he was human.

Kurt, however, wasn't so easy to hide. He towered over the goblins, most of whom weren't any taller than Lexi. Even with a cloak on, he clearly didn't fit in with the rest of the group.

Hop immediately saw the problem. "*Ahka*. You're too tall to fit in with the rest of us and too short to pass as *kijakgoben*. Scrunch yourselfs down and try to look goblinish."

Coached by Hop, Kurt took up a wide-legged, bent-kneed stance that better imitated goblin posture. But Kurt wasn't happy. "Look," he whispered to Billy as he adjusted his cloak, "I say we run for it. Ditch this freak parade and go back down into the caves. Find our way home."

"What about Lexi? You want us to leave her here?" Billy couldn't hide his contempt.

"We need to get help. I don't trust these monsters. Do you?"

"I have big ears, you know?" It was Hop. Apparently he'd heard every word. "Well, at least the one big ear. But it let me hear *maja* good, *zaj*."

"Sorry. We're just . . . nervous," Billy said. "We don't know how we got here, and we really want to find a way home."

"You saying you do *nai* want to be here?" Hop seemed puzzled.

"We got lost in that cave. We don't even know where 'here' is."

"I told you. It're Kiranok. The greatest city in the Seven Lands."

Kurt scoffed. "So far all I've seen are tunnels, tunnels, and more tunnels."

"Heh. Then you need to see this." Without any further explanation, Hop poked his head through a nearby archway, peering into a larger chamber beyond. Once he was satisfied it was safe, he went through the archway. The other goblins, including the pair of burly males carrying Lexi, filed after him.

Billy looked at Kurt. "They're taking her with them." As far as Billy was concerned, that decided it. "Do what you want. I'm gonna see what the big deal is."

Billy strode toward the archway, trying to project a confidence he didn't feel, only remembering to slouch at the last second. After a moment of indecision, Kurt followed, reluctantly bringing up the rear.

It was, quite simply, the most amazing thing Billy had seen in his entire young life. It was more breathtaking than the Golden Gate Bridge on a perfect sunny day. It was more intimidating than a chaotic downtown street at rush hour. It was like the Grand Canyon and New York City and Carlsbad Caverns all rolled into one.

"The Underway. That're what we call the center of

Kiranok," Hop said. "It're the beating heart of *goben* civilization. They say if you do *nai* love the Underway, then your soul are maked of stone. Get a quick look. We can *nai* stay long."

Billy looked out at the Underway over a wrought iron railing on the edge of a cobblestone avenue three lanes wide. The railing fenced him off from a plummeting central chasm that dropped as far as he could see, an impossibly large cavern with countless stone streets and buildings carved into its steep sides. Above and below, left and right, the underground city stretched off into the distance. Arching bridges made of stone and iron crisscrossed the chamber, connecting one side of Kiranok to the other. Street after street, each lined with numerous buildings, were stacked one atop the other like ancient Native American cliff dwellings. Billy recognized shops and houses, saw what looked like banks, temples, and even police stations, all of which created a dizzying number of windows, doors, balconies, and passageways in the cavern's stone cliff face.

And every surface of this seemingly endless cavern, every cobblestone street and precipitous platform and impossible bridge, was full of goblins, goblins of every age, shape, and size.

There were old goblins hobbling along with canes and baby goblins being carried in their parents' arms. There were goblins riding unicycles, goblins pushing handcarts, even goblins mounted on giant rams. Billy saw a pair of goblins almost ten feet tall carrying huge barrels of scrap metal across an iron bridge. Outside a stone storefront, a circle of miniature goblins decorated goblin baby clothing with intricate needlework. There was even a goblin band playing for donations from the many passersby.

In addition to the chasm-spanning bridges, a network of

what looked like ski lifts moved goblins quickly about the Underway. Goblins rode in wooden cars that hung precariously from metal cables, jerking and creaking from one part of Kiranok to the next. Billy worried that the delicate-looking cables would break, sending the goblins plunging to their deaths. But surprisingly, the clacking, whining gondolas puttered along without catastrophic incident.

Somewhere in the distance, a gong rang. Immediately, the street musicians took up a new tune. Billy could hear the same song echoing from all over the city, played on rattling drums and echoing pipes, on high-pitched tin whistles and deep haunting horns. And weaving through it all, a skirling mournful drone that could only be bagpipes, rising from the very bottom of the Underway. The music built, deliberately, inevitably. As it crested, all at once, all over the city, the goblins began to sing. Not just a few. Not just a hundred. To Billy, it sounded like every goblin in the city was singing, from the smallest shrill-voiced child to the oldest crackling crone, from the impossibly high notes of the tiny miniature goblins to the thrumming bone-quaking bass of the hulking giants, tens of thousands of voices joined together in inhuman harmony.

Come the darkness
Come the night
End the day
Douse the light

The sun are gone, fleeing west
Now come the hours we love best
Feel the mist's gathering tide
See the crescent rise
In the darkened skies

Let the goben *roam far and wide*

Good are the hunting
Now in the glooming
Hided and safe, cunning and strong
We ride in the black
With the moon at our back
And nai *human can work us* nai *wrong*

Come the darkness
Come the night
End the day
Douse the light

Once all the world were goben *lands*
We holded all in goben *hands*
We feared nai *when the sun shined*
But then comed the sails
Humans riding the gales
And bringing death and war unkind

Now all through the daylight we hide
In woods, in caves, on mountainside
We dwell in the reaches
Far from their sight
We wait for the night
And the secrets she teaches

Come the darkness
Come the night
End the day
Douse the light

But one night up we'll rise
As the last daylight dies
And all of the humans are sleeping
From ocean to tarn
We'll take what are our'n
'Til all of the humans are weeping
'Cause the debt we are owed
We'll collect, heads unbowed
And that what we take we are keeping

Come the darkness
Come the night
End the day
Douse the light

The song was mesmerizing, sad, brave, angry, and joyous all at the same time. For a moment Billy forgot all his troubles—this strange world, Lexi's leg, his various bumps and bruises, his father's illness, all of it—and stood there soaking in the music, knowing it was an experience he'd never forget as long as he lived.

Then the song ended. Billy snapped out of his reverie and realized he was alone. The others had moved on sometime during the song, but he'd stayed behind, compelled to listen a little longer. Billy pulled his hood farther over his face while looking around for his companions. But all he saw were goblins . . . goblins bustling to and fro, goblins carrying packages and bundles, and goblins with weapons, moving slowly through the crowds, scanning for trouble. Police?

"*Ahka.* There you are." Billy nearly jumped out of his robe as Hop slipped up alongside him. "We feared we losed you. You *nai* hear me tell you it're time to move on?"

"Sorry," Billy said, still distracted, "I . . . What was that music?"

"It're the Night Song. We sing it every night as the sun go and the stars come."

"It's beautiful."

"It're *nai* supposed to sound beautiful. *Nai* for humans. It're supposed to scare the vinegar outa you. Now hurry. We need to get you someplace safe."

Without another word, Hop dashed off. Billy pulled himself away from the astounding view and hurried to catch up.

But in his rush, Billy's hood fell away from his face.

The reaction was instantaneous.

"*Skerbo!*" The first shout came from an old goblin woman bent with arthritis but still, unfortunately for Billy, sharp-witted and alert. Soon the cry spread all through the Underway.

"*Skerbo! Skerbo! Skerbo!*"

Billy wasn't sure what it meant, but it didn't sound good. The crowd surged around him. The old she-goblin poked at him menacingly with her walking stick. "Bleedy murdering *skerbo!*"

Billy backed away, confused. He hadn't killed anyone. Why was she so angry? All he wanted was to get away from her, but the crowd was closing in. He was surrounded.

"*Skerbo!* Call the Copperplates! *Skerbo!*"

It was Billy's secret fear come to life. Ever since he could remember, Billy had had nightmares about being singled out as an outsider and a freak. Hunted like a monster or surrounded by a hostile mob for being different. Billy's bad-dream-come-true paralyzed him; just like in a nightmare, he was desperate to run but unable to move.

"Go!" Hop doubled back and pulled Billy away from

the old goblin woman, jamming his hood back over his head and yanking him down the street. In a flash, Hop and Billy plunged through the growing crowd of goblins, broke free, and ran for all they were worth.

The crowd set off in hot pursuit, crying, "*Skerbo*" and swelling in numbers by the second.

"What's a *skerbo*?" Billy asked as Hop shoved a surprised goblin out of their way so they could continue their sprint.

"It mean 'human.' Only *nai* in a nice way."

Billy and Hop dashed through the street. They dodged past handcarts and kiosks, through plazas and around fountains. Their pursuers fell behind, unable to keep up in the packed streets. More goblins took up the cry of "*skerbo*," but the Underway was so crowded it was impossible for anyone to see where the commotion had started.

As Billy followed Hop, he realized that Lexi and Kurt were nowhere in sight. "Lexi . . . Kurt . . . Where are they?"

"Taked to safety by Frost if he have any brains. Time to worry later! Now save your skin!"

Hop led Billy across a bridge, up a staircase, through a side tunnel, and down a ladder. Finally he pushed Billy into a small alcove cut into the cave wall. Billy nearly fell into a wide hole in the alcove floor, but Hop grabbed his collar just in time.

"Trash chute," Hop explained. The alcove stank of refuse, but it was out of the way and hard to see from the street. Billy and Hop crouched inside and waited for the cries of "*skerbo*" to fade. As he hid, Billy felt the fear and adrenaline from the chase drain away and something new creep in. Despair. Billy feared he'd never find Lexi and Kurt now, never get home. He unconsciously edged a little closer to Hop, not wanting to lose his only remaining ally.

But Hop wasn't in a reassuring mood.

"Stay put." Leaving Billy in the alcove, Hop went to the railing. Billy could see him studying the milling crowd with a critical eye. At first Hop seemed satisfied that they'd lost their pursuers. Then the one-eared goblin spotted something that made his yellow eyes narrow with worry. Billy followed Hop's glance and saw a group of armed goblin soldiers pushing toward them through the crowd, meticulously checking every side passage, nook, and door along the way.

"Sawtooth's folk," Hop said, returning to the trash chute, obvious concern in his voice. The goblin looked around, seeming to weigh his options, then came to a decision.

"Follow me!" Hop darted back into the street—

And jumped right over the railing.

Billy froze. Follow him? Was he crazy? But the soldiers were getting closer. Billy didn't have much choice. He ran to the railing. And leaped.

To his surprise, Billy didn't die. He landed almost immediately on a tarp hanging over a vegetable stand a level below. He slid off the tarp and landed on his feet. A few yards away, Hop was haggling with a harried goblin wearing thick, padded leather clothing, heavy gloves, and what looked like a leather pilot's cap from the First World War, complete with earflaps.

Billy adjusted his hood to make sure it was hiding his face. He had to wonder, why was Hop going to such great lengths to help him? He got the feeling the goblin wanted something from him and his companions, but he had no idea what.

Hop slipped the cap-wearing goblin his last two gold rings and stepped onto a small balcony that projected out into Kiranok's central chasm. "Hurry!"

Billy swallowed hard and followed Hop. The balcony had no railings of its own. Away from the shelter of the streets, Billy could feel a strong, cold wind whipping through the chasm. Billy had never liked heights. Now, standing at the edge of the Underway's seemingly bottomless abyss, the fierce wind grabbing at his cloak, he was convinced that any second, he'd lose his balance and fall screaming to his death.

"Get ready, *zaj*," Hop said.

Billy looked at Hop. Get ready for what?

The goblin in the pilot's cap blew a whistle. Billy couldn't actually *hear* the whistle, but he could *feel* it. The not-quite-a-sound made his teeth hurt.

In response to the inaudible whistle, a huge bat rose up out of the depths of the Underway. The thing was the size of an elephant, maybe even bigger counting its massive flapping wings. Billy managed to contain a shout of surprise. He knew drawing attention to himself now would be bad. Very, very bad.

The bat turned slowly in the air, aligning its backside to the balcony, then hovered, its wings in constant motion as it fought to maintain position. The goblin pilot walked confidently onto the bat's back, then plopped himself into a saddle mounted behind its neck, part of a riding platform with room for three or four passengers.

"On you go," Hop said, shoving Billy forward.

Billy stumbled onto the back of the bat and half fell, half sat onto the riding platform. Hop followed, more sure-footed, and squatted next to Billy.

"Smile, pup. You're traveling fancy now."

With a powerful surge of its wings, the bat rose gracefully from the balcony. The wind blew the hood from Billy's face. An approaching soldier spotted him and shouted in alarm. The cries of *"skerbo"* started again, but receded quickly as their goblin pilot guided his bat over a gondola cable, under a bridge, and then into the open air in the center of the chasm.

Billy gulped in awe. He was soaring through the heart of the mountain, surrounded on all sides by the swarming goblin city. He could see tens of thousands of goblins on hundreds of streets on dozens of levels, bustling about their business.

Once, when Billy was young, his father had shown him a print by an artist named M. C. Escher. Escher had drawn four or five interlocking stairways going off at impossible angles, with the top of one stairway turning into the bottom of another. The picture featured dozens of tiny men walking on the stairways, sometimes on one surface, sometimes on another, eating, shopping, and carrying groceries. Billy had spent hours studying that picture, counting the men, delighting in the way Escher had used optical illusions to turn walls into floors and ceilings into walls. From the back of the bat, Kiranok looked like that drawing come to life, only there were hundreds of stairways, bridges, and passageways, and more tiny men than Billy could count in a lifetime.

"Traveling fancy," he said. "That's one way to put it."

The bat leaned into a slow banking turn, and the impossible city of Kiranok stretched out all around Billy, a wonder to behold.

CHAPTER FOUR
Just a Stranger Here

Billy and Hop made their way down a shadowy street in the farthest depths of the Underway. Unlike the bustling, prosperous neighborhoods higher up, this area, appropriately called "Rockbottom," was dirty, grim, and dour. Here, Kiranok's central chasm narrowed so much that Billy thought he could almost jump from the railing on one side of Rockbottom to the other. That is, where there was a railing. In much of Rockbottom, it appeared the iron balustrades had long since rusted through and never been repaired.

Between the two sides of Rockbottom, the cavern floor turned into a narrow gorge filled with drainage water and waste from the upper levels. The wastewater gurgled slowly past the poorly maintained streets, reeking of corruption and decay.

Billy and Hop were searching for Frost's place. Hop had confessed that he had no idea where Frost lived. He'd only just met the little wizard. So it had taken several tense meetings between Hop and various shady characters to get this far. Still, if Hop's informants were right, Frost's place was nearby. The one-eared goblin rechecked a note he'd scribbled to himself.

"Five doors downstream of the Old Quarry Pub. *Nai* far now."

Hop picked up the pace, and Billy dutifully followed along. The streets of Rockbottom were recessed under the layers of city above. Low stone archways supported the ceiling, and Billy had to keep ducking his head to avoid bumping into them. The last thing he needed was to bash his face in again. Doing his best to ignore his throbbing head and aching ribs, Billy tried to take in his surroundings without revealing his battered but all-too-human face. Tiny houses cut into the cave wall lined the covered streets. Many looked abandoned, their doors and windows bricked over. There were poor, ragged goblins everywhere, huddling in alcoves, begging for food. Billy shuddered when he saw a few fishing in the polluted stream running down the center of the chasm. Nothing that came out of that vile-smelling water could possibly be healthy to eat.

"Who are these people?" he asked Hop.

"You *nai* have poor folk where you come from?" the goblin replied.

"Some," Billy said. "In the city. But not this many." Billy had seen a few homeless people living in the parks back home, and more downtown, but in Rockbottom, they were everywhere. "What happened to them?"

"It're the war."

In a low voice, Hop explained that the goblins had

recently fought, and lost, a brutal war against the neighboring human kingdom of Gran Hanor. Many goblins had died. Even more had been displaced by the vengeful Hanorian army, which was advancing relentlessly into goblin territory. Unfortunately, even a city as big and prosperous as Kiranok didn't have enough jobs, food, and homes for the numerous refugees who'd flooded through its gates. Hop had been one of the lucky ones. He'd found work and a place to live. The less fortunate ended up in Rockbottom.

Finishing his sad tale, Hop finally located the entrance to the Old Quarry Pub. Billy glanced inside the dark, dingy bar, surveying its patrons, a surly collection of refugees and war veterans.

"Keep your head down," Hop said. He hurried Billy past the entrance, then counted doors. "*Enik, menik, mynta, mogh, katcha.* Five doors. This're it."

Hop and Billy arrived at a low, battered wooden door hanging slightly askew in a cracked brick archway. Hop stood outside the door and loudly announced, "*Wazzer.*"

Billy heard a muffled response from inside: "Coming."

Billy looked at Hop. "Goblins don't knock?"

"Na. Why bang up a poor defenseless door? We say '*Wazzer*' instead. It mean 'Here're I' or 'Watch me.'"

"*Wazzer!*" tried Billy.

"I're coming, I sayed." From inside, Frost cracked open the door and peered out cautiously. "*Ahka,* good. It're you."

"Lexi? Kurt? Are they here?" Billy said in a rush, hoping Hop's guess had been right.

"*Zaj.* They're here." Frost muttered a hasty, ritualized greeting. "I, Atarikit Bluefrost, in the name of me and me family, welcome you to me house. You're at home here so long as you treat it as your home. You're family so long as you act like family."

"Which mean you can come in," Hop added by way of explanation. "But do *nai* break nothing."

Frost opened the door wider so Billy and Hop could step inside and then quickly shut it behind them. Billy found himself in a small entry room. A very, very large goblin filled most of the vestibule. The giant towered over Frost, who stood between its legs.

"Sorry about the neighborhood," Frost said. "Hard to get folk to rent to a wizard. They're always afeared we'll blow up their house or something."

"Frost *nai* ever blowed up a place," the big goblin said in a deep, powerful voice. "Blowed a place down once. But *nai* up."

Frost glared at the huge goblin. "This're Bohorikit Leadpipe. Me little brother."

"Good to meet you," Leadpipe boomed.

Leadpipe was easily ten feet tall. His dark green skin was thick with bony growths. Horny spikes projected from his knuckles, elbows, and knees, and huge razor-sharp canines grew from the sides of his mouth like giant tusks. He had much more hair than either Frost or Hop, worn in thick dreadlocks decorated with gold and silver rings.

"Little brother?" Billy said.

"Goblins're like that," explained Hop. "Most times we grow normal. But sometimes we grow extra small . . ." He nodded to Frost. "We call *goben* like Frost here *jintagoben*, 'tiny goblins,' *zaj*. In the other fist, a few *goben* get *maja* big, like Lead."

"*Skerbo* folk call me a troll, but it're *nai* true. I're just a big goblin. A *kijakgob*."

"Do *nai* call these humans '*skerbo*,' Lead," Frost corrected his brother. "It're *nai* nice."

"Sorry." Leadpipe looked genuinely apologetic.

"It's okay. Pleased to meet you, Bohorikit." Billy was proud he'd managed to remember the giant goblin's first name.

But the huge goblin bristled. "Who you think you are, me mother?"

Frost quickly stepped between his brother and Billy. "Leadpipe! He do *nai* mean nothing by that. He're just a stranger here."

Frost turned to Billy. "You should *nai* ever use a *gob*'s true name unless it're a trial or a marriage or whatnot. Otherwise it're an insult."

"I . . . I didn't mean it," Billy said. He knew that the giant goblin could probably rip him in half with his bare hands. Billy looked up at Leadpipe. "Now it's my turn to be sorry."

"Then we're even," said the giant. "Call me Leadpipe. Or Lead."

"There," Hop said, "that're settled."

But as distracting as meeting Lead had been, Billy hadn't forgotten the reason they'd come to Frost's home in the first place. "Lexi," he said to Frost. "Have you fixed her up yet?"

Frost shook his head. "*Nai*. Just about to try. This way . . ."

Frost walked between his giant brother's legs through a curtain and into the main room of his house. Leadpipe scrunched himself back into a corner, allowing Hop and Billy to follow.

Skerbo, Sawtooth fumed. There was a *skerbo* in Kiranok. A dirty, night-blind, hairy, blunt-toothed human in his city.

Sawtooth listened to his enforcers with growing frustration. Apparently the thing had walked brazenly right through the Underway. A male, dark-haired, brownish-pink, not much more than a child, it had somehow evaded the mob, escaped his elite guards, and vanished into the city.

Sawtooth tried to keep his considerable temper in check as his enforcers sputtered excuses for letting the human escape. He'd once seen a puppet show where the villain had executed his followers for failing to capture the hero. At the time, he'd found it annoying and amateurish. If a leader killed his loyal retainers whenever they let him down, he'd soon have no supporters left. But for once, Sawtooth sympathized with the villainous puppet. It would feel good to kill someone right about now, and not just because he hated humans with all his heart and soul. The general's plan for Kiranok was at a critical juncture, and a human in the city threatened everything, his position, his power, his very life.

All because of some worthless prophecy.

Better than executing his own soldiers, Sawtooth wished that he could go back in time and kill a few prophets. In his experience, all oracles did was fill folks' heads with false hopes, overblown expectations, and dangerous dreams.

A small part of Sawtooth wondered what that said about him. After all, weren't his dreams and his hopes rooted in the prophecies of the Dark Lady? But he'd met the Dark Lady himself. She was different. She was real. He'd seen her work miracles. And he was determined to make everything she'd promised come true. If he had to kill a *skerbo* or two to do it, so much the better.

"Find him," Sawtooth ordered his soldiers. "Find this human boy. And bring me his head."

The main room of Frost and Leadpipe's small home was a cramped chamber that served as a combination living room, kitchen, dining room, and library. Mostly library. There were books everywhere, scattered across the simple wooden table, piled on the two chairs (one tiny, one extra large), stacked along the mantle of the sputtering, smoky fireplace, and filling every available inch of the three bookcases jammed into the tiny space. Billy found Kurt sitting on the floor, crammed between the books, eating what looked like oatmeal. From his expression, it didn't taste very good. Seeing him miserable made Billy smile. But not for long.

"Lexi?" Billy asked again.

"In the bed nook," said Frost, moving across the room to the far wall. Sweeping aside a ratty drape, the tiny wizard revealed a bed-sized cubbyhole carved into the stone. Lexi was inside, dozing on a simple mattress of layered blankets.

"I gived her a potion to help her rest and reduce the pain and fever. Cleaned the wound and washed it with poultice so her blood will *nai* go to poison. Now I just have to do the spell. Problem are, it're a nasty tough one. I're only good at dark magic. That'll work to make her sleep or stop bleeding. But it're *nai* so good at healing and growing and such."

Lexi's leg still looked terrible. Though Frost had cleaned up the blood and rewrapped the break, Billy could make out gashed skin and protruding bone even through the bandages. It made him feel nauseous.

"Still, if you *nai* try, you *nai* win. So everyone join hands. I're going to need all the energy I can get," Frost said.

Billy gently took Lexi's hand. She stirred a little,

half-asleep, and squeezed his hand back. She looked so helpless, so unlike her usual spunky self.

"It's going to be okay, Lexi," Billy said.

Hop took Billy's hand. The goblin's hand felt like a worn leather glove full of marbles. Hop held out his hand to Kurt, smiling. Kurt looked at Hop's hand like it was poisonous.

"You're *nai* afeared, are you?" Hop asked slyly.

With an angry glare, Kurt got to his feet and took Hop's hand, then joined hands with Leadpipe (who had to crawl to get into the main room). Lead reached out and put a single massive finger on Frost's tiny back.

With that, Frost reached into the bed-nook and carefully placed his hand on Lexi's broken leg, completing the circle. Immediately, the room grew colder. Billy felt a deep chill. The light faded as dark energy gathered around Frost. The goblin wizard whispered an incantation, intense but too quiet for Billy to make out the words. Then, in a burst, the dark energy rushed down Frost's body and poured through his hand onto Lexi's broken leg.

Billy felt his own various bumps and bruises chill and fade as Frost's healing magic rippled through the circle. But that was nothing compared to what was happening to Lexi. Her bandages unwrapped on their own accord as darkness played across her wound. Amazingly, pieces of shattered bone pulled themselves back into place and began knitting together. Lexi gasped a little, her eyes fluttering open as the magic worked to heal her leg.

But the process was slow. Halting. Uncertain. The little wizard redoubled his efforts, visibly straining from the energy required to maintain the spell.

"Concentrate!" Leadpipe said as his tiny brother's chanting became even more urgent. "Think healing thoughts."

Billy closed his eyes and tried to do just that. He thought about Lexi's leg. Thought about it repairing itself, the bone sinking into its proper position, the flesh and veins and nerves and muscle and skin all growing healthy. Perfect again.

"Harder!" Leadpipe bellowed "*Maja!* Give it all you can!"

Billy wished with all his might that Lexi would get better. He knew she would get better. She was already getting better. He had to convince himself of that. *She's getting better. She's better now!*

Frost stopped his incantation. Light and heat returned to the room. The spell was done.

Billy could no longer feel his own injuries. Frost's magic had certainly done him some good. But what about Lexi's leg? Billy cautiously opened his eyes and looked at Lexi.

She wasn't better. Well, she was slightly better. She was awake, though groggy. The bone had sunk back beneath the skin. But it was still shattered, and Lexi's skin and leg muscles were still torn.

Frost slumped in exhaustion, looking crestfallen. "I're sorry. It're the best I can do."

Billy started to let go of Lexi's hand, but to his surprise, Lexi gripped him even harder.

"More," she muttered, as if still in a dream.

"Wait," Billy said to the others. "Don't let go. We have to keep trying."

To Billy's surprise, everyone listened to him, keeping their hands linked. But Frost shook his head, sadly. "It're *nai* good. I can *nai* fix—"

Before he could finish his sentence, there was a bright flash and a rush of hot wind. Billy broke out in a sweat. The hearth fire, once smoldering, roared up into an inferno. Overpowering waves of light and heat filled the room.

Lexi's hand felt red hot; it was all Billy could do to keep his grip. Trying to ignore the heat, Billy looked at her injured leg. He could see a fiery red light playing over the wound and the bone *growing back together*. Before his eyes, the break repaired itself, then the muscles and flesh and skin sealed shut.

The light and heat faded away. Lexi's hand felt normal again. Billy realized he'd been holding his breath. He let it out in a slow exhale of relief.

"She's okay." Billy could barely believe what he was seeing. "She's going to be okay." Billy turned to Frost. "You did it."

But the little goblin looked every bit as stunned as Billy. "It are *nai* me. That are the white. Light magic. Fire. I're *nai* capable of such things."

"*Nai* goblin're able to work light magic," Hop explained. "Only humans."

Frost picked up a small brass compass from a shelf, muttered a spell over it, and then pointed it at Billy, watching the needle with a critical eye. "It're *nai* you." He moved the compass toward Kurt.

"It sure wasn't me," Kurt said. "I have no idea how any of this stuff works. I just keep hoping I'll wake up, and you'll all turn out to be a seriously weird dream."

Frost shook his head. "This're *nai* dream." He double-checked the compass. "But you're *nai* light-worker neither."

Billy jumped to the obvious conclusion. "So if it wasn't me or Kurt . . ."

"It're her," Frost confirmed, holding the compass over Lexi, who had lapsed back into a deep sleep. Billy could see the needle spinning rapidly in the casing. "She used light magic to heal herself."

Billy looked at Lexi. She seemed healthy and whole, completely recovered from everything she'd been through.

"Lexi?" Billy said, trying to absorb one final shock in a long day full of unbelievable events. "Lexi is a witch?"

As the fire guttered out and the room grew dark, Hop watched the humans sleep, absentmindedly flicking back and forth from normal vision to redsight. Hop liked the way redsight made the world look. It blurred the edges, dispelling the darkness and imbuing his vision with a soft, warm glow. Somehow, everything looked more peaceful through redsight. But it lacked detail, precision. Hop crinkled the muscles around his eyes, restoring his normal vision. Shadows replaced the glow. With day vision, he could see less, but what he could see was clearer. And much less reassuring.

The sleeping human children, soft red-orange glows in redsight, looked all too young with day vision, all too fragile. It was hard for the one-eared goblin to believe that his future, the future of his entire people, might depend on them. Confused, lost, and weak, how could they possibly free Kiranok from Sawtooth and his mad plans? Could they really prevent the goblins' impending destruction?

Hop tried to convince himself that all was not lost. The big yellow-haired male, Kurt, showed promise. Add in the fact that the small female could work light magic, and there still might be hope. It all came down to prophecy, prophecies centuries old and half remembered. If the stories were accurate, if the ancient oracles spoke the truth, if the prophets and their cryptic predictions hadn't been misinterpreted, then the goblins' salvation was in this room, sleeping.

But the Dark Lady had claimed prophetic insight too. And look where that had gotten folks. Hop knew his people's situation was grim and getting worse. The Hanorian Army of Light marched closer to Kiranok every day. The goblins were dispirited and broken, their Warhorde shattered, their hopes frayed to the breaking point. Sawtooth's grandiose plans for a counterattack guaranteed more death and defeat. Whether the prophecies were real or not, Hop's people needed a miracle.

So Hop would give them a king.

A king to save them. That's what the opening of the Eye had promised, and that was what Hop planned to deliver. If that meant risking the lives of three human children, possibly even sentencing them to death, well, what were the lives of three outlanders compared to the survival of his entire race? It was a cost he'd have to pay.

So why was he having such a hard time falling asleep?

Lexi dreamed of fire. Not a nice, tame fire like the ones her father would build on foggy nights to warm their house. She dreamed of blazing infernos that devoured everything in their paths. In her dreams, though she walked through the raging fire all around her, she didn't burn. The flames destroyed everything around her, but they tickled when they touched her. Inside the fire, Lexi felt safe, comfortable, and warm.

And in the crackling and hissing, Lexi could hear a faint, scratchy voice. The flames were speaking to her: "Let us in. Let us out. Let us out, let us in."

Billy woke to the smell of frying eggs. Kurt was already up, sitting in a corner, surrounded by books, looking surly and miserable. Billy avoided eye contact with the quarterback. Though part of him blamed Kurt for the events that brought him here, he didn't want to get into it right now. All he really cared about was Lexi. Was she okay? Had the strange events of the previous night really healed her? Billy checked the sleeping nook. Inside, Lexi was just opening her eyes.

"Do I smell eggs?" were the first words out of her mouth.

In response, Hop called out from across the room, "Just the one egg, but it're from a mountain *arrok*, so it're plenty big."

Lexi's eyes went wide when she saw Hop, who was using a large iron pan to cook a single huge egg over Frost's simple wood stove.

"Am I really seeing that? It's not shock or something from the broken leg?"

"Your leg's not broken," Billy said. "Not anymore."

Lexi felt the spot where the break had been. It was completely healed, though there was a long, somewhat ragged scar. "I remember . . . a cave? Then goblins. And a city. I thought it was a dream."

"It was all real."

Billy brought Lexi up to date on their adventure so far. She had been semiconscious for some of the time, and though she'd initially dismissed what she'd experienced as a fever dream, it didn't take long for her to get used to the idea that everything she half remembered since breaking her leg had actually happened.

Unfortunately, that also meant it didn't take her long to start asking uncomfortable questions, starting with, "How do you think we got here?"

I brought us here, Billy thought. But he didn't say it. It sounded too crazy. Plus, Billy didn't want to admit he was responsible for stranding himself, Lexi, and Kurt in this bizarre alien world. So instead, he sputtered, "I don't know."

Lexi's response surprised him. "Maybe it was me."

"You?"

"Well, you're saying I'm a witch or something. So maybe I magicked us here somehow, without even realizing it."

"*Nai.*" Billy and Lexi turned and saw Hop splitting the huge scrambled egg into segments and spooning it onto battered metal plates. "It're *nai* you. It're the King."

"The King?" Kurt asked. Apparently he'd been listening attentively to the conversation as well.

"The *Heir* to the King, are more precise," Frost said. "The priestesses and prophets say only the Heir of the King can bring folks from your world to our'n." Frost grabbed a plate of egg for himself. "*Yob'rikit*, that smell good. *Ganzi.*"

"Bring me some," said Leadpipe, poking his head in from the entrance hall.

"So us being here. A goblin did that?" Billy said, trying to get the conversation back on track.

"A human," Frost said. "The Goblin King are always a human."

"Wait, but if this king is always human, then why were those goblins trying to kill me?" Billy asked.

"'Cause our war with the humans are a fresh wound, and the Goblin King are an old legend. One *nai* everyone believe these days," Hop explained. "Eat. I'll tell you the tale, *zaj.*"

Hop handed out breakfast. He'd sautéed the giant egg with mushrooms, then spiced it with salt, garlic, and a little bit of hot pepper. It was delicious.

As they ate, Hop told the story of the Goblin King. "Once, long ago, our folks ruled all of the Seven Lands.

From the Mother Mountain all the way east to the Endless Water, from the Erg of Lost Years in the south to Hartwood in the north. Then the humans comed. They sailed here from o'er the sea, in their thousands and tens of thousands. They sayed they needed a new place to live, that they only wanted the coastlands. Us *goben* do *nai* like living near the waters much. So we welcomed them, at first. Then they started taking more and more. Until we haved *nai* choice but to fight back . . . to go to war.

"Back in the old times, we goblins only maked things out of stone and bone and such. But they haved iron and steel. They haved horses and engines of war and sailing ships. They winned that first war. Many goblins died.

"Then when things looked darkest, a man appeared from the depths of Mother Mountain. His name were Piast Kolodziej. He were a stranger in this land, human, but *nai* Hanorian. He were lost, alone, and afeared. He goed to the Hanorians for help, but they thinked him an evil sorcerer and tryed to burn him at the stake.

"We saved him. And good thing too. Turned out, even though Piast were just a peasant where he comed from, he were smart and strong and best of all, he were a wheelwright. He knowed how to make iron and wagons and such. Since we helped him, showed him hospitality and such, he teached us his knowledge, helped us fight, gived us tools and weapons to match what the Hanorians used against us. Thanks to the Wheelwright, we holded on to the hills and forests, the high plains and mountains. In gratitude, we maked him king.

"After that, he leaded us for many years. There were peace and happiness and all the like. Finally, though, the Wheelwright decided to go back home, to his own world and his native land . . . a place called Pole-land."

"Pole-land?" Kurt perked up when he heard that. "You mean Poland? This guy Piast was Polish?"

Frost answered, "*Zaj*. Polish. From a town on Goplo Lake."

"Goplo Lake? I've been there," Kurt said, surprised. "My dad is half-Polish. He made us go there on vacation."

Hop nodded. "Piast the Wheelwright, he promised that whenever we needed help, *zaj*, one of his sons or grandsons or grandgrandsons or so forth would come to Mother Mountain and lead us against our enemies. Ten times now, that're happened. Ten sons of Piast have appeared in our times of need. Ten times they've saved us."

"More or less," Frost muttered. No one but Billy seemed to hear the little wizard, but Billy got the impression there was more to the story than Hop was saying.

"You keep saying sons or grandsons," Lexi said. "So it's always a boy?"

"Course," Leadpipe said. "Kings're boys, *zaj*?"

"Typical," Lexi groused.

"Wait. You think one of us . . ." Lexi looked at Kurt and Billy skeptically. "One of them . . . is the heir to this King Piast of yours?"

Frost nodded. "Us *goben* have *nai* layed eyes on *nai* Goblin King in over two hundred years. But we're in bad trouble. The humans have decided to kill us all, to finish the war now and forever. If we ever needed one of Piast's heirs, it're now."

"So that mean our savior are here," said Hop confidently, locking eyes with one of the boys. "Right in front of me."

Kurt swallowed nervously. Hop was looking right at him.

"It're you, Kurt. You're the Goblin King."

CHAPTER FIVE
Making Someone King Isn't Easy

L exi was losing patience. She'd been hiding in a narrow tunnel for over an hour now. It was cold and wet and the ceiling was low and her feet were getting tired from standing on the uneven stone. "This may be the stupidest thing I've ever done," she grumped to Billy, who was crouched just ahead of her.

"It'll all work out," Kurt assured her. He was a few yards ahead of Billy at the front of the line.

"Sure, now that you're going to be king, everything is great," Lexi sniped back. Kurt turned toward her angrily, but Lexi didn't back down. "Try it, jockboy. I wonder if I can turn you into a frog or something." Lexi wiggled her fingers. "Alakazam!"

Despite himself, Kurt flinched. But nothing happened; Kurt remained decidedly un-frog-like.

"Sucker," Lexi said evilly. She had to admit, being a wizard was fun. Even if she had no idea how it actually worked.

"Leave him alone, Lexi," Billy said. Lexi couldn't believe it. Was Billy actually defending Kurt? "He's actually being pretty brave," Billy continued. "I mean, he's the one they're going to come after first if this all goes wrong."

Kurt paled a little at that. Everyone went quiet. Even Lexi withheld her instinctual snarky reply. She'd expected Billy to join her attack on Kurt, and her new friend's honest appraisal of the arrogant quarterback took the wind out of her sails. Lexi knew that they were about to do something extremely dangerous, and if everything didn't go exactly as planned, they'd be in a lot of trouble.

After all, making someone king isn't easy.

"It's going to be fine," Lexi said to Kurt, who was looking increasingly doubtful. "You'll be wearing that crown in no time." But her reassurance fell flat. Billy and Kurt were lost in thought. Lexi suspected they were doing the same thing she was—going over all the ways their plan could fail.

It had seemed reasonable when Hop first presented it. The large, uncut ruby set in the Goblin Crown was supposed to glow when it was worn by a true descendent of Piast the Wheelwright. It had already pulsed to announce their arrival in the cavern. The goblins' bullying military dictator, General Sawtooth, hadn't dared put it on himself. Hop said the ruby in the Crown would only shine for the true King, and Sawtooth knew that didn't mean him. So the Crown sat on its shelf in the Hall of Kings, untouched and unworn. All Kurt had to do was put on the Crown. The ruby would shine with a bright red light, and the goblins, even Sawtooth, would acknowledge Kurt's royal majesticness.

Hop said the biggest problem would be getting Kurt into the chamber where the Crown was kept. After the near disaster with Billy on the Underway, Hop didn't want to take chances trying to disguise the humans. Unfortunately, the Hall of Kings, where the Goblin Crown was on display, was heavily guarded, protected by both *Glinkspangen*, literally "Copperplates," the Kiranok City Guards, of which Hop was a member, and by soldiers owing allegiance to General Sawtooth. Billy had said the whole thing was like a boss level in a computer game. Unfortunately, there were too many patrolling monsters to risk a direct assault.

Hop agreed. "Time for the creepy-crawly," as Hop had put it.

Hop had led Lexi, Billy, and Kurt to this passageway, explaining that it was an old servants' entrance to the Hall of Kings. The passageway ended in an old metal door, welded shut, still sturdy despite decades of disuse. Hop planned to report for duty at his guard job in the Hall. Frost, Leadpipe, and some of their goblin friends would enter as pilgrims. As soon as the way was clear, Frost would blast open the sealed door, Lexi, Billy, and Kurt would rush into the Hall of Kings, protected by Hop, Leadpipe, and their allies, and Kurt would don the Goblin Crown. The ruby would shine red, everyone would hail Kurt as King, and Kurt, following Hop's "suggestions," would save the goblins from destruction. Epic win.

Which is why they were in this tight little passageway. Waiting.

Lexi hoped Hop knew what he was doing. The goblin Copperplate seemed smart and competent, and the plan made sense, but even though Hop was a goblin, he was still a boy goblin. And boys, in Lexi's experience, weren't nearly as smart as they thought they were.

Plus, Lexi worried that Hop's fear for his people might be making him reckless. Lexi knew that if some terrible doom were threatening every human on Earth, she'd willingly risk the lives of three goblins if it might make a difference.

Still, Hop, Frost, and their allies had rescued Lexi, Billy, and Kurt from the cave. She'd probably be dead right now if not for their help. In the stories Lexi had read, the goblins were always the villains, but Lexi felt confident that *these* goblins were the good guys. Sure, they had yellow eyes and fangs. Some of them even had horns. But Lexi knew better than to judge them just because of the way they looked. If anyone knew what it was like to be prejudged for being small and dark-skinned, it was Lexi. That was one thing she figured she had in common with the goblins . . . and Billy. They were all different. Outsiders.

According to Hop, the Hanorians wanted to exterminate the entire goblin race. So if Lexi had to pick sides, she figured she should help the people being threatened with genocide, not the ones trying to commit it. If things were really as bad as Hop said, helping the goblins was the right thing to do.

So long as it didn't get them killed.

Hop surveyed the Hall of Kings. He didn't like what he saw. Sawtooth had ordered the ten royal statues draped in black cloth, concealing their human features. Hop figured Sawtooth didn't want any reminders of what the previous Kings had actually looked like. The general had packed the room with dozens of soldiers, armored in plate mail, great helms, and kite shields, and armed with brutal barbed maces. Sawtooth himself sat on the throne, holding court with his key advisors. His personal bodyguards, five huge *kijakgoben*, stood close at hand. In addition to the general's personal retinue, twenty Copperplates kept guard around the Hall—two at each door, another six patrolling the crowd, and four, including Hop himself, stationed by the throne.

Hop could only count on maybe half the Copperplates to fight for him. Aside from that, Hop's "army" consisted of the twenty-three goblins who'd been with him when he'd found the humans. They were scattered through the crowd, waiting for the action to start. The odds were definitely not in his favor.

He glanced at Frost, standing by the sealed servants' entrance, waiting for Hop's signal. Leadpipe was at Frost's side, along with ten of Hop's followers. Once Frost began the spell to blast through the old metal door that protected the entrance, the little wizard would need all the help he could get. Everyone in the Hall of Kings would sense the spell's gathering power, and it wouldn't be hard to spot Frost when the dark energy began swirling around him. Wizards were powerful, but fragile. One lucky arrow shot or a well-placed mace blow and Frost would be dead before he could trigger his spell.

Hop did the math again. Four heartbeats or so for Frost to blast open the tunnel. Another five heartbeats for Kurt to rush the throne and put on the Crown. A few more beats for the crowd to react to the light of the Eye. They'd need to survive for ten or maybe fifteen heartbeats.

Hop figured Sawtooth's senior advisors would stay out of the fight; they were soft old *goben*, armchair generals, merchants, bankers, and politicians. Still, Sawtooth was a formidable warrior. He had forty-five soldiers. The five *kijakgoben* bodyguards. Nine or ten Copperplates would probably back Hop, but the other nine or ten would side with the general. That gave Sawtooth sixty-one backers against Hop's thirty-five. Nearly two-to-one odds, favoring Sawtooth. Hop assumed the crowd of civilians milling about the hall would mostly run for it. The chaos would help. But as badly outnumbered as they were, Hop and his allies would be hard-pressed to buy the fifteen heartbeats they needed.

Still, Hop thought they had a chance . . . if they took Sawtooth and his supporters by surprise. If Frost got his spell off. If the little wizard's magic was powerful enough to blast open the old passageway. If Kurt was able to get to the throne in one piece. If . . . if . . . if . . .

Frost caught Hop's eye from across the room. *Are it time?*

Hop shook his head. Better to wait a little longer. Maybe Sawtooth would leave or some of his soldiers would go off duty or . . . or, well, anything. Anything that would increase the chances even a little.

Back at the throne, Sawtooth decisively slapped down a map of the Mother Mountain and her foothills. "Charge to meet 'em, I say. Take 'em afore they ever catch sight of Kiranok."

Sawtooth looked pleased with himself. His cronies nodded and praised his wisdom.

"Sun and Moon," Hop cursed under his breath. Hop had to admit, it was a brilliant plan . . . if the goal was to shatter what was left of the Warhorde and leave Kiranok utterly defenseless against the humans' vengeance. Hop struggled to keep his expression neutral in the face of such monumental stupidity. If Hop couldn't crown Kurt and depose Sawtooth, the general's plan would lead to the destruction of the entire goblin race. At times like this, Hop wished he actually believed in the gods. Then at least he could pray to calm his nerves. But Hop didn't have faith in anyone but himself. And even on that regard, he had his doubts.

So Hop clenched his teeth and watched and waited for the perfect moment.

Sawtooth felt good. The line of petitioners coming to beg for his indulgence stretched out the door. The rich and powerful of Kiranok vied for his attention. And the surviving officers of the Warhorde were slowly coming around to his idea of sallying out from Mother Mountain to meet the invading humans. Drive them back with a decisive battle, that was the surest path to victory.

True, they hadn't found the human boy. His soldiers had scoured the Underway, searched random houses, and questioned anyone remotely suspicious, all without success. The intruder was gone, but Sawtooth wasn't particularly worried. If the *skerbo* boy had disappeared, then he wasn't a problem anymore.

Runned away, probably, Sawtooth told himself. *Humans'll nai ever fight excepting they have a clear advantage. Them* skerbo *are afeared of their own shadows. Just like their bleedy Army of Light. Take 'em by surprise, throw 'em off guard, put the fright in 'em, and they'll run, sure as Night.*

Sawtooth felt confident in his plan, secure about his backers, and safe in his position. Mostly, though, he felt good because of the crowd. It didn't matter why they were here, in the Hall of Kings, whether they supported or opposed him. The important thing was that they were *here*. In their hundreds. And with so many people around him, Sawtooth could never be completely alone.

The goblins' fearsome general secretly hated being alone, had ever since childhood, when he'd been abandoned by his parents and consigned to the silent, solitary meditation of the monastery. He'd escaped that solitude by joining the Templars. He'd loved the bustle of the barracks, the formations, and even the long muddy marches, all forms of soldierly camaraderie.

Once he'd met Cutty, things had gotten even better. Others might have criticized her incessant talk, but he found it comforting. With Cutty, he never felt isolated or unloved. She was always there, always talking, nagging, and chattering.

Her untimely death had paralyzed Sawtooth with grief. He'd been unable to leave his quarters for months. Not even their daughter had been able to move him. With each day of crushing isolation, he'd sunk further into a deep, unshakable abyss.

Then the Dark Lady had entered his very soul, filled his mind with her visions, and saved him from his loneliness.

Until Solace Ridge.

After the disastrous battle, Sawtooth experienced his third and most terrible period of isolation. He'd lost both his army and his prophetess. For months, he'd skulked and scavenged, trying to escape from human lands back to his native mountains. And always, he'd been alone. In the long, desperate flight back to Kiranok, it'd been every *gob* for himself.

But now he was back where he belonged, leading his people, surrounded by his army and the crowd.

"The key to victory are numbers," Sawtooth said, pointing to an organizational chart. "We need to bring ever *gob* what can fight, and even some what can *nai*. Bring enough to terrify the *skerbo* cowards and make 'em break."

Bring so many that I'll nai *feel alone ever again,* nai
even in death.

Billy was awesome at video games. Real-time strategy,
massive multiplayers, first person shooters, he loved
them all. In their manufactured worlds, he never felt
different, never worried that he didn't belong. He appre-
ciated how the video game characters always did exactly
what they were programmed to do. Even the real people
he'd interact with online were better, somehow. Easier.
His fellow players never asked awkward questions about
Billy's parents; they didn't know about the cancer eating
away at his father; they were still there no matter what
city he and his family moved to; all they cared about
was how skillfully Billy manipulated his online avatars
to complete quests or defeat the opposition. And that
was one area where he excelled. He could expertly
organize digital armies, navigate imaginary mazes, and
coordinate multiplayer raids against mind-bogglingly
complex, computerized archnemeses. Online, Billy was
everyone's best friend.

His father didn't approve, of course. After a lifetime
working in construction, William Senior didn't put any
stock in things you couldn't touch. "Frittering." That's
what he called video games. But the sicker his father got,
the more Billy fled to the refuge of his virtual worlds.

In times of stress, Billy often imagined that his reality
was a game. Doing homework became a quest. Complete
the task to get rewards from his parents and teachers.
Navigating a new school was like entering a virtual city in
an online game. Identify and avoid the hostile characters;
find and try to befriend the helpful ones.

So while he waited in the cramped tunnel, Billy found himself mapping his current situation onto his online experiences. He, Lexi, and Kurt were about to go on a raid, like the ones in a massive online game. The object of the encounter was to put the Goblin Crown on Kurt's head. Kurt was the leader, Lexi was the wizard, and Billy—

Billy was useless. He felt like one of the nonplayer characters who'd rush into battle alongside the player-controlled heroes and immediately die at the hands of the computerized monsters. He was just cannon fodder, destined to be slaughtered in a cut-scene.

Billy looked at Kurt, who absentmindedly chewed at a cuticle as he waited next to the old metal door. Despite his handsome features and broad shoulders, at the moment, the quarterback came across more like a nervous kid than a prophesized savior. Lexi fanned herself, sweating in the warm, stuffy tunnel. She looked tiny, vulnerable, and more than a little scared.

If this had been a game, Billy would've logged off right then. He didn't want to play. His team wasn't ready. The quest was too hard. But he couldn't just hit Quit. They were stuck here. They'd made a promise. The goblins were counting on them. They had to play it through.

Even though, in this game, if they died, they wouldn't get another life.

Hop thought he'd finally found his moment. Two of Sawtooth's giant *kijakgoben* bodyguards had left the room on some errand. The general himself was busy fending off an especially insistent merchant who wanted to give him a sample of her wares. Frost had positioned himself perfectly, a few feet away from the sealed servants'

entrance but completely hidden from the remaining body-guards by one of the draped statues of the Goblin Kings. Hop was just about to give the signal . . .

When everything went wrong.

The priests and priestesses of the Night Goddess paraded into the Hall of Kings in one long, black-cloaked column. Armed Templars marched at their flanks, dressed in black tabards with a distinctive crescent moon insignia. The clerics themselves were swathed in black, with black capes, black robes, and black hoods. The only parts of them that were visible were their eyes, peeking out through tiny slits in their hoods. Hop couldn't even tell which black-robed figures were male and which were female.

The Templar at the head of the line was clearly female, though. So much so that Hop couldn't help but stare. Under her tabard, the female goblin wore fine steel chain mail, thick leather gloves, and iron-shod boots. She carried a glaive, a wicked-looking polearm with a sword-bladed head. But unlike the other Templars, she'd removed her helmet so that everyone could see her face. And what a face it was. With her dark, glossy skin, she looked like a sculpture carved from obsidian. Her features were perfectly formed, from her long, thin, elegantly pointed ears to her pale purple eyes to her strong, sharp chin. Her mouth was set in a sly grin, showing just a hint of her almost dainty fangs. When she spoke, her voice had a musical quality that made Hop want to soak in every word.

"*Wazzer*, Papa," she said, locking eyes with Sawtooth.

Hop was shocked. General Sawtooth had a daughter in the Templars?

Sawtooth's tense reply betrayed his irritation at her arrival. "Ishkinogi Slipshadows," he said.

"That're me name. Rude as it are for you to say it," the general's daughter answered, defiant.

"What do you want, Shadow?" The way Sawtooth spit out his daughter's calling-name was every bit as disrespectful as when he'd used her full name. Hop could only admire the female Templar's cool demeanor as she stood firm under her father's withering gaze.

"*Nai* what I want," she said calmly. "What they want." Shadow nodded toward the long column of waiting priests. "Appear that someone think he are a king?"

"*Ahka!* I are the King!" roared Sawtooth.

"Well then," Shadow said, "why are you *nai* wearing your crown?"

All eyes went to the Goblin Crown, sitting untouched on its shelf above the throne.

All eyes but Hop's. He looked around the room, trying to contain his panic. His plan wasn't going to work. Not with the priests here, every one of them a wizard. Not with their Templar guards putting Sawtooth on edge. Not with everyone looking at the Crown.

And then Hop realized . . . Not *everyone* was looking at the Crown. Shadow was looking at him, studying his face with a thoughtful expression.

She knew. She knew he was up to something. He had to get out of here. Make sure his followers got away. Get the humans out of the tunnel. But before he could move, before he could even take a step toward the door . . .

His world exploded.

Lexi felt flushed and feverish. The narrow tunnel had been warm and stuffy to begin with, and now, after the long wait, she felt like the walls of the tunnel were closing in around her. And the more claustrophobic she felt, the hotter it seemed to get.

"Hey," she finally broke down and asked, "is it getting hot in here?"

But before Billy or Kurt could answer, Lexi heard, "*Ahka*, you hear something?"

It was a distant goblin voice, coming from the entrance to the tunnel, unnaturally deep, reminiscent of Leadpipe's rumbling bass.

"*Zaj*. Some kinda noise up there," replied a second goblin, his voice even deeper than the first. "See anything?"

Lexi froze. Next to her, she could sense Billy and Kurt trying to stay as still and quiet as possible.

"*Ahka*," said the first goblin. "Redsight this. There're someone up there. More than one someone from the heat I're seeing,"

"Should *nai* be anybody up there. That tunnel dead-end right outside the Hall of Kings," said the second goblin. "*Wazzer*!" he called out. "What're you doing up there?"

No one was foolish enough to answer. Lexi hoped the goblins would lose interest and go away.

"*Nai* answer," said the first goblin. "*Zajnai* it're just some giant bats or something. Hard to tell from just redsight. Whatever are up there are packed so tight I can *nai* make out what glow are what."

"We should fetch 'em out, *naizaj*?" said the second goblin.

"That're a pretty tiny passage for you and me," responded the first.

If the passage was too small for them, that meant the goblins at the tunnel entrance must be giants, like Leadpipe, big and strong enough to tear Lexi, Billy, and Kurt to pieces. Lexi felt hotter than ever.

"True. But I do *nai* think that're bats. And the Tooth sayed be *maja* careful about anything out of the ordinary," said the second goblin.

"Second glance are first vision," agreed the first. Then he shouted up the tunnel, "*Ahka!* That tunnel are a dead end. So better come out now or me and Roofscraper are gonna send for some friends. Which mean we're gonna have to wait around and miss our lunches. When we get hungry, we get pretty angry, *zaj*. You do *nai* want us to get hungry, do you?"

"Maybe we should rush them," Kurt said. "I'll try to hold them off while you two run for it."

"Are you nuts?" Lexi said. "They'll kill us."

"We can hear you, idiots," barked the first goblin. "Scraper, go find us some *jintagoben* what can fight in tight tunnels. Make sure they're nice and mean."

"*Zaj*, Rumblejaw," said the other goblin. "I know just the pair."

Lexi could hear one of the large goblins, presumably Roofscraper, thudding off down the corridor. It suddenly felt ten degrees hotter in the narrow tunnel. Lexi could feel herself flush; she was having trouble breathing.

Great, we're facing down a giant goblin, and I'm having a stupid panic attack.

"Listen," Billy called to the remaining goblin, "we're not going to hurt anyone. Why don't you just leave us alone?"

"You *nai* sound like a *goben*," replied Rumblejaw thoughtfully. "Thing are, you sound kinda like a *skerbo*."

"*Nai*," said Lexi, doing her best to sound goblinish. "We're just *goben* here. *Ahka! Zaj. Ahka?*" Lexi wasn't sure about that last *ahka*, but she figured every bit helped.

Lexi heard Rumblejaw taking in a deep sniff.

"You smell like *skerbo* too," said the giant goblin. "All sweaty and clammy and moist."

Lexi realized she *was* sweating. A lot. The air around her felt like an oven. She had to get out, but there was nowhere to run. The giant goblin blocked the bottom of the tunnel, and the exit door was sealed.

"Smelling you are making me mouth water," rumbled Rumblejaw. "I *nai* have a good munch of human meat in forever."

"Meat?" Kurt said. He sounded panicky, his usual macho facade shattered. "They're going to eat us?"

The heat was unbearable now. Sweat ran down Lexi's forehead. She felt like she was going to pass out.

"So you *are* a *skerbo*!" roared Rumblejaw triumphantly.

At that moment, inside Lexi, something clicked. Or more accurately, something sparked. It was like the first time she rode her bike without training wheels, in that moment when all her nervous energy had vanished and she'd suddenly found herself flying down the hill, away from her proud father. Now, in the tunnel, despite the blazing hot air around her, Lexi felt calm, centered, the eye of the firestorm.

Lexi spoke in a tense, fierce voice, "Kurt. Duck."

"Duck?" Kurt replied, confused. He was standing behind her, between her and the sealed door.

"Duck!" Lexi shouted as her entire body burst into flames, heat whipping around her like a bonfire.

Kurt ducked.

Just in time.

A stream of fire blazed from Lexi's eyes and blasted into the sealed door. The old metal door buckled, bent, boiled . . .

Then it disintegrated with a fiery roar.

CHAPTER SIX
The Foolishness of Trying to Change the World

The door exploded into a thousand pieces. Not from inside the Hall of Kings, as Hop and Frost had planned. And not with ice. Instead, it exploded *from the outside*. With fire.

Panic spread quickly through the Hall. Ordinary goblins, come to pay homage to Sawtooth or to plead for favors or just to see the self-proclaimed Goblin King, fled in a crush for the exits. The general's followers reacted to the explosion with confusion. A handful ran toward the shattered door. More moved to guard Sawtooth himself, while still others fought to maintain order among the terrified petitioners. Across the room, the Templars of the Night Goddess closed ranks. On Shadow's order, they formed a circle, interlocking their shields to create a protective wall around the Goddess's black-clad clergy. Shadow slammed on her helmet and readied her glaive, fixing her eyes on the smoking hole in the wall where the old servants' entrance had been.

To Hop's relief, his own allies remained calm. Though the explosion wasn't quite what they were expecting, they stuck to the plan and quickly took up their assigned positions. Leadpipe stepped forward to shield his smaller brother from potential attacks while Copperplates loyal to Hop rushed the blasted doorway, ready to protect the emerging humans. Recovering his balance, Hop put his plan into action. Ready or not, it was time.

"General!" he shouted, moving toward Sawtooth. "We need to get you outa here. It're *nai* safe!"

Sawtooth's giant bodyguards obviously had the same idea. The three remaining *kijakgoben* were already at their master's side.

"The Copperplate're right. Time to go," said the lead bodyguard.

Sawtooth looked around. Hop held his breath. Everything was riding on this. If the human children were still alive, Hop had to get the general away from the Crown before they came out of the tunnel. But Sawtooth hesitated. Hop could tell that the crafty old general didn't want to look cowardly by leaving in the middle of a crisis.

"This're a possible *skerbo* attack!" Hop said loudly. "General Sawtooth are going to check the entrance fortifications and rally the Warhorde. Everyone make way!"

Sawtooth nodded at Hop. The Copperplate's announcement gave him an excuse to leave gracefully. "Everything are under control," the general said to the crowd. Then, with his *kijakgoben* around him, Sawtooth strode purposefully toward the main exit from the Hall of Kings.

Which is when Kurt charged into the room.

Billy rushed to Lexi's side as soon as the heat faded from the blast. Lexi slumped to the floor, out of breath and glassy-eyed.

"What did I do?" she gasped.

"Magic," Billy explained. "Again."

"Oh, good." Lexi looked relieved. "You saw it too. I thought I was going crazy."

"The door. It's open," Kurt said, stunned.

Billy realized instantly what that meant. Just like a multiplayer video game, once someone on a team attacks a monster, the encounter starts whether the other players are ready or not. Lexi had triggered Hop's plan. There was no time to lose.

"You have to go!" Billy shouted to Kurt. "Put on the Crown. Now!"

To Kurt's credit, he didn't hesitate. "I got this." The quarterback charged through the door.

Billy could hear the resulting shocked cries of "*skerbo*" from inside the throne room, but to be honest, he was more worried about Lexi than Kurt.

"Can you stand up?" he asked.

"I think so."

As the sounds of fighting echoed from the Hall of Kings, Billy helped Lexi rise unsteadily to her feet. Then Lexi gasped in alarm, looking behind him.

"They're coming!"

Looking back, Billy saw two small goblins moving up the tunnel toward them. Though the *jintagoben* were no bigger than Frost, each carried a pair of wicked chopping knives, and they looked eager to use them.

"Dinnertime!" shouted one of the tiny goblins in an unnervingly high-pitched voice.

"Yum," his companion agreed as he advanced rapidly up the passageway.

Billy and Lexi exchanged a quick look. They both knew that, whatever was happening in the Hall of Kings, it had to be better than facing these two savage little goblins in the cramped space of the tunnel.

As Lexi staggered out of the tunnel supported by Billy, she saw Leadpipe grab a hapless soldier and hurl the unfortunate goblin into a crowd of Sawtooth's followers. Just behind his hulking brother, Lexi could make out Frost standing in the center of his own personal blizzard. Wind and snow swirled around the little wizard. A sheet of ice spread from his feet, covering the stone floor and making everyone near him slip and fall. To Lexi, the entire battle seemed surreal. Channeling heat and fire through her body may have reduced the door to scrap, but it had left her dazed. In her eyes, the world was obscured by a wavering heat shimmer, and the people moved in herky-jerky slow motion.

Trying to focus past her exhaustion, Lexi watched as Kurt dashed toward the Crown. Using all his quarterback moves, Kurt dodged one goblin soldier, stiff-armed another, ducked under a thrown spear, and juked his way past a third charging enemy. Then Lexi saw a giant goblin in heavy armor coming up rapidly behind him. The icy floor didn't slow the giant at all. Heavy feet shod in hobnail-studded boots crunched through the ice like it wasn't even there. In four thundering strides, the thing was almost on top of Kurt.

Billy shouted a warning before Lexi could even react. "Kurt! Look out!"

Kurt turned and saw the massive goblin looming over him. But it was too late. There was no way he could escape.

Lexi tried to summon more fire to save the quarterback, but whatever power she'd channeled in the tunnel didn't respond this time. She couldn't summon the fire, and because of that, Kurt was going to die. Lexi staggered dizzily, too spent to help, too tired to cry.

Then Hop charged the giant with his long barbed spear, impaling Kurt's attacker in the right thigh. The big goblin howled in pain.

"Protect the human!" shouted Hop to the crowd and his fellow guards. "He're the Wheelwright's Heir!"

The Hall of Kings was already in chaos, but Hop's pronouncement made the place go completely mad. Goblins who'd been trying to flee suddenly rushed back into the room, shouting, "The Goblin King" and "The Heir! The Heir!" The Copperplates loyal to Hop redoubled their efforts to keep Sawtooth's soldiers away from Kurt. Some guards fighting for the general even switched sides in the middle of the battle, suddenly battling to protect Hop and Kurt instead of trying to keep the human boy from getting to the Crown.

"Traitor!" Sawtooth roared at Hop, using his gigantic sword to cleave through the shield of one of the turncoat guards. "You side against us with the *skerboen*? You're dead! You hear me? I'll make you wish you stayed in your mother's womb!"

Hop already regretted a lot of things, but being born wasn't at the top of his list. Luckily, Sawtooth wasn't anywhere near him . . . yet. Unfortunately, Hop had other problems. He ducked as the giant goblin he'd speared swung a huge fist at his head. Another narrow escape. Hop reminded himself there was a reason he usually hid during battles.

To make matters worse, Hop's spear was stuck in the giant goblin's leg, so he was basically unarmed. He considered drawing his boot dagger, but the thought of facing an enraged *kijakgob* with such a tiny blade made him feel like a mouse trying to bite a hawkbear. Better to concentrate on defense. On the bright side, at least having a spear stuck in his leg was slowing down the giant . . . a little.

As Hop dodged another attack from the hobbled giant, he felt a cold wind rising at his back. A few yards away, Frost redoubled his efforts to protect the humans. Snow and wind whipped around him. The wizard sent tendrils of ice creeping across the floor, reaching as far as the priests and priestesses of the Night Goddess, still ensconced behind the shield wall of their Templars. But a black-swathed priestess stepped forward and glared at the ice. It stopped expanding as if terrified to go any farther.

Which was when Hop's towering opponent reached down and yanked the barbed spear out of his leg. The *kijakgob* grinned, showing off an impressive set of fangs. "I're going to eat you without salt," he rumbled as he swung the spear shaft at Hop's head.

"Over here, quick," Billy said, pulling Lexi toward a tall, draped stone statue. It wasn't much shelter, but it would have to do.

Lexi followed as best she could. And a good thing too. The second she moved toward the statue, a huge javelin thrown by one of Sawtooth's soldiers clanged off the wall. Billy swallowed hard. If Lexi hadn't moved, the spear would have hit her right in the head.

More stones and spears lashed toward them. Frost directed a freezing wind to deflect the missiles. The wind caught the draping over the tall statue and blew it away. To Billy's surprise, the statue portrayed a British soldier from the First World War, complete with wide-brimmed helmet, rifle, and digging tool.

But Billy didn't have long to process this strange sight. Seconds later, he spotted the two vicious little goblins with the knives emerging from the melted door. Billy ducked behind the statue of the British soldier as the *jintagoben* scanned the melee for their intended victims.

"Where're our dinner?" said one.

"And what're all the fuss about?" said the other.

"*Ahka.* Why worry? Start stabbing folks!" the first replied with a nasty grin.

"*Yob'rikit!*" said the second, gleefully wading into the crowd, slashing about with his chopping knives, seemingly unconcerned with the allegiance of his targets.

"This is not good," Billy said to Lexi as the battle raged around them. "Seriously not good at all."

Sawtooth could feel it all slipping away. His plans were dissolving, his followers turning against him. The walls of isolation were closing in.

He knew, however, that to survive a battle, a good soldier needed to exist only in the moment, to put the future out of his mind and focus on the now. Sawtooth spotted one of his *kijakgob* bodyguards battling the one-eared Copperplate who'd tried to trick him into leaving the throne room. The

Glink turncoat seemed to be the leader of the rebels. The coward dodged around the Hall of Kings, shouting orders to the humans and their traitorous goblin allies.

Live in the now, Sawtooth told himself. He decided that even if it was his last action on the face of the world, he would kill these *skerboen* invaders and *goben* traitors. Starting with the Copperplate. Sawtooth was not going down alone.

"One-Ear!" he bellowed. "I're coming for you!"

Hop reflected on the foolishness of trying to change the world. It had seemed simple enough: crown Kurt, get rid of Sawtooth, avoid a disastrous climactic battle with the humans, and hopefully save Kiranok from destruction. Unfortunately, he probably wasn't going to live long enough to save much of anything. Sawtooth was fighting furiously to reach him, determined to wreak his vengeance on Hop personally. Not only that, the general's *kijakgob* bodyguard was doing his best to make sure there wouldn't be much left of Hop by the time his master reached him.

Reluctantly, Hop finally drew the long knife he kept tucked into his boot. He knew what he had to do. The one-eared goblin dodged and ducked as best he could, then he charged the furious giant.

Hop's enemies never expected that. He spent so much time avoiding combat that whenever he attacked, they always ended up off balance. Taking a glancing blow to his shoulder, Hop closed in on the *kijakgob* and stabbed upward with his knife. He connected with a meaty thunk. He pushed the knife deeper, and the giant goblin's blood gushed out over his arm. It gave him no pleasure to take the giant's life. The *kijakgob* bodyguard was just doing his job. But given a choice between his life and another's, Hop selfishly preferred his own.

Then Sawtooth's huge sword came down right on top of Hop's head.

Hop staggered. By instinct, he'd twisted away at the last moment, so Sawtooth had hit with the flat of his blade instead of the edge, but the blow still made Hop's ears ring. Blood ran down his face from a cut to his forehead, he felt like he had to vomit, and his legs were so rubbery he could barely stand.

Hop reeled aside as Sawtooth's sword whooshed through the air again, nicking his one good ear. Goblin ears are particularly sensitive; pain shot through Hop's body, and he fell to one knee. The general raised his weapon again.

"Fire burn your soul," Sawtooth cursed.

This was it. Hop was certain he was going to die. Then he heard Kurt shouting at the top of his lungs.

"Goblins! *Wazzer!*" the human boy yelled. "Look at me!"

Sawtooth couldn't help himself. He turned from Hop toward Kurt. The human boy was standing triumphantly atop the throne, holding the Goblin Crown.

"Touchdown, baby!"

Lexi couldn't believe her eyes. The heat haze in her head had finally lifted, but she had to wonder for a moment if she was back in her fever dream. Kurt was standing on the throne with the Goblin Crown in his hands, just like Hop had planned it. Everyone in the room was staring at him, but Kurt looked right back with a confident smile. He had their attention, and he knew exactly what to do with it.

"Goblins. I am Kurt Novac, called the Quarterback. Son of David Novac, son of Robert Novac of America and Helen Krajenski of Poland, the land of Piast the Wheelwright. And I come to you as the Wheelwright's Heir."

This set off a ripple of mutters across the room, both disbelievers and believers alike whispering, "Piast" and "the Wheelwright" and "the Wheelwright's Heir."

"These are troubled times," continued Kurt. "But my ancestor promised you that whenever you were in need, one of his descendants would come to save all of goblinkind."

Lexi thought Kurt was hamming things up a bit, but it seemed to be working. The goblins around her murmured in approval. There were even a few muted cheers.

"He really likes to hear himself talk, doesn't he?" Lexi asked Billy.

"You okay?" Billy asked in turn, looking down at her with concern.

Lexi hated it when people worried about her, even though, given how she felt, Billy was probably right to wonder. Still, Lexi was more interested in what was going on with Kurt. She could see he wasn't done yet. The jock drew himself taller, getting ready for his big moment. "Shh. I want to hear this."

"So now I come to claim my rightful place," Kurt said. He was speaking more softly now, making certain that everyone had to be quiet to hear him. Despite herself, Lexi couldn't help but admire Kurt a little. He really knew how to command the spotlight. "To take my throne. To save my people." Now his voice grew loud again, triumphant, certain. "To be your king!"

With that, Kurt plunged the Goblin Crown dramatically down onto his head.

For a long moment, no one moved. Everyone just stared at Kurt, standing confidently astride the throne, grinning, the Crown on his head.

Then, finally someone spoke. To Lexi's surprise, it was one of the little goblins from the corridor.

"*Ahka*," said the tiny goblin with the giant knives. "Why're the Eye *nai* glowing?"

Indeed, the central ruby of the Goblin Crown, which Hop had said would blaze like the sun when worn by the Wheelwright's Heir, was still a dark, shadowy red. There was no glow. Not even the faintest glimmer.

"Imposter!" shouted a huge, armored goblin who could only be General Sawtooth. "Imposter!"

All eyes went to Sawtooth. "Kill him," the goblin general said calmly. "Kill the humans. Kill their allies. Kill 'em all."

Lexi tried to find the fire inside, but she was spent. There would be no explosions to save them this time. No light. With a bloodcurdling scream, the crowd of goblins surged toward Kurt, who was still standing on the throne, stunned.

"You mean . . . I'm not the King?" he asked.

Then he disappeared under a tidal wave of frenzied goblins.

CHAPTER SEVEN
Look You on the Accused

B illy awoke in complete darkness. He didn't know
where he was, how he'd gotten there, or how much
time had passed. He had vague memories of being
swarmed by goblins, of trying to protect Lexi, of seeing
Frost collapse and Leadpipe surrender, but it all seemed
distant and unreal. Billy's entire body ached, and his head
felt like it was full of mush. He tried to get up, but he
quickly realized someone had tied him up and gagged
him. From the echoes thrown off by his struggles, the
room he was in was huge, at least as big as the Hall of
Kings. The floor felt smooth and hard, like marble, and
the air smelled of incense.

Billy heard a groan and some thrashing nearby. It
sounded like Lexi. Billy scooted in her direction and
bumped into another prone body. From the masculine

grunt that Billy elicited with his awkward flailing, it had to be Kurt. So his two schoolmates were there too, tied up and gagged just like him. He found that reassuring. At least he wasn't alone.

More time passed. Billy wasn't sure if it was minutes or hours. He drifted in and out of sleep. At one point, he dreamed of his father. He saw his father wandering through the fog by the ocean, looking rail thin, even worse than after his last chemo treatment. He was carrying an old-fashioned train engineer's lantern and calling Billy's name.

"Billy! Where are you? Billy? Come home."

Billy tried to run to his father, but the fog held him back, like a million wispy ropes. He tried to shout, but the fog rushed into his mouth, filling his throat and choking off his breath. Then his father disappeared into the mists. Gone.

Billy woke up again, thrashing and sputtering into his gag. There were tears in his eyes. He told himself that the vision of his father had been a dream. But it still hurt. *Dad could be dying back home, for all I know. I may never see him again.*

As he lay on the hard floor, trying to shake off his nightmare, Billy heard a crowd of what he assumed were goblins file into the huge room. None of them spoke, but from their footfalls against the marble, Billy guessed there were hundreds of them. Maybe even thousands. It took them a long time to fill the room. Billy sensed Lexi and Kurt stirring nearby, roused by the goblins' arrival.

Once the room was full, an authoritative female voice barked, "Sit yourselfs down."

As the crowd settled to the marble floor, the female goblin continued, "This're a tribunal of the Night Goddess. There're *nai* light allowed in Her temple. *Nai* speaking or singing or interrupting or any of that nonsense. If you disturb this hearing, we'll chop you up and feed you to the poor. *Zajnai* we'll even take a bite or two ourselfs."

There were scattered chuckles at that, but the female goblin didn't sound amused. "*Ahka*, that're the only laugh you get. Now shut your chewers and open your listeners. This tribunal are beginned. The Great High Priestess Ulgarkiren Starcaller presiding."

The chamber—*The temple*, Billy thought to himself—went completely silent, except for the quiet sound of slow measured footsteps, someone walking with difficulty. Billy could hear the footfalls getting closer until they stopped only a few feet from his head.

From the vicinity of the footfalls, Priestess Starcaller spoke, her voice cracked with age. "Hear the words of the Night Goddess." Then she began to sing, surprisingly sweet and strong:

> *A bond are braked*
> *An injustice maked*
> *Peace are our birth right*
> *Safe home and hearth light*
> *Let all who witness*
> *Speak to the fitness*
> *Of the Goddess' truth-seeking*
> *Of the Goddess' law speaking*
> *And let the punishment*
> *Lead to abolishment*
> *Of all what would do us wrong.*
> *Goddess Night, hear me song.*

Starcaller's final note reverberated through the vast temple, then faded. Even Billy, tied up and on trial for his life, had to admit it was hauntingly beautiful.

"A crime're committed," Starcaller continued. "Look you on the accused."

Billy tried to straighten up and look innocent, even though he had no idea how anyone could see his expression in the darkness.

"Now hear you the particulars," Starcaller said. Then, "Shadow."

Shadow, it turned out, was the name of the female goblin who'd first addressed the crowd. Billy recognized her voice when she spoke again.

"*Wazzer*," Shadow called out. "These three humans trespassed in Kiranok. With the help of traitors among us, they blasted their way into the Hall of Kings by means of forbidden light magic, in the process of which one *gob* were killed and many more hurt. One of the humans then taked the Goblin Crown itself and putted it on his head. But the Eye *nai* glowed.

"As to the rest afore us," Shadow continued, "them are those what helped, *goben* great and small. What betrayed us to the humans. And that're the particulars."

"And this're the responsibles?" Starcaller asked.

"All but one what getted away," Shadow replied, sounding a little embarrassed. "The one what killed another *gob*. A Copperplate named Korgorog Hoprock. This Hop were the ringleader, seem like. We're looking for him now, but *nai* luck yet."

So Hop had gotten away? Billy could vaguely remember seeing the goblin leaping from the huge black throne in the Hall of Kings. *Guess that's how he got his calling-name*, Billy thought. He's a hopper. Billy figured he should be angry with the goblin soldier for abandoning them. But truthfully? He was glad at least one of his new friends had made it out.

"Are there *nai* a wizard as well?" Starcaller asked.

"This little one here. Atarikit Bluefrost."

"Casting magic what harm other *goben* are a serious crime. Add that to the particulars."

"*Zaj*, ma'am," Shadow said.

"So, are there anyone what want to speak for the responsibles?"

"I want to speak," said a small voice from the back of the room.

"I redsight you there, Zororashtag Grindacorn," Starcaller said. "How're that little daughter of your'n, Acorn? She all recovered from the croup?"

"She're right as Night, *ganzi*," Acorn answered.

Blinded by darkness, Billy had to imagine what Acorn looked like. Male. Dark-skinned, quiet, serious if a bit scattered. Then Billy realized that he was imagining his father as a goblin. It was almost comical, picturing William Senior with pointy ears and shiny yellow eyes . . . except that it reminded Billy how much he missed his dad and how badly he wanted to be home.

"You want to speak, Acorn? Speak," Starcaller said.

"Me nephew, Hammerkettle, are up there," Acorn said. "He are a good lad, underneath it all. But his father are dead, killed in the war. Like so many others. And that make Kettle angry, *zaj*? He're always going on and on about righting wrongs and bringing justice and such. So if some Copperplate asked him for help to set the world right, Kettle are the kind what'd jump to it. If you know what I're saying, ma'am."

"Them're good words, Acorn. Anyone else?"

The crowd came to life. Billy heard bodies shifting, voices calling out.

"I see," Starcaller said. "We can tell that all these *goben* have their defenders. Are there any *gob* up here what *nai* have someone to speak for 'em?"

"Surely," said a commanding voice from near Billy, "*nai* one will speak for a *gob* what used magic against his fellow *goben*." Billy recognized the voice from the battle in the Hall of Kings. It was General Sawtooth.

Despite Sawtooth's assertion, Billy heard an unmistakable bass voice boom out. "I want to say something." It was Leadpipe.

Sawtooth grumbled at that. "He are a responsible. He get nothing to say."

"Perhaps *nai*, General," Starcaller said calmly, "but I will hear him still. Speak, Bohorikit Leadpipe."

"All I want to say are that whatever happen to me brother, I want the same to happen to me," Leadpipe said. "Where he go, I go."

"Fine with me," Sawtooth said.

"This're *nai* your tribunal, General. This're the Goddess's," Shadow said with an edge in her voice.

Starcaller's response was more measured. "You're a good brother, Bohorikit Leadpipe. I promise to consider your request." Billy heard robes rustling, as if Starcaller had turned back to the crowd. "I'll rule first on the *goben* what helped, excluding Leadpipe and Frost, and the fugitive Hop. All you others, listen to me justice."

The temple went so quiet that Billy could hear his own heart beating.

"All you *goben* are good *goben*," Starcaller said, "but you maked mistakes. You looked for a hero, and you trusted wrong. Folk do that from time to time. Especially when they are afeared. But none of you touched the Crown, so you're *nai* guilty of sacrilege. And none of you killed, so you are *nai* murderers either, praise the Goddess. That leave only bad judgment. More *maja* bad judgment than an old *svagob* like me care to see in her dotage. Such foolishness need a penance or more foolishness will come, *zaj*? So I rule this. Each and all of you must leave Kiranok and go to the Fastness at Coaler's Break. There you're to work for the Goddess until I say you have your heads fastened back on right."

Billy felt a surge of relief. If he understood Starcaller, that meant the goblins who'd tried to help crown Kurt would be going to a kind of prison. It might not be very nice, but it was better than getting killed.

"That're all?" Sawtooth said unhappily. "Sewing robes and cleaning cells and growing food for monks are barely a punishment."

"I promised justice, *nai* one *jeg* more nor less," Starcaller said, daring Sawtooth to object.

No objection came. Starcaller continued, "Now, as to the brothers, Frost and Leadpipe, I rule this. Magic are a mighty and deep responsibility. Use it wrong and it make you go mad. Fling it about like it're nothing, and the madness will come sure as daybreak. The law are clear. If you use magic without thought, you're a danger to everyone around you. And you must die to protect 'em. You hear me, Atarikit Bluefrost?"

"I do," Frost said, speaking for the first time. "And I accept your justice."

"Right you should," Starcaller said gravely. "I send you and your brother to the Fastness as well. There to wait 'til the signs are right for execution by the Goddess's embrace."

"Better," Sawtooth said.

"Enough from you," Shadow snapped. "This're the Goddess's house and you are but a guest."

"Apologies. I're just expressing me appreciation of the priestess's fair and just ruling."

"Keep your appreciation to yourself."

As the goblins bickered, Billy tried to keep from shaking. "Execution." That's what Starcaller had said. Frost and Leadpipe were going to die. Because he'd brought himself, Kurt, and Lexi here. It was all his fault.

"And finally to the humans," Starcaller said, her voice grave. "Will anyone speak for them?"

Billy knew what was coming. Death. Death for him, death for Lexi and for Kurt. To his own surprise, he shouted out loud, trying to make himself heard through his gag. He was trying to say, "Let me talk, let me talk." But all that came out was, "Lll meh lk, lll meh lk."

"Let the human speak," Starcaller said.

Billy felt rough hands on his shoulders, then someone yanked away his cloth gag.

"Name yourself, boy," Starcaller ordered, not unkindly.

"I'm William Tyler Smith Junior," Billy managed. "They call me Billy."

"Speak, Wilyamtylersmith Junyer. Called Billy."

Billy swallowed nervously. It was strange, speaking to a huge crowd and not being able to see anyone. On the other hand, *not* seeing the goblins made it easier for Billy to trick himself into thinking things were more normal than they really were. All he had to do was pretend he was talking in class or at the school auditorium. Then Billy remembered . . . he hated talking in class.

"Umm . . . uhhh . . ." Billy sputtered.

"*Nai* much of an argument so far," Starcaller said.

"Wait. No. I have something to say." Billy spit out the words as quickly as he could, hoping the goblin priestess would listen. "We only want to go home. That's all. We don't even know how we got here. We were lost and freaked out, and Hop found us. So when he said that Kurt was a king, and we had to get him crowned, that it was important and would save people, we believed it. But we weren't trying to hurt anyone or break any laws. We realize now that we shouldn't have done what we did, and we're sorry. We just want to go home."

Billy braced himself for Starcaller's response, praying what he'd said would make a difference.

"Fate're funny," said Starcaller after a long moment. "It send us strange places and make us do strange things. But at the end of the night, it're always *us* what're doing the doing, *us* what make our own actions and what must live through the consequences. I know you are young and *nai* from this land. I even know you probably meant to do good. But your actions are rash and dangerous. And a *gob* died because of you. If you kill a *gob* by accident or ignorance, he're still just as dead. A crime are a crime. And justice must follow."

The goblin priestess paused. Billy imagined she was looking out over the crowd, impressing on them the seriousness of her decision. That is, he tried to picture it. But mostly what he saw in his mind's eye was his own head being sliced from his neck.

After an agonizing delay, Starcaller spoke again. "So hear me now. The three humans are likewise sended to Coaler's Break, there to wait until signs are right for their deaths."

Billy tried to shout in protest, but before he could get a word out, he felt a firm hand clasp over his mouth. He fought back, but he knew it was hopeless. He heard sounds of struggles from nearby, but they didn't last long. Weak, tired, lost, and unable to see in the unrelenting darkness, he, Lexi, and Kurt were quickly subdued.

As unseen goblins regagged Billy and threw a burlap sack over his head, he heard Starcaller issue a final ruling.

"I have one last judgment," she said. "And it're for Korgorog Hoprock, the one what started all this trouble, the only *gob* what taked another *gob*'s life in what followed. Now *zajnai* he could argue self-defense if he were here. *Zajnai* he could explain why he doed what he doed. That're why we have a trial, but he're too *maja* a coward to attend. I say if he are *nai* here to speak for himself, and *nai* other *gob* will speak for him, I have *nai* choice but to rule against him. So hear me, any *gob* what find Hoprock. I say there're *nai* appointed time for a coward like him to die. *Nai* need to wait for omens or such. You find Hoprock, you kill him.

"And if he're *nai* guilty, then the Goddess protect him. Because I will *nai*."

Starcaller was looking right at him. Hop knew it. It wasn't possible, of course; faces in redsight were just blobs of heat even a few feet away. So there was no way anyone should be able to recognize a specific goblin in a crowd this big with only redsight. Except the heat glow of Starcaller's face was pointed at him and him alone. The fierce fires that were her eyes flared so brightly in Hop's redsight, he felt like she could burn a hole right through his skull.

"So if he are guilty, he'll get catched. And killed. And if he are *nai*," Starcaller continued, "well then, he best run."

Hop didn't need to hear her warning twice. He dashed through the curtains of the Night Temple before the echo of Starcaller's voice could even fade away. He emerged into the deserted streets of Kiranok. Then the High Priestess's words echoing in his mind, Hop ran. He didn't plan to stop running anytime soon.

Through a haze of exhaustion, Lexi felt herself being lifted into the air by a giant goblin with hands big as doormats. Part of her was just awake enough to be annoyed. *Why do people keep carrying me? I can walk for myself.* Lexi struggled briefly, but the ropes around her ankles and wrists wouldn't budge. Someone lowered a hood over her head, then the giant tossed Lexi over one shoulder and jogged through the darkness. After a dozen or so unnaturally long strides, they passed through three layers of heavy leather curtains. Lexi could feel the thick material dragging across her body. After the third curtain, light seeped through Lexi's hood. She felt relieved; she'd been afraid she'd never see light again.

The giant goblin's jostling run continued for a while longer. Lexi's ribs thumped repeatedly against the giant's bony shoulder, adding new bruises to her already battered body. She was briefly tempted to use her newfound abilities to burn the giant, but she remembered the goblin priestess's words. If she were caught using magic indiscriminately, especially to hurt anyone, the goblins might not wait to execute her. Plus, in her condition, she'd probably only make the giant goblin feel a little warm. It was all ridiculously unfair. *I will not cry*, Lexi thought fiercely to herself. *I will not cry.*

As the jostling, torturous journey continued, Lexi found herself thinking of home. At home, she often felt powerless, her every moment structured and planned by her omnipresent mother. Lexi hated that. And now, here she was, in a whole other world, suddenly blessed with the ability to do amazing things, and she felt just as powerless as ever.

Finally, the giant unceremoniously dumped Lexi onto what felt like a net. The tightly woven mesh cloth bounced noiselessly as she thumped down. Two more impact waves followed, no doubt Billy and Kurt being thrown onto the netting nearby. Lexi lay still as the undulations dissipated, aching in dozens of spots, too worn out to even try to escape.

She must have slept for a while. The next thing she remembered was a female goblin voice saying, "They're all aboard. Make way."

More shouts followed. "Make way!" and "Cast off" and "Ya! Ya! Go, you bug eaters!"

Suddenly the net flooring under Lexi lurched and jerked. Then it started to sway. At first the netting moved in a herky-jerky, side-to-side motion. But after a short time, the movement became more regular, a gentle swaying to and fro.

Lexi had been on a catamaran once, on the Bay, with one of the rich girls from school. It had swayed a lot like this. *A boat*, she thought, *we must be on a boat.* She guessed that the netting probably stretched out over a cargo hold, like on an old sailing ship. For a while she lay there, trying to understand what was happening around her. Maybe if she could figure out where they were and where they were going, she might be able to make an escape plan. Visions of leading a grateful Kurt and Billy to safety danced in her head. She would show everyone that she could make a difference.

But her visions were more dreams than plans. Soon, Lexi succumbed to her exhaustion and the gentle rocking of the netting and fell back asleep.

She didn't open her eyes again for a very long time.

The dream was always the same. Sawtooth stood on a vast sun-bleached plain, alone. All around him, countless thorny plants thrust themselves up from the bone-dry soil, growing in seconds into spiky trees bearing innumerable round white fruit. Feeling a sudden hunger, Sawtooth walked up to the closest tree. Fighting past the thorns and brambles, he plucked one of the fist-sized white globes, anticipating a juicy, satisfying meal. But as he brought the fruit to his mouth, the orb turned into a skull, opened its mouth, and screamed.

With a chorus of agonizing howls, the fruit of every spiky tree on the plain likewise transformed into skulls. The trees' thorns dripped red sap like blood.

Usually that was enough to wake Sawtooth. But not this time. This time she was there, the Dark Lady, with her decidedly un-goblin-like features—ivory skin, midnight hair, and startling moon-silver eyes.

"We can plant a hundred trees, but years must pass before we eat," she said, transfixing him with her silvery stare. "A gallon splashed to the ground yields a single drop of juice. And the earth is ever thirsty."

"Tell me what to do," Sawtooth said. "Tell me."

"If ordered to do so, would a thornbush produce apples?" came the answer, in a voice of painful beauty. "Every tree follows its nature. And bears in kind."

With that, the wind became a gale, and the Dark Lady turned to dust. The entire plain, the trees, the fruit, even Sawtooth himself, broke apart into sand and blew away.

Sawtooth awoke, covered in sweat. But he had his answer.

The treacherous Copperplate Hop and his human allies had failed. There would be no human king to save his people, no miracles. There was only Sawtooth.

And the fruit of Sawtooth's tree was death.

CHAPTER EIGHT
An Empty Jar

Lexi woke feeling much, much better. Had she healed herself with her newfound magic? It certainly felt like it. She rolled over, surprised to find that someone had removed the various restraints that had kept her immobilized.

Then she saw Billy. She remembered how, in the throne room, he'd thrown himself over her, trying to protect her from the onslaught of angry goblins. Despite his best efforts, she'd gotten pretty banged up. But from the look of things, he'd gotten it a lot worse. His hoodie was spattered with dried blood, and there were cuts and bruises all over his face and arms. He moaned in his sleep, in obvious pain.

Lexi would have to do something about that.

"Billy. Billy?" Billy woke to someone shaking his shoulder and calling his name. It was Lexi.

Billy opened his eyes. He was lying on some sort of net floor, which was rocking gently. It was night and foggy, but he could just make out his surroundings by the feeble light from a row of flickering lanterns strung along a nearby railing. He seemed to be on some kind of boat. Lexi was kneeling over him, a worried look on her face.

"You okay?" she asked.

"Yeah," Billy answered after a moment's consideration. "I feel better."

Which was true. Billy's bumps and bruises were gone. He sat up, setting off a small wave of motion in the netting.

"I did some of that magic stuff. To fix you up," Lexi said. Billy could see dark rings under her eyes. She looked drained.

"You didn't have to do that," Billy said.

"Yeah, I did. You looked terrible." Lexi studied him. "Better now, though. I mean, you're still a skinny geek, but at least there's less blood."

"Yeah. Thanks." But though Billy really did feel better, he didn't like the fact that patching him up had made Lexi feel worse. "Look, maybe you should go easy on the spells. I don't think they're good for you."

"So I should've just left you lying there moaning?" Lexi sniped back, her temper overcoming her exhaustion.

"Billy are right," Frost interjected, emerging from the darkness and the fog, carefully balancing on the springy net floor. "The boy woulda healed without your help. And you shoulda let him."

"I'm not going to let people suffer if I can fix things," Lexi said.

"But at what cost, youngling?" Frost said. The little

goblin looked worn from his own spellcasting. His ears drooped, and his eyes seemed less bright. "That're the problem with magic. It give you much, but it take *maja* much in return."

Lexi bristled. "I know what I'm doing."

Frost shook his head sadly. "All young wizards think like you do now. And all of 'em are just as wrong. Magic are power, *zaj*? But power are a tricky thing. The more you use, the more you want. It're like strong drink. A sip every now and then are *nai* too bad. But drink too much, too often, and it'll rot your brain."

Billy could tell this wasn't what Lexi wanted to hear. "All I've done is help," she said. "I healed myself, got us out of that tunnel. And now I made Billy feel better."

"That're a stack of spells packed into less than two days. Let me ask you something. How're you feeling right now? Good?"

"Tired," Lexi admitted. "Like I haven't slept for a week."

"*Zaj*, and I feel worse," Frost said, frowning. "But there are ways to fix that. Magical ways. And let me tell you, I want to use 'em right now. A simple spell and I're right as rain. But I knowed a wizard what went down that path, *zaj*. A pretty little *svagob* named Moonfall what were just finishing her apprenticeship when I started mine."

The memories seemed painful to Frost, but he forced himself to continue. "All of us young wizards looked up to Moonfall. She were bright, pretty, sweet. And when it comed to magic, Moonfall were the best. She could work any spell, do anything she liked. But *zajnai* that're the problem. Because she could do it, she would do it. Whenever life would *nai* go Moon's way, she used a spell to fix it. A spell to wake her up, a spell to make her breakfast, a spell for energy, a spell to sleep.

"It only taked a few years 'til Moonfall's whole life were spells, 'til her mind fried like an egg, leaving her with glazed-off eyes and *nai* a thought in her head. A *graznak*, we call that. A soulless one, an empty jar. A *graznak* are dead inside, keeped alive only by magic, working spells without even thinking. That were Moon, in the end. When Moonfall getted hungry, food rained down from the sky. If a door were in her way, cold winds teared it to pieces. And if someone maked her angry . . . well, that someone died.

"In the end, all the other wizards, including me, were forced to hunt Moonfall down. We used all our powers against her. And we killed her. Although the truth are . . . by then Moonfall were already dead. It're the magic what killed her. Us wizards just finished the job."

Frost rubbed his face, surreptitiously wiping away a tear. "But this're sour talk," he said, eager to change the subject, "and it're *nai* everyday you get to ride a batreme. Which are a rare and amazing thing. We should see what we're missing."

Billy looked around, confused. "See what we're missing? But we're prisoners."

"And *naizaj* tomorrow we're dead. But right now we're as free as we're likely to get anytime soon. So if you want to sit there feeling miserable, you're welcome to it. But I are going to enjoy meself 'til I can *nai* enjoy meself *nai* more." True to his word, Frost walked carefully away across the net, heading toward the lantern-lit railing. In a few seconds he was lost in the mists.

"Maybe he's right," Billy said. "We're alive for now. And this batreme thing sounds like it's worth checking out."

Lexi nodded, but she didn't look happy. "Billy?"

"Yeah?"

"You don't think I'm gonna turn into a grassneck or whatever Frost was talking about, do you?" Lexi's voice sounded small, hesitant, not her usual forceful self.

"No," Billy said, "you're way too cool for that."

He and Lexi got unsteadily to their feet and tried to follow Frost. It wasn't easy. Walking on the net floor took some practice. And aside from the flickering lanterns, there wasn't much light. Between the darkness and the heavy fog, it was hard to get a sense of their surroundings. Now that he was standing, Billy could feel a wind whipping across the deck from the front of the boat. Either the wind was blowing hard or they were moving at a pretty good clip. Or both.

As he and Lexi moved around, Billy, by necessity, mostly kept his eyes on the net floor, a tightly woven mesh of cables similar to bungee cords. Every few feet, Billy could see a loop sticking out of the net. Emergency handholds, Billy guessed, though he wondered why the boat needed so many of them.

The fog parted a bit, and Billy saw that the netting was surprisingly crowded. Nearby several goblin prisoners clustered together, commiserating. At the prow, a small group of priests chanted and prayed, shrouded under thick black cloaks. A scattering of goblin soldiers kept watch, while others played dice or kept warm by a hooded copper stove at the ship's stern.

A dozen or so small, agile goblins dashed to and fro about the deck, securing lines, working winches, and generally keeping things running. *Sailors*, Billy supposed. The sailors went barefoot, the better to grip the net floor with their toes. They wore simple gray uniforms and wool caps to protect their ears from the cold.

And it was really cold. Kansas winter cold, which was

about as cold as Billy could ever remember being. Billy zipped up his sweatshirt and was just about to pull up the hood when he noticed Lexi. Unlike Billy, she only had her light red sweater. And she was wearing a skirt. She had to be freezing.

"You, uh, want my sweatshirt?" Billy asked.

Lexi seemed touched by Billy's gesture. Then she glanced at Billy's sweatshirt and smiled sadly. "I'll pass, thanks."

Billy followed Lexi's glance. His sweatshirt had been clean when he put it on. Two days ago. Or was it three? But that was before he crashed into Kurt and spilled spaghetti sauce all over it. Before he'd fled through a muddy culvert, or carried Lexi with her bloody broken leg, or dug around in fungus-infested caverns looking for an exit. Or run from a goblin mob. Or ridden a bat-taxi. Or crept up an old tunnel full of spider webs. Or gotten attacked by yet another mob.

Billy's sweatshirt was filthy, covered in dried tomato sauce, dried mud, dried sweat, and dried blood, plus cobwebs, more sweat, dust, and more blood, all caked together into one continuous blot. Under the dirt, the fabric was ripped and frayed, the right cuff was missing, and the drawstring had gotten twisted and tangled until it was one big knot.

"Yeah, it's pretty gross. Now that you mention it." Then Billy managed a smile in return. "Well, at least it's warm."

Lexi chuckled a little at that. Then a worried expression crossed her face. "Hey, Billy, this is a boat, right?" Lexi peered into the thick fog.

"Yeah, of course. What else would it be?"

"It's just . . . I don't hear any water." Lexi glanced up at the misty sky. "I think it's getting lighter out. The sun must be coming up. Maybe we can see where we're going."

Lexi moved toward the side of the ship, easily keeping her balance despite the awkward swaying of the net floor. Billy followed at a considerably slower pace. Still, after a few stumbling, bouncy steps, he managed to join Lexi at a railing made of a light, yellow wood similar to bamboo. The sway of the ship was more noticeable now. He gripped the railing tight as he looked around.

"There's still too much fog," he said. "I can't see a thing."

Billy looked down, trying to catch a glimpse of the strangely silent sea. But all he could see was more fog. Fog off the bow. Fog ahead of them. Fog behind them. And most disturbingly of all . . . fog below them.

"Uh, Lexi." Billy tried to keep the fear out of his voice. "Do you see any water?"

"No, the fog is too . . ." Then Lexi trailed off, realizing what she was seeing. "That's not fog, is it?"

"I think it's clouds," Billy said. "We're flying?"

"Not us." Lexi's voice was filled with awe. "Them."

With the dawn, the fog burned off enough that Billy and Lexi were finally able to see what was propelling the boat forward. Frost had called the ship a "batreme." And now Billy knew why.

The ship was being carried by bats.

The clouds parted, and sunlight revealed a huge boat-like craft. Meshwork netting stretched across an oval wooden framework, creating two trampoline-like decks, one up top and one below. Passengers filled the top net; cargo packed the lower "below-decks" netting. Beams and crossbeams extended from the ship, front, port, starboard, and aft, like horizontal masts. And strapped to the beams by an elaborate system of leather riggings were sixteen giant bats.

Four bats in front, four on each side, and four to the back, each with a single goblin riding its back. The bats were gargantuan, two or three times as big as the taxi-bat Billy had ridden in Kiranok. Together they sped the batreme through the clouds like a team of galloping horses pulling a carriage.

"Wow," said Billy as the lead handler shouted a series of commands, guiding her bat into a gradual turn. The other handlers followed suit, and the entire ship banked gently to one side.

Billy gripped the railing a little tighter to compensate for the lean of the deck. He couldn't help but admire the nimble bat-handlers as they guided their giant mounts. Only a single delicate-looking safety line protected each rider from certain death if he lost his footing. Using a combination of their voices and long poles, the bat-handlers goaded their bats, and the bat ship gracefully corrected course in response to their commands.

"I want to do that," Lexi said. "It looks like a blast."

Billy watched as a bat-handler leaned hard to one side, encouraging the bat to turn. "Scary."

"Yeah," Lexi said. "But sometimes the things that scare you are the most fun things you can do."

"Like standing up to Kurt?" Billy grinned.

"That *was* fun," Lexi said. "Hey, where is King Jock?"

"Hey, squirt," Kurt said. "Feeling better?"

Lexi and Billy found Kurt sitting on the opposite railing, staring at the clouds rushing past below them. He looked pretty banged up. For a moment Lexi thought about using her newfound abilities to make him feel better, but then she remembered Frost's advice. Maybe she *should* cool it when it came to magic.

"Yeah," Billy answered. "Lexi patched me up."

"I'll bet she did."

Lexi saw Billy's ears go red at the implication. She could tell he was trying to think of something clever to say in response, but nothing came out. Lexi suppressed a snide comment of her own. She didn't want to make Billy feel worse. But she was glad she hadn't helped Kurt. Let him suffer.

Just then, the ship broke through the last of the clouds. All three of them gasped in amazement as the world unfolded below them.

The batreme was navigating a high mountain pass. Steep slopes rose precipitously on either side. The ship was high above the tree line, which explained the cold air and the fact that Lexi was feeling short of breath. Below them, a long narrow valley wove between two towering, snow-capped mountains. A glacier-fed stream rushed and tumbled through the valley, roaring down a series of cascades.

"Beautiful," Lexi said.

"Yeah," Billy agreed. But then he added with a frown, "Almost makes you forget they're going to kill us all when we get where we're going."

"Way to bring down the mood," Kurt said.

For once, Lexi found herself agreeing with Kurt. "Billy. Can we just pretend everything is going to be okay? That we're not a million miles from home and surrounded by goblins and sentenced to death. Can we maybe not think about that? Just for a while."

"Sure. Whatever you want." Billy looked embarrassed again . . . and a little ashamed. It made Lexi feel a little better. He actually cared what she thought. That was a first.

For the next few hours, the batreme maneuvered through a series of interlocking mountain valleys, each one more beautiful and remote than the next. Billy, Lexi, and Kurt sat at the rail and watched in awe as waterfalls, forests, and glaciers rolled by. The view never got old. There seemed to be wildlife everywhere, herds of deer, a family of beavers laboring away at their dam, a solitary moose. Once Billy saw a herd of what looked like sheep or goats. As the batreme got closer he realized that they were actually giant rabbits the size of cows, grazing voraciously on hillside plants. It was a bizarre sight, and reminded Billy how far he was from home.

As the sun reached noon, Frost brought the three of them steaming cups of soup. Billy, suddenly aware of how hungry he was, slurped it down. It tasted of onions and carrots. Down below, an animal that looked like a bear covered in feathers splashed into a stream, coming out with a mouthful of flopping fish.

"That're better, I bet," Frost said as Billy drank his soup. "Life're almost never completely bad, *zaj*? The good're always somewhere if you can step back and take it in."

Billy realized the little goblin was right. He'd forgotten his troubles for a while. Looking at the mountains and the woods and experiencing the batreme in operation had been an amazing experience. One he'd never forget as long as he lived.

Which, he reflected, *might not be very long.*

"Thanks for the soup," Kurt said to Frost, gulping the last of his share. "I'm beat. I'm gonna rest a bit." Kurt walked away, limping visibly.

"I could've helped him. But I didn't. Because of what

you said," Lexi admitted once Kurt was out of earshot.

And because he's a jerk, Billy thought. But he felt guilty for thinking it. Kurt had risked his life to help Hop and the other goblins. Now that they'd failed, he was sentenced to death just like the rest of them.

"We do what we can do," the goblin wizard replied philosophically, then wandered away across the deck.

Billy and Lexi went back to sharing the view. It was nice, the two of them sitting there like that. Billy was tempted to reach out and take Lexi's hand, but he restrained himself, not sure how the hot-tempered girl would react. Then, to his surprise, Lexi put her hand gently on his. At that moment, Billy forgot all about his guilt over bringing the three of them to this strange world and the death sentence awaiting them at their destination. At that moment, he was happy.

A little while later, the batreme crested a small ridge and descended into yet another valley. But this one was different. While the other valleys had been uninhabited, this one held a small town, surrounded by terraced slopes of carefully maintained farms, nestled up against a dark blue mountain lake.

As they got closer, Billy saw the smoke.

The village's cottages, its barns, its grain silos were blackened and burned. Even the fields had been scorched. The buildings were still smoldering. Whatever had happened here was recent.

It wasn't long before Billy and Lexi saw the first dead body lying in the ashes.

Hop hadn't run nearly as far as he'd hoped. Sawtooth, curse him, had sealed the city tight. No one could get in or out without showing a stamped metal disk that allowed people to travel. Even the secret ways through the deep caverns had been secured. And not by the usual Copperplates either. The city guards had new overseers, big, battle-scarred goblins equipped with heavy truncheons and no-nonsense iron armor. Combat veterans personally loyal to Sawtooth, the new overseers wore pendants around their necks decorated with giant bat fangs. It wasn't long before people were calling them the Teeth.

A few hours after the Teeth appeared in the streets, crews of goblins plastered up a series of notices around the city. Hiding in the shadows of Rockbottom, Hop sounded out the notices to himself as criers and sages recited them aloud for the less educated. One poster declared:

THE LORD PROTECTOR SAWTOOTH

Declare Kiranok under Martial Law 'til Further Notice.

Nai Goben *to Congregate in Groups of Three or More.*

Nai Goben *to Enter or Leave the City without a Proper Permit.*

Any Gob *Disobeying an Order*

From the Lord Protector or his Deputies to be

EXECUTED.

Hop shook his head in disgust. Apparently in deference to the priests, Sawtooth wasn't calling himself the King anymore, but that didn't make his declaration any easier to swallow. No coming or going, no gatherings, and no disobeying? Disobeying orders was practically a goblin tradition. Executing a *gob* for doing what he wanted instead of what he was told? That was the way *humans* did things.

The first poster horrified Hop. The next left him seething with anger:

THE LORD PROTECTOR SAWTOOTH

Hereby Command Any <u>Gob</u> *Strong Enough to Carry a Spear*

To Report for

COMPULSORY MILITARY TRAINING

For the Preservation of the Goben Race.

Hop had no objections to the "preservation of the *goben* race." In fact, he was entirely behind the concept. But Hop knew the truth of the goblin saying: "Generals order, sergeants rule, and deserters vote with their feet." No one could "command" a goblin to fight. Goblins fought for glory, for their beliefs, to defend their homes, for fun, for plunder, or even for pay. Hop himself had volunteered for the Warhorde because it had provided him with a family, a cause, a place to sleep, and food to eat. But as grateful as he'd been to the military, in Hop's mind, if a *gob* didn't think a fight was worth fighting, he had every right to run for it. So whatever "Compulsory Military Training" was, Hop wanted no part of it.

The final poster didn't bother Hop philosophically, nor was it particularly surprising. In some ways it was even flattering. But on a personal level, it was by far the most alarming of the three.

Wanted for Treason
KORGOROG HOPROCK,
Former City Guard
Offender Are Dangerous and Well-Armed
Contact Proper Authorities
Reward Payed
DEAD OR ALIVE

This last poster featured a woodcut portrait of Hop, reasonably accurate, with an especially detailed rendering of his mangled ear. It went on to detail his height (just over nine span), weight (eleven stone two), and eye color (bright yellow). The poster didn't specify the reward, which irritated him. If Sawtooth was only offering a few steel *jegen*, Hop might have a chance of getting out of Kiranok alive. But if Sawtooth was paying in gold *krognen*, Hop was probably as good as dead.

For once in his life, Hop found himself hoping that people didn't value him particularly highly.

"*Nai* sign of the Copperplate, General Sawtooth," Rumblejaw reported, looking downcast.

Sawtooth gazed from his office window into the courtyard of the Fist, a fortress carved out of a large cave which served as the headquarters of the Warhorde. Below him, raw recruits fumbled with spears in response to the shouted calls of their sergeants.

"Dress that line, you *zigparen*," Sawtooth bellowed through a narrow window. Hearing their general's voice, the infantry goblins shuffled and fumbled anew. Eventually, their ranks approximated a proper formation. "Better, lads," Sawtooth added, not really meaning it. Still, it helped to encourage them from time to time.

"You want we should keep looking?" Rumblejaw asked sheepishly.

"For the Copperplate?" Sawtooth shook his head dismissively. "He are likely run someplace far off. And it'll *nai* matter soon enough. The Warhorde are coming back together. The ranks are filled. All that're left are the marching."

"And the fighting," Rumblejaw reminded him.

For a brief minute, the dream flashed before Sawtooth's eyes. The same dream as always, rendered all the more horrific since it came upon him unbidden, hours from his last sleep. A hundred thousand skulls impaled on trees howling in agony. And for once, he could make out the words of their anguished cries.

The skulls were screaming his name.

Sawtooth blinked, and the vision passed. Down below, the troops continued their drill. Ready spear. Raise shield. Single step forward in ranks. Double step. Triple step. Lunge. Step. Charge!

"If we catch the Copperplate, we catch him. If we do *nai*, it're still too late for him," Sawtooth said calmly. "Too late for any *gob* to stop what're coming now."

Even me, he added silently to himself. *Especially me.*

The bat-handlers called out a signal, and the batreme lifted slowly away from the fire-blackened field.

Starcaller had ordered the prisoners locked below decks so the batreme could land and its crew could help survivors from the burned town. But there were no survivors. The entire population of the village had been massacred, leaving nothing but death and cinders. From inside the cargo deck, Billy had seen dozens of dead and burned goblins, from giant *kijakgoben* corpses to tiny charred lumps that Billy hoped were *jintagoben*. There were also dead pigs, dead riding bats, dead livestock of every kind. As the ship's guards searched the village, they'd startled an injured giant rabbit out of a burning barn. The rabbit was missing a leg, and terrible wounds crisscrossed its bulky body. It lunged at the guards, then fell to the ground a few yards from the batreme and thrashed silently on the burnt field. The Templars had no choice but to put it out of its misery.

It was an image Billy knew he would remember for a long, long time. Even now, as the batreme rose into the air, Billy's eyes remained fixed on the burnt remains of the village. He wanted to look away, but he couldn't. Part of him knew it was necessary for him to see this. It was important.

Once the batreme was away from the ground, the Templars unlocked the cargo hatch, allowing Billy and the rest of the prisoners to return to the top deck. No one hurried. The prisoners were as grim as their guards.

"Humans are responsible for this," grumbled a goblin prisoner as the smoldering wreckage dwindled beneath them. *"Skerboen."*

Hearing the insulting word from a fellow prisoner startled Billy. After all, wasn't this one of the goblins who'd tried to put Kurt on the throne?

"How can you be sure?" Billy asked, trying to keep the anger out of his voice.

"The ground were all teared up by hooves, *zaj*," the prisoner answered. Judging from his smooth skin and tall, upright ears, he was a younger goblin, probably no older than Billy. "Hooves shoed with iron. Us *goben* do *nai* ride horses. Humans do."

An older female prisoner nodded in agreement. "*Nai* to mention they destroyed everything. All the buildings, the barns. They even slashed up that poor *kijakhof*. Killing the livestock, burning up the grain, that're destroying *food*. For us *goben*, ruining good food are an unforgivable waste. Even when we raid the humans, what we can *nai* steal, we leave behind. So *zajnai* we can steal it another day.

"*Nai*, mark me," she continued, "it were humans what attacked that town."

From the hostile looks the rest of the prisoners were giving Billy, Lexi, and Kurt, they agreed with their more vocal companions. Billy shifted uncomfortably, not sure how to reply to the accusations.

"If it was humans, then we're sorry," Lexi said. "We're sorry if people like us did that to people like you. It's wrong."

The younger prisoner still looked angry, but the female goblin's expression softened slightly. "We know you're *nai* the ones what attacked that village, deary. Human you are, but you're only children. It're just that right now, we're tired and afeared. Same as you."

The other goblins nodded in agreement. All but the young male goblin who'd originally challenged Billy. Instead, he glared at Kurt, his anger mixed with hurt and disappointment. "We believed in you," he said to Kurt. "We thinked you our king. We risked everything for you. But you're nothing. Nobody. And now we're all fated to die. Acause of you."

With that, he walked away to the stern of the cargo hold, the better to watch the burned-out village recede into the distance.

The old goblin woman turned to Kurt, "Do *nai* mind Kettle. He're a good lad. He're hurting are all."

"Yeah. I get it." Kurt walked away, quiet.

To Billy's surprise, he actually felt sorry for the quarterback. Kurt was beating himself up for everything that had gone wrong. And Billy knew exactly how that felt. "Let me talk to him."

Before Lexi could object, Billy joined Kurt by the railing. "It's not your fault," Billy said tentatively. "You were trying to help."

"That's what I keep telling myself. You know what my dad would say right now, if he were here?"

Billy didn't know Kurt's father, but based on the SUV the football player drove and the expensive clothing wore, he figured Kurt's dad must really care about him, the way he spoiled him rotten. "He'd probably say the same thing. Go easy on yourself."

Kurt snorted in disgust. "My father never said anything like that in his entire life. He would've been all over me, telling me what I did wrong, dissecting every decision, every move. It'd be like those three interceptions I threw against Bellside last year. My dad never lets me forget that. He made me spend the entire summer working on ball management, accuracy drills. 'No more Bellsides,' he kept telling me. 'Division One colleges don't recruit quarterbacks who throw interceptions.'" Kurt looked troubled. "Maybe he's right. Maybe I'm just a walking choke-job."

Billy couldn't believe what he was hearing. The quarterback seemed so confident, so sure of himself. But underneath it all, he was just as self-doubting as Billy. At least Kurt had his father to blame. Billy's parents were great. He managed to run himself down without any help from them.

"My dad would say that mistakes are the only way we learn anything. That they're opportunities for growth."

Kurt turned from the railing to study Billy. "Your dad sounds cool. You're lucky."

Billy thought about how sick his dad had been lately, how little energy he'd had for anything but doctor's visits and his half days at work. He couldn't keep the edge out of his voice. "Yeah, we're real lucky."

Kurt looked confused so Billy explained, "He has cancer. He's probably going to die. Soon."

"I didn't mean . . . Sorry."

Billy realized it wasn't Kurt's fault. There was no way he could have known. "No. I'm the one who's sorry. I came over here to make you feel better, not dump on you." Billy gave it another try. "Look, you did everything right. You got to the Crown, you put it on. If you *were* the King, the eye-thingy would have glowed. And Hop's plan would've worked."

"I guess. But what I don't get is . . . if I'm not the King, how did we get here?"

I did it, Billy thought. *I brought us here. I got us trapped in that cave and got Hop's hopes up. I let you take the risk of putting on the Crown instead of trying it myself. And now we're prisoners and stuck on this weird boat, sentenced to die. If there's anyone to blame, it's me.*

He couldn't bring himself to say it. All he could manage was, "I don't know."

But that was a lie, a lie that haunted Billy through the rest of the day and well into the night as the giant bats flew relentlessly onward.

CHAPTER NINE
Dance of the Uncrowned Flowers

A s the sun rose on a new day, the batreme crested a final ridge and began its descent into a gap between the mountains.

"This're it," Frost said, "Coaler's Break."

Lexi stood with Frost, Leadpipe, Kurt, and Billy at the bow of the ship, taking in the sights. Playing tour guide, Frost explained that Coaler's Break was a fortunate accident of geography or a gift from the Night Goddess, depending on whom you asked. The Break cut through the heart of the Ironspine Mountains, forming a natural gateway to the Westreach, a sprawling, untamed wilderness blessed with rich deposits of gold and diamonds, shaded by majestic old growth forests, and bounded by a long fertile coastland teeming with fishing grounds. For centuries, the goblins had controlled the pass with a combination of spells and fortifications, blocking human expansion into the Westreach. But a generation ago, the Hanorian army had pushed the goblins to the margins of the Break, allowing the humans to establish colonies in the west and gain access to new farmland, mines, and lumber.

Frost sighed. "You can still feel 'em, in the bones of the land. The old protective spells. But they're mostly breaked now. Old and weak. Fading just as we *goben* are fading. Until it're all just memories."

Lexi tried to sense what Frost was talking about. She squinted and thought she could just make out a network of spidery blue lines crisscrossing the landscape below, faintly glowing, connecting one ruined tower to another. Magic, Lexi knew. Magic only she and Frost could see.

"*Nai* all disappeared just yet," Leadpipe said, providing a counterpoint to Frost's melancholy. "There're the Fastness. You can eyeball it already."

Leadpipe pointed into the distance. Lexi spotted a huge complex of walls and palisades, towers and keeps, and earthworks and embankments that crept from the valley floor all the way up a distant ridge. With walls fashioned from blackish green granite, the Fastness had a sinister, threatening appearance. Underneath the fortifications, Lexi could perceive more of the glowing blue lines, weaving the dark green stones together like a web. It was haunting . . . and a little scary. This was where the goblins were taking them to die.

But as they flew closer, the Fastness began to look less like a fort and more like a city. Lexi could see hundreds of buildings nestled amid the walls and towers. There were shops and homes, grain silos and windmills. The slopes beneath the fortifications were thick with vegetable gardens. Entire courtyards were planted with fruit trees. Blackberry vines covered huge sections of the walls.

Lexi's fear began to subside. How could you be afraid of a place where they grew blackberries and laundry flapped on lines strung between watchtowers? Where tiny bells hung from the trees, chiming gaily in the wind? And where goblin children chased giant pet rabbits through the streets?

As the batreme soared low over the walls, more goblin children poured out of the buildings, waving at the ship and cheering as it flew overhead. Slowing their bats, the handlers piloted their huge airship to a large field at the very top of the Fastness. Unlike the other open spaces in the fortified city, nothing grew here. Instead, soldiers dressed in Templar gear were using the area to drill and train. On a shouted signal, they cleared the field, making way for the batreme.

For something so large, the batreme settled to the ground with surprising grace. Lexi felt only the slightest bump as the ship touched down. The huge bats continued gently flapping their wings until their handlers disconnected them from their harnesses. Then the bats, tired from their long flight, used a few final powerful wing beats to propel themselves into a windowless stone building that abutted the field. The building looked like a gothic church crossed with an airplane hangar, with a single huge door and a massive, arching ceiling. The handlers sang a chant praising the bats, then ordered the door closed on their loyal mounts. Time to rest after a job well done.

Once the bats were in their nests, the crew extended wooden ramps from the upper deck down to the ground. Guards ordered the prisoners to stand back as the other passengers disembarked. Shadow, the female Templar who'd stood up to Sawtooth at the trial, led the way. On the batreme, Leadpipe had told Lexi, Kurt, and Billy that Shadow was actually General Sawtooth's daughter. Lexi hadn't seen much of the goblin dictator, but she could tell that Shadow shared her father's intimidating presence. Shadow marched ahead of a column of her Templars, elegantly confident in her spotless black armor.

Together, the batreme's Templars and the soldiers from the field formed ranks to greet the priests and priestesses of the Night Goddess as they returned to the Fastness, shrouded in their black robes. As the first priestess put her foot on the ground, Shadow barked, "*Wazzer!*" and the soldiers snapped to attention. They held their stance until the last priest filed into the main part of the Fastness.

Once the clergy left the batreme, its crew set about unloading cargo, strapping down riggings, and generally making the flying boat ship-shape. Eventually, the guards ordered the prisoners to prepare to disembark. Lexi lined up with Kurt, Billy, Frost, and Leadpipe, half expecting to be shackled and frog-marched into a dungeon. But instead, a young female goblin in a simple black dress boarded the ship and shyly approached.

"I're Novice Yesigerath Silkturn," she said, bowing. "Folk call me Turner."

Lexi and her companions introduced themselves. Turner seemed pleased. "You humans are to come with me, *zaj*," she said and headed down the ramp.

"Wait!" Billy called after her, looking to Frost and Leadpipe. "What about our friends?"

Were they going kill Frost and Leadpipe? Right now? Lexi felt the fire deep inside her spark to life, but Frost shook his head gently. Not now. Lexi tried to keep the fire down and hear Turner out.

"They're to have their own quarters, near the temple, where Frost's magic can cause *nai* mischief. But Priestess

Starcaller instructed me to bring you to a place where you'd be comfortable."

"It're all right," Leadpipe reassured Lexi, Billy, and Kurt. "We can take care of ourselfs."

"Yeah, but can we?" Billy asked.

"You'll do fine," Frost said.

Kurt looked at Turner, who was waiting patiently. "Looks harmless enough," he said.

Sure. To you, Lexi thought. *Except you were wrong about being king, about the plan, about everything. That goblin girl could be leading us to our death. And even if she isn't, following her won't make us safe, won't get us any closer to home.* Lexi wanted to lash out, to burn down the entire Fastness, starting with Turner. To do anything except act like a nice little lamb walking cooperatively to the slaughter.

Then Billy caught her eye. Lexi got the message. Calm down. Go with it. Don't do anything stupid.

Okay. For you.

Lexi, Billy, and Kurt said their reluctant good-byes to Frost and Leadpipe, then followed Turner off the ship.

But part of Lexi was still looking for something to burn.

Billy, Lexi, and Kurt cautiously followed Turner as she led them through a labyrinth of gates, alleys, and passageways. At one point she took them into an old building and down a spiral stairway until it felt like they were several dozen yards underground. She guided them through a long, tight tunnel, down another staircase, through a door, and they emerged into bright sunlight on a hillside overlooking the valley. As Billy's eyes adjusted to the light, he realized their underground journey had taken them halfway down the mountain, though they still hadn't left the fortress.

Unfortunately, Billy soon realized that meant they had to go uphill again. They climbed three long stairways that scaled the side of a ridge, arriving in a narrow passageway between two walls. By the time they finished their climb, Billy was thoroughly out of breath. Lexi, still drained from her spellcasting, had to lean against a wall to keep herself on her feet. Billy was glad to see that even athletic Kurt was huffing and puffing a little.

Turner didn't even look winded. "Almost there," she assured them.

But before they could resume their travels, Billy heard goblin voices approaching from around the next corner, along with strange thumping, clacking sounds. A worried look disturbed Turner's previously placid expression.

"Outriders," Turner said. "Make way. Now."

Following Turner's example, Billy, Lexi, and Kurt pressed themselves against the walls of the passageway. The goblin voices grew louder, as did the strange sounds. Soon the approaching goblins rounded the corner. There were four of them.

But they weren't alone.

Each goblin rode a huge animal, a giant, panting monstrosity. At first glance, the beasts looked like wolves . . . pitch-black wolves, eight feet long and five feet high at the shoulders, with prominent horns growing from their muzzles. Lion-like manes framed their enormous heads, and the monsters' eyes glowed an eerie red. Massive, padded paws thumped on the paving stones, followed by the clacking of the creatures' formidable claws.

"Careful you," joked an outrider. "They bite."

The wolf-monsters were equipped with sleek saddles, chain mail armor across their chests, sides, and backs, and leather wrappings to protect their hocks. They had no bridles or bits; the goblins controlled them with whistled commands and pressure from their knees.

The outriders themselves carried long lances and wore black leather armor decorated with gold filigree. Compact curved bows sat in cases on their saddles. The four goblins looked sharp, confident, and dangerous.

One of the monsters snorted in Billy's face as it shuffled through the narrow passageway. Its hot breath smelled like raw meat. As it passed, the creature's thick black mane brushed across Billy's cheek, surprisingly smooth to the touch.

"What are they?" Lexi whispered to Turner.

"*Vargaren.* Most times us *goben* ride *bokrumen.* Like giant sheep, *zaj*? But *bokrumen* are shy and *nai* good in battles and such. The blood and the noise afear 'em. So for war, the *goben* ride *vargaren.*"

The last rider in line, a wiry goblin sitting easy in her saddle, smiled and looked down at Billy and his companions. "Do *nai* worry. They only eat humans when we tell 'em to."

The outriders and their *vargaren* mounts disappeared around a corner. As soon as the way was clear, Turner was on the move. "Just through this gate."

Billy, Lexi, and Kurt followed Turner through a final portal, a massive stone archway with impressive iron-studded wooden doors. The gate led to an unexpected oasis, an expansive courtyard tiled with red marble and planted with dozens of thorny pomegranate trees heavy with fruit. An intricate network of irrigation channels crisscrossed the courtyard, conveying water to the trees from a central fountain.

But it wasn't the trees, the marble, or the fountains that drew Billy's attention. Rather, it was the inhabitants of the courtyard.

They were human.

But the people in the courtyard didn't look like anyone Billy had ever seen before. They were dressed in simple clothing in muted colors, rough-spun cotton tunics, wool pants, and calf-high boots. Men and women alike wore round knit caps atop loosely curled hair in various shades of light brown, red, and blond. They had brownish skin, almost as dark as Billy's own, and their eyes were light like their hair, tending toward blue, green, or hazel.

When Billy, Kurt, and Lexi entered the courtyard, its residents were busy harvesting the pomegranate trees. But as soon as they saw the new arrivals, they broke off their work and gathered around them. After an initial rush of children, the adults quickly moved to the forefront. A tall, white-haired man with an air of authority addressed Billy, Lexi, and Kurt in a quiet, confident voice.

Unfortunately, they couldn't understand a word he was saying.

"Okay, that's not Spanish. Or French," Lexi offered.

"Or Latin," Billy chimed in.

"Or Polish," Kurt said.

"Or even Tagalog," Lexi added.

"It're *Hanoryabber*. Hanorian," Turner said. "These folk are refugees from Gran Hanor."

Billy was confused. "Refugees? I thought the humans won the war."

"True, true. But these are Celestials. Heretics. They're the only folk the Hanorian leaders hate more than us. In the Hanorian Empire, they burn Celestials at the stake. So they comed here. And Priestess Starcaller sayed they can stay, so they stayed."

The white-haired man said a few more words, something formal sounding.

"This're Donegan Darrig. He're the Elder here," Turner translated. "He welcome you to the Court of the Orbs and bid you treat this as your home for as long as you need."

Donegan continued to speak, launching into a grand soliloquy. He went on for a few minutes. By the end of his speech, Turner looked more than a little confused.

"He sayed . . . uh . . ." Turner trailed off, not sure where to start.

"This is a waste of time," Lexi said impatiently. Suddenly the air around her glowed. Bright lights flashed from Donegan and Turner to Lexi and then to Billy and Kurt. Turner screamed and went down, covering her eyes. Billy felt like he was breathing lava.

With a hissing *whoosh*, the pomegranates on the trees near Lexi exploded, popping like overheated corn and spraying the courtyard with thousands of superheated seeds. The onlookers panicked, shouting and scattering. Scorching pomegranate seeds rained down on Billy, stinging his skin like an angry swarm of bees.

Lexi cried out in pain and collapsed to the ground. The heat lingered for a moment, then vanished as quickly as it came. Billy staggered, trying to get his bearings as the burning sensation faded from his brain, mouth, and ears.

"Are you mad, girl?" Donegan roared at Lexi.

Billy understood every word. Lexi had worked the same spell Frost had used to teach them *Gobayabber*, but this time her spell had given them the ability to understand and speak Hanorian.

Except it looked like Lexi's spell had almost killed her.

Lexi lay in the middle of a spray of smoldering pomegranate seeds. Her clothing was seared and charred. Her body was steaming, pouring off heat into the cool mountain air. Billy rushed to her side.

"Don't be angry. She was trying to help," he said.

"You can speak Hanorian?" Donegan said, surprised.

"Thanks to her." Billy turned his attention to Lexi. "Lexi! Lexi, are you okay?"

Lexi started to snicker. The snicker became a chuckle, then a giggle, and soon Lexi was rolling back and forth, laughing until her tears filled her eyes and she was gasping for breath. The Celestials who'd run from the exploding pomegranates slowly returned, curious to see what was making this strange girl laugh so hard.

Finally Lexi caught her breath. She looked up at Billy and smiled. "That was fun. Can we do it again?"

"You think this is amusing?" Donegan asked with a glare. "You could have killed yourself with your little trick, with the rest of us thrown in as part of the bargain. And for what? To learn our language? We could have taught it to you, if you'd had a little patience."

"Loosen up, old man. No one is dead, and at least now I can understand you when you get all in my face like that." Though clearly weakened from her efforts, Lexi had something in her eyes that startled Billy. Defiance. And maybe a little madness.

"Lexi. Empty jar," Billy whispered.

"I'm fine," she snapped back.

"Are you? Look at Turner."

Lexi shifted her attention to their goblin guide, who was still holding her face. Seeing Turner in pain sobered Lexi. "Are you all right?"

Turner looked up. Her eyes were watering, their yellow

shine dull and dim. "I . . . I can't see."

Lexi's smile vanished, replaced by a look of determination. "I can fix this."

Donegan shook his head. "I think you've done your share of miracles today." Something in Donegan's expression brooked no argument.

"I didn't mean to. It was an accident."

"How do we know you won't have another accident trying to fix your first one?"

Lexi had no answer for that. Billy gave Lexi's shoulder a quick squeeze of reassurance. Lexi looked up, grateful.

Donegan called out across the courtyard, "Alyseer!"

A girl about Billy's age came running. She was pretty, with copper red hair and bright green eyes. "Yes, Father?"

"Bring this young goblin to see your mother. Explain what happened. The heavens will set things right."

"As you say." Alyseer took Turner gently by the hand. "Don't worry. My mom is sun-touched. You'll be good as new."

"Sun-touched?" Billy asked as Alyseer led Turner away.

"Blessed with the power of the day sky. Like your irresponsible friend," Donegan explained. Then Donegan seemed to realize something. He turned to Lexi. "Girl, you were trained by someone, right? A lightworker? You've had your apprenticeship?"

Lexi looked at Donegan, confused. Billy answered for her. "We just got here a few days ago. From a long way away. Lexi never had any special abilities until then."

Donegan's expression softened. "That explains it. I'm sorry, girl. I shouldn't have lost my temper like that. I didn't realize you were a spark."

"A spark?" Lexi asked. "What's that?"

"An untrained lightworker. Someone who never knew

they had the touch until they started using it. Like a spark on the wind." Donegan considered the situation. "My wife, Sarlia. She can teach you how to use the touch. Train you. If you'd like."

"I . . . Thank you," Lexi stammered. "I'd like that."

"It's settled then." Donegan smiled and turned to Billy and Kurt. "As I was saying before . . . you are welcome here." He nodded at Lexi. "All of you. This is your home. For as long as you wish it to be so."

"You mean, until they execute us," Kurt muttered.

Donegan's smile faded at Kurt's grim expression, but his eyes stayed bright. "All our songs have a final refrain, but only Father Day and Mother Night know the count. So until the last note fades, might as well enjoy the dance."

With that, the other Celestials gathered to welcome them, warmly and genuinely. Soon it seemed as if Lexi's moment of madness had never happened. For the first time in days, Billy felt . . . safe. He suspected the feeling wouldn't last, but he decided to accept Donegan's advice and enjoy it while he could.

"Stand tall, soldiers," Sawtooth shouted to his newly reconstituted army assembled outside the gates of Kiranok. In response, the Warhorde snapped to attention. As best they could. Goblin attention wasn't particularly straight or snappy. It wasn't even all that attentive. Still, it would do.

Sawtooth continued. "Soon we march out to face those what would destroy us. But afore we do, I want you to think on the faces of your loved ones, of your neighbors, of all you hold dear. Picture 'em in your minds. And remember, if you shirk your duty, it're their blood what'll spill. If you fail, it're them what'll die."

Sawtooth let that sink in. He wasn't particularly specific about why the deserters' friends and families would bleed or who would kill the loved ones of those who failed. Best to keep them wondering.

"So I say to you, fix your hopes on one thing only. Victory. Because only in victory will you and those you love survive." Sawtooth smiled broadly. "So . . . which one do you choose? Victory? Or death?"

There were a few scattered shouts in response, but nothing unified, nothing with any power. Sawtooth would fix that.

"Victory!" Sawtooth shouted. "That're your answer. Say it loud. Like you mean it. Like it're already cooked up and on your plates. Victory! VICTORY! VICTORY!"

The new recruits took up the shout, hesitantly at first, but with increasing gusto: "Victory! VICTORY! VICTORY!"

Sawtooth turned to his lieutenants. "March 'em out," he snarled. "Afore the excitement wear off and they start to think too much."

And off they marched, to victory or death.

More likely death, Sawtooth reflected. *But better to die in battle than hiding in a hole. Aside,* naizaj *the Dark Lady'll grant us one last miracle. Night know we need it.*

If rumors are true, then the Warhorde are marching about now, Hop thought. *Glad I are* nai *with 'em.* Hop downed his mushroom wine, sitting in a dark corner of an out-of-the-way pub, wishing, not for the first time, that he'd never marched anywhere. For anyone.

Shoulda stayed at Tower Gulkreg, he thought, fingering the simple copper band he wore around his right wrist.

Shoulda deserted afore the first war.

Hop threw back another gulp of *zobjepa*, trying to shrug off his dark thoughts. He'd been happy at Tower Gulkreg. It wasn't much, just a stone fort and a small walled village, like a dozen other goblin outposts in the foothills. But he'd served there long enough to earn a promotion to sergeant, so he'd had a room of his own, three meals a day, and just enough responsibility to feel like his life meant something.

Hop oversaw Tower Gulkreg's complement of sentries, twenty or so goblin soldiers who stood watch on the fort. It was soft duty, much safer than being a ranger or an outrider. Most of Hop's charges were raw recruits, snot-nosed *goben* fresh from their nowhere villages in the mountains. Still, Hop did his best. He instilled a bit of discipline, showed them how to fight, and generally taught them what it meant to be a soldier.

Hop reported directly to Tower Gulkreg's commander, Mattock, a sleepy old officer who'd taken over the fort as a compromise between retirement and soldiering on until the bitter end. Mattock had been a fearsome warrior in his day, but by the time Hop got his promotion, he'd been content to nap away his final years and trust his new sergeant to do the actual work. Under Mattock's sleepy neglect, Hop's life had been free from care, light on responsibility, and completely devoid of actual combat.

Not only that, Hop had taken the fancy of a nice *svagob* who worked in the laundry shop. Cotton was her name. She was pretty, if a bit shy. She and Hop had eaten a few dinners together, watched the traveling players when they came through the village, and enjoyed several memorable walks in the countryside. Hop had even gone so far as to awkwardly initiate the first stages of courtship, gifting her with flowers, mushrooms for the stewpot, and a simple gold necklace.

Then the war broke out.

It had all started when some *duenshee* witch woman had had a vision of the Night Goddess. The *duensheen* (or "elves," as the humans called them) were powerful creatures of magic. Which meant most of them were raving mad from entire lifetimes steeped in spells and enchantments. They were thin, elegant, and deeply dangerous, like beautiful knives with a tendency to nick anyone who touched them. Luckily, they were also extremely rare. They lived on the southeast coast, in their own isolated kingdoms, hidden in the dunes and the sea mist. They rarely emerged, and then only one or two at a time, following their own peculiar, incomprehensible agendas. Until the war, Hop had never laid eyes on one.

This particular *duenshee* called herself "Dance of the Uncrowned Flowers." She came drifting into Kiranok one day, her eyes burning with religious zeal. The goblins had let her be. Everyone knew it was a bad idea to interfere with a *duenshee*. They were powerful wizards and tended to turn people they didn't like into burnt piles of ash. So for days, Dance of the Uncrowned Flowers had stood in the middle of the Underway, babbling strange prophecies to anyone who came close. Eventually, a few goblins gathered to listen. And then more. And more.

What prophecies they were. The goblins would be great again. They would ride forth from Kiranok and reclaim their lands. All the humans would pay them tribute and honor them.

Then there were the miracles. Diseases cured. The blind made to see. Food for the hungry. An old polluted well enchanted to run pure and clean.

The *duenshee* soon attracted a huge following. The goblins

began calling her "The Dark Lady" and flocked to her side.

A few months later, Sawtooth arrived in Kiranok. He'd been the Fastness's commander for almost fifteen years, loyal, methodical, practical, a model soldier. Starcaller herself had sent him to Kiranok to investigate the Dark Lady, to see if the *duenshee* was truly touched by the Goddess or merely acting from her own unfathomable impulses. Following his orders, Sawtooth went to the Underway and listened to the Dark Lady for several days.

He became a believer. More than a believer, he became a fanatic. Taking it on himself to bring her prophecies to fulfillment, Sawtooth seized control of the Warhorde. Supported by the Dark Lady, he recruited tens of thousands of new soldiers, swelling the ranks of the army. Then, certain that the Dark Lady's prophecies guaranteed his victory, he'd marched the goblins off to war.

Hop's garrison had been called up for the war effort. Cotton kissed him good-bye, wished him luck, and gave him a copper band from her dainty upper arm to remember her by. It was too small for Hop's arm, so he placed it around his right wrist.

And off they marched.

Hop and his soldiers had been there for Sawtooth's first heady victories, the storming of Fellentor, the crossing of the Venstell, the wild descent into the Uplands. In the rugged frontier between the goblin mountains and the human plains, the Warhorde had won battle after battle. Hop gorged himself on grain and pork stolen from human farms, drank his fill of human wine, and watched the goblins' *vargaren* devour entire herds of cows.

Then everything had started to go wrong. Hop lost two of his young watchmen at the human frontier town of Bastinge, where the Hanorians put up their first organized resistance. The town had fallen, but only after hundreds of the attacking goblins had died at the hands of its desperate human defenders.

At Pollard, the goblins had suffered their first outright defeat, driven back from the walls by wave after wave of human cavalry. Hop and his comrades killed five humans for every goblin that fell, but the humans just kept coming. Hop buried seven more of his band that day. Sawtooth's grand crusade to drive the humans into the sea was quickly turning to *duenshee* madness.

Eventually even Sawtooth realized that the goblin lines were overextended. When news came that three more regiments of human cavalry were on their way, the outnumbered Warhorde had no choice but to retreat.

Sawtooth fell back to Bastinge, where the goblins dug in to wait out the heavy autumn rains. It was there that Hop first saw the Dark Lady. He found her distant, alien, and terrifying in her stark beauty. She spoke rarely now, and then usually only to Sawtooth. Her voice was like music, her every word tinged with madness. Still, her powers were great. When the soldiers complained of hunger, she caused the fields to sprout new grain even as the rain poured down. She cured the wounded, made the crippled walk. Without her, even more goblins would have died that wet, miserable fall. Of course, without her, there never would have been a war at all.

Hop avoided her as best he could. She terrified him. But late one night, as he staggered out of his barracks, drunk from some particularly powerful human alcohol, he literally walked right into her. The Dark Lady was standing in the middle of the muddy street, silent in the rain, and in his drunken haze, he hadn't seen her until it was too late.

Hop backed away as quickly as he could, muttering

apologies. But to his horror, she noticed him. She looked down at him with her silvery, demented eyes, trapping him with her gaze. Hop knew instantly he'd never be able to forget those eyes. Looking into them felt like falling down a mineshaft, plummeting endlessly with no hope of survival.

She spoke then, simply and quietly. "The greatest beast crushes the bravest man. The bravest man slaughters the wiliest fox. The wiliest fox preys on the most elusive bird. The most elusive bird pecks up the smallest insect. And with a single diseased bite, the smallest insect brings down the greatest beast. We are all carrion and eaters of carrion, fertilizer for the wheat that makes our bread. Place a crown over it. And call it paradise."

With that, she walked away into the pouring rain, turned a corner, and was gone.

The next day the rains ended and a cold frost set in. The roads froze hard and the Warhorde marched out.

They were barely a mile from town when Hop heard the news. A week earlier, human raiders, striking deep into the hill country, had attacked Tower Gulkreg. They'd breached the walls, overrun the garrison, burnt the town . . . and slaughtered every single goblin inside.

Which meant Mattock was dead, along with the small skeleton crew left behind to guard the walls. Redfist, the old blacksmith who'd forged Hop's spear and shield, was dead. The cooks, the laundry-goblins, and the gardeners, the weavers, the stonemasons, and the millers, they were all dead.

And sweet, innocent, shy little Cotton? Cotton was dead. Hope was dead. Hop's heart was dead.

When he learned what had happened, all the strength went out of Hop's body. He wanted to fall to his knees in the middle of the frozen road and weep. But the Warhorde was marching toward their final confrontation with their human foes. And the Warhorde wouldn't wait for Hop and his tears.

As he marched, Hop felt the copper band around his wrist. It was ice cold.

Hop didn't need to be a prophet to hear the future that freezing fall day as they marched toward Solace Ridge. He could hear it in the thump of his shield against his backpack, in the rhythm of the drums that measured the march, in the synchronized clattering of twenty thousand goblin soldiers' hobnailed footfalls.

"*Doom-doom,*" Hop heard. "*Doom-doom. Doom-doom. Doom-doom.*"

Hop broke from his reverie. He realized he was deep in his cups, lost in too much mushroom wine and too many memories. He'd come to this particular pub because it was dark and unpopular. But even an unpopular pub in Kiranok filled up after work times. Hop's little corner wasn't so quiet anymore. A half-dozen miners had taken over the next table. They were a sullen lot, glaring at the other patrons as they nursed their watered-down redbeers. One miner looked Hop up and down, peering at the former Copperplate in the dim light.

"Do I know you?" the miner asked.

Hop kept his head low. He was wearing a battered old bat-handler's cap, complete with earflaps. Hop had stolen it to disguise his mangled ear. But it was still possible that the miner had recognized him, either from the wanted posters or his days as a City Guard.

"*Na,* just one of them faces," Hop said.

That seemed to satisfy the miner, at least for a moment.

Hop wanted to run for it, but he knew rushing out would only create suspicion. So he forced himself to finish his drink, then he settled his tab (had he really downed two entire *duenen* worth of *zobjepa*?), and threw down a few *jegen* for a tip. Moving as calmly as he could, Hop pushed himself up from his seat and walked toward the door.

Once he reached the street, Hop exhaled in relief. The miner hadn't asked him any more questions or tried to follow him. The post-work rush was over, so the streets were fairly empty. Everyone was already home or at their favorite pub. Hop stumbled through Rockbottom, weaving more than he would've liked to admit. His surroundings appeared blurry and out of focus. Two silvers bought a lot of booze.

Luckily Hop didn't have far to go. A few days earlier, he'd found a small hiding space under an old broken-down fountain. Now he was using it as an impromptu bedroom. It wasn't very comfortable, but it was warm and well concealed. All he had to do was stagger a few hundred feet, slip under the fountain, and sleep off the mushroom wine.

He only made it a dozen steps before someone grabbed his arm from behind.

"*Ahka*, you," said a gruff voice.

Hop spun around drunkenly. "I told you, I never seed you afore in me—"

But it wasn't the miner. It was a squad of Sawtooth's enforcers, the Teeth, three heavyset goblins armed with truncheons. Hop tried to pull himself free, but two of the goblins slammed him against the nearest wall and held him there. The third, the biggest of the lot, loomed over him.

"You're coming with us." The leader of the Teeth raised his truncheon, brought it down, and Hop's world went dark.

CHAPTER TEN

A Tightrope Walk

As he spun two weighted chains through the air, Billy thought about how much he missed home. He missed his mom and dad; he missed television and the Internet. He missed his video games, his music, and his books.

They'd been at the Fastness for almost a week now. As far as Billy could tell, Starcaller wasn't in any hurry to execute them, so their stay had turned into a kind of exile. Thanks to the Celestials' hospitality, he, Kurt, and Lexi were well taken care of. They'd been given new clothes and even a small house to use as their own. Still, they *were* prisoners. They weren't allowed to leave the Fastness, and Billy knew that sooner or later Starcaller would order their deaths. Which meant that every night Billy went to bed fervently wishing that they could somehow get transported back home.

But every day he'd wake up in his simple bed in the human quarter of the Fastness. He'd splash his face in the washbasin, clean off his teeth by chewing a minty-tasting twig, and join the Celestials' communal breakfast in the courtyard. Then all through breakfast (which was usually cheese and some kind of fruit), he'd wait for the dreaded news that this was the day that he, Lexi, Kurt, Frost, and Leadpipe were to be executed.

The order still hadn't come. Instead, he, along with Lexi and Kurt, spent their time with their human hosts, learning about the Celestials' culture and traditions. And waiting to die.

Whack. Billy hit himself with the weight at the end of the chain. It hurt. Not a lot, just enough that he didn't want to do it again.

"Concentrate," advised Alyseer. "And try not to think about it."

"How can I do both?" Billy wondered as he started the chains spinning again.

"That's the trick, isn't it?"

Billy concentrated. Rotate the wrists while holding the chains lightly. Use the weight at the end to control the speed. Establishing a rhythm, he tried to relax his mind and maintain the spin without thinking about it. Concentrate. And relax.

The Celestials followed their own peculiar religious tradition. Unlike the Night-worshipping goblins or the Day-worshipping mainstream Hanorians, the Celestials believed that Day and Night, Light and Darkness, Fire and Water had equal value. That life should be a harmonious balance between the fiery and the cool, between anger and love, aggression and passivity.

Donegan explained it like this: "Night is never truly dark. There are always the moon and stars, always a little light. Day is never entirely light. There's always the cool shelter of shade, the blessed relief of a passing cloud or a rainstorm. In every situation, the opposite is always present. True happiness comes from understanding that both are necessary. That success is not measured in destroying your opposite, but by acknowledging it and accepting it."

His daughter, Alyseer, put it more simply: "Life is a tightrope walk. That's what makes it fun."

Because of their beliefs, the Celestials had been forced to flee their homeland and live as refugees. For the life of him, Billy couldn't understand why anyone would want to kill Donegan, Alyseer, or their friends. They were kind people, generous, slow to anger, quick to forgive. Most of their spiritual teachings consisted of games. There was actual tightrope walking. Kurt spent hours at it; excelling as usual, thanks to his mix of strength and athletic grace. They also played a game like Blind Man's Bluff, where one person would be blindfolded, and everyone else would surround him while singing, playing an instrument, or clapping. The blindfolded person would try to tag the others by following the sounds alone.

Then there was juggling. The Celestials loved to juggle. Balls, clubs, even knives. And most impressively, fire. At night, they would light burning balls of pitch at the ends of chains, then spin the chains to make fiery patterns in the darkness.

"Better," Alyseer said. "You can do this. Just feel the motion. Try the weave."

The weave? Great, Billy thought. *Turn the wrists, cross the arms, move everything in a figure eight. Turn the wrists, cross the arms, figure eight.*

Kurt had learned the trick in just a few hours. He was already spinning real fire. Billy still hadn't moved past the unlit practice chains.

Wham! Billy lost control again and the weight on one of his chains thumped into the back of his skull. Days of work and he was still hitting himself on the head.

"I'm never going to get this," he grumped.

"It just takes time. Like everything worth doing. Watch me."

Alyseer spun her own practice chains with ease. Her lines were graceful and effortless. Billy couldn't help but notice how cute she was. She was about Billy's age, friendly, and constantly upbeat. Plus, she didn't look at Billy like he was some kind of freak. With his skin tone and hair, he actually looked more like the Celestials than either Kurt or Lexi. In the Court of the Orbs, Billy was the one who fit in. It was a nice change.

Except thinking about Lexi gave him a brief pang of guilt. "Hey, how's Lexi doing?" he blurted.

Alyseer's spin hitched a little as she lost concentration. But unlike Billy, she recovered without hitting herself. She turned the hitch into a twirl, then resumed weaving her two chains around each other.

"Mom says she just needs time and practice. It's dangerous being a spark or a shadow. But now that she's getting some training, she should be fine."

"That's good to hear." Billy started his chains spinning again.

But Alyseer had something else on her mind. "Lexi, is she your intended?"

"Intended? What does that mean?"

"It means . . . is she promised to you? When you come of age, you'll be married?"

Billy's spinning chains became hopelessly entangled, and he managed to hit himself with both weights.

"Uh, that's not how things work where I come from," he said as he unraveled himself.

"How do they work?"

Luckily for Billy, before he could answer, there was a disturbance at the courtyard gate. Through the pomegranate trees, Billy could see several goblins on *vargaren*-back riding into the human quarter.

Billy turned to Alyseer. "What's that about?"

"The Sunchase," Alyseer said excitedly. She dropped her practice chains and headed for the gate.

"The what?"

"Come see!"

This are getting silly, Hop thought as he stared into the huge tent. While he was grateful to still have his head firmly attached to his body, he couldn't help but worry that his continued survival against impossible odds was stretching the law of probability uncomfortably thin. If Hop were the religious sort, he would have offered the Night Goddess a prayer of thanks. But he was reasonably certain that if the Night Goddess existed, She had more important things to worry about, and the fact that he was still breathing was attributable solely to luck.

He was equally certain his luck was due to run out. Probably very soon.

Take his current situation. When Sawtooth's enforcers had nabbed him, he'd figured they were taking him straight for the executioner's axe. But the Teeth had never realized that Hop was a wanted *gob*. Instead, they'd fixated on the bat-rider's cap hiding his mangled ear. Apparently Sawtooth was desperate for experienced riders and had ordered his thugs to kidnap any they could find.

Which explained why Hop was now, despite a total lack of experience or qualifications, an aerial scout in Sawtooth's newly reconstituted Warhorde. Certainly it was a promotion from the last time he'd been in the army. Aeronauts were well treated and well paid. They were even allowed a level of eccentricity, which came in handy as far as hiding his identity was concerned. No one expected a bat-rider to mingle with his fellow soldiers. And if Hop chose to leave his cap on all the time, even when he was eating or sleeping, well, everyone knows flyboys are crazy, right?

Still, Hop had a serious problem. Eventually he would actually have to pilot a bat. He'd avoided flying duty so far by faking a hacking cough, all the while pretending he was furious that his feigned illness was keeping him from getting "skyward." His enforced grounding gave him a chance to study the other aeronauts, hopefully to learn the basics of bat-riding before his cough wore out its welcome. Currently that meant standing at the entrance of a huge bat-sheltering tent, watching the other bat-riders tend to their mounts. Hop was a quick learner, but he was still confused by the complicated tack and gear, the intricate whistles used to signal the bats, and the various tricks for maintaining balance and control while the bats swooped and dove, climbed and banked. It took years to properly train a bat-pilot.

Hop had, at most, a few days.

By calling on the allegiance of his veterans, exploiting the patriotism of the naive, and bullying and press-ganging every remaining able-bodied male left in Kiranok, Sawtooth had assembled a decent-sized army. And Hop knew the general wouldn't build an army unless he intended to use it. That meant the war would be heating up again. Once that happened, Hop would be expected to pilot his bat and its crew into combat, assuming he could figure out how to rig his gear, mount his bat, whistle it skyward, and stay on the thing for more than a split second. Not an easy task.

To make matters worse, humans had learned the hard way that goblins on bat-back were dangerous foes. The warbat crews could snipe at officers, drop rocks on enemy formations, spy out hidden ambushes, and generally wreak havoc if left unmolested. So when the warbats appeared on the battlefield, the humans did everything in their power to bring them down. That meant arrows and crossbow bolts, but mostly, it meant spells—horrific bolts of fire and light that turned the bats, along with their pilots and crews, into cinders and brought them plummeting from the sky. If Hop didn't learn how to avoid that, and soon, he was as good as dead.

"Afeared, are you?"

Hop turned and saw an old, battle-scarred goblin wearing an aeronaut's cap standing behind him in the tent entrance.

"Why you say that?" Hop asked as calmly as he could manage.

"'Cause you appear like a *gob* with some sense. Any *gob* with a brain atwixt his ears are afeared to ride a bat when the fighting get hot, *zaj*." The old aeronaut looked Hop up and down, then added, "Especially one what're never piloted one afore."

"Me, *nai* pilot?" Hop tried to look offended.

"You think you can fool *us*, lad? Wearing a flappy cap do *nai* make you *nai* rider. *Nai* matter what them idiot Teeth think."

Hop's mind raced. He could continue to bluff and bluster, but the old *gob* clearly wouldn't buy it. He could run, but if the old rider shouted for help, he wouldn't get far. Or he could try to overpower the perceptive flyer, but the veteran aeronaut probably wouldn't go down without a fight. Unfortunately, Hop's only viable option was his least favorite . . . telling the truth.

"I finded the bleedy cap in a ragmonger's shop," Hop muttered.

"Then the press gang catched you," the aeronaut nodded knowingly. "But why *nai* tell 'em the truth?"

Because I're a wanted gob *and they woulda chopped me head off?* Nai. *That are enough honesty for one day.*

Hop put on his best embarrassed expression. "The thing are," Hop said, "I always wanted to learn to fly. That're why I buyed the skycap in the first place. So when the Teeth catched me, I figured, *zajnai* it're destiny or something."

The wily old bat-rider didn't look entirely convinced.

"That and I do *nai* want to march in the mud *nai* more," Hop blurted, making it sound like he was confessing his darkest sin. "I getted enough of that in the last war. You swoopers have it easy."

"Easy? Are you touched in the head, boy? Bat-riding are the most dangerous job in the Warhorde."

"Do *nai* look so hard. Seem to me the bat do all the work." Hop smiled, hoping he hadn't overplayed his hand. The old *gob* was proud of his profession, sure. And he hadn't called for the Teeth yet. But would he take the bait?

"Tell you what, boy. We're short riders right now. Since Solace Ridge, we're always short." Hop had seen what had happened to the bat-riders that day. Dozens killed, falling burning from the sky. The old rider continued, "And you're the first *gob* I meeted in weeks stupid enough to want the job. So I'll show you what it take. And then you can tell me if it're easy."

"Deal. You have me gratitude. *Ganzi.*" Hop tried to keep his expression neutral despite the feeling of triumph flowing through his veins.

"We'll balance accounts if you live, Borrowed Cap. You're a bat-rider now. And bat-riders have the life expectancy of a fat *kijakhof* the night afore a feast." Chuckling, the old aeronaut ambled into the tent with a rolling, bowlegged gate caused by decades sitting astride a giant bat. "Do *nai* dawdle, Borrowed Cap," he called back to Hop. "You've much to learn and *nai* time to learn it. Just listen to old Sergeant Flyrat, do what I tell you, and *zajnai* you'll get your chance to die properly in battle."

Hop followed Flyrat, feigning enthusiasm. Maybe he should have run after all.

Lexi tried very hard not to set the building on fire.

"Just the smallest spark, little one. That's all we need. A whisper. Not a shout." Donegan's wife, Sarlia, reminded Lexi a lot of her aunt Jo. She was in her late thirties, slightly plump, with an easy laugh and a kind voice. Sarlia was a lightworker, an accomplished healer, and, it turned out, an amazing teacher. In only a week or so, she'd taught Lexi a hundred different things about how to harness the magical heat inside her. How to cure various ailments, bake mud into clay, melt metal, create light, even, theoretically, how to fly. But all of Sarlia's light spells relied on one ironclad requirement . . . self-control.

Lexi was terrible at self-control. She was always acting on impulse. She spoke without thinking, changed her mind constantly, and had a hard time concentrating on any one thing for long. Sometimes she wondered if she had ADHD or whatever they were calling it these days, but her parents weren't big fans of giving kids pills, so they'd never had her tested. They insisted that whatever was wrong with Lexi, she could manage herself with a little effort, a little forethought, and a little self-awareness.

Easy for them to say.

Right now, all she was supposed to do was light a candle. Sarlia had explained the trick many times. Use the least possible amount of energy to heat the wick slowly until it ignited. Lexi had been working on it for days, and every single time, the result had been the same . . .

Whoosh. The candle went up all at once, turning into a column of fire that shot right up to the roof.

"Better," Sarlia said, focusing her own energies to absorb the flames and douse the candle.

"How was that better?" Lexi slumped.

"The wick smoldered for a moment before it exploded. You almost had it. But you lost patience."

"Story of my life."

"The story of your life has barely begun. You've been working with me a week and you're already improving. You should be proud."

Lexi shook her head. "Why are you so nice to me?"

Sarlia smiled. "Being nice is easy. Hating those around you, carrying anger and resentment, that takes effort. Self-control isn't about clamping down on something unnatural. It's about moving through life with ease and grace."

"Easy for you to say," Lexi almost snapped back, her usual reply to parental advice. But for once, she stopped herself. Or rather, she let the impulse go without acting on it. *Ease and grace? Couldn't hurt to try.*

"You see." Sarlia gave Lexi a gentle kiss on the forehead. "Better."

Just then Donegan entered, smiling slightly, as he usually did. "Wife and Love, you should set your lessons aside for a bit."

"Should I, Husband and Home?"

Lexi managed not to make a face at Sarlia's and Donegan's pet names for each other. *Ease and grace. Ease and grace.* She repeated it like a mantra. It helped, a little.

"It's the Sunchase," Donegan said. "They're doing the choosing. And I know how much you like to pet the *vargaren.*"

In the stories Billy had read, goblins had always been pretty simple. They were stupid and mean, they worked for the bad guys, and they ate people. So it still surprised him whenever these goblins, *his* goblins, turned out to be as strange and complicated and surprising as . . . well . . . people. Complete with their own language, culture, cooking, music, and, he was now learning, crazy religious holidays.

From what Billy could tell, the goblins' Sunchase was like Mardi Gras, Thanksgiving, and the Kentucky Derby all rolled into one, a huge race up and down the nearest mountain on *vargar*-back. The lead outrider explained the basics, then announced the Chase would take place in five days, and that the contestants would be chosen today, as per goblin tradition.

Billy, Kurt, and their Celestial hosts gathered around the outriders and their *vargaren*, eager for more details.

Then Billy heard, "Hey, Freckles. Jockboy."

Lexi joined them, obviously a bit spent from her latest lesson. "School's out. Hear it's some kind of holiday."

Billy hadn't seen Lexi in days. "Lexi!" He rushed over and gave her a hug. Then he realized he may have gone a little far. "Uh, sorry." He let go.

"No. It's okay. I don't mind. Glad to see you too."

"You good?" Billy studied Lexi. There were lines around

her eyes as if she hadn't been sleeping much.

"Yeah. Just been working really hard. There's a lot to learn." She looked around the Court of the Orbs, taking in the scene. "So Donegan said this Sunchase thing is some kind of race? A bunch of goblins ride those giant wolf things up a mountain as fast as they can, then race down?" Lexi said. "Sounds dangerous." She looked nervously at the *vargaren*.

"It's terrifying," Alyseer admitted, stepping closer to the three outsiders. "We got here last year right before the Chase, so it was our first experience with a goblin holiday. From here, you can only watch the last few hundred yards of the course, and that's pretty flat. But I still saw a half dozen riders fall off their *vargaren*. Or get shoved off."

"They fight each other? That's legal?" Kurt asked.

"Goblin games don't have a lot of rules. They fight, push, shove, whatever they can get away with. I hear it gets pretty rough up on the mountain, under the trees where the judges can't see. Sunchasers get hurt every year. Sometimes they even die."

"Then why do it?" Lexi asked, backing away as an outrider paraded her mount uncomfortably close.

"What're the point of living if you spend all your time safe in a bed?" answered the keen-eared outrider. "Them Celestials juggle fire; other humans dance with swords. On *Genzirjad*, us *goben* race our *vargaren* up and down the mountains. It get the heart pumping, make the blood hot, so you feel every breath and taste every moment."

"And it honor the spirits of the mountain and the *vargaren*," another outrider interjected. "It celebrate the end of fire time and the start of the harvest."

"That too. But mostly it're *maja* fun. *Yob'rikit!*" The first rider grinned, flashing her sharp teeth.

The second outrider looked over the crowd of humans. "So, time to find out which of you get to ride in the Chase."

Even Alyseer looked surprised by this. "None of us rode last year."

The first rider's grin widened. "Last year you were guests, *zaj*. Newly arrived. But this year you're part of the community, *nai*? Starcaller sayed so. And every courtyard in the Fastness provide three riders. So now we find out who ride for the Court of the Orbs."

"I'll do it." Kurt stepped forward, his face set and determined.

"Do *nai* work that way. Otherwise, everyone want to do it, *zaj*. So we draw stones."

The first rider pulled a leather sack from her saddle bag. "Everyone draw a rock. If you get a white one with a number painted on it, you get to ride. Number are the order you choose your *vargar*. Now, this're only for young folk. *Nai* children. *Nai* what have a family to feed. So if you're old enough to have hair below your neck, but still do *nai* have children of your own, file up."

The young humans from the Court of the Orbs formed a line, some eagerly, some with considerably more reluctance. Billy had learned that the Celestials tended to marry fairly young, at eighteen or nineteen, so most of the people in line were his age, more or less. Only he, Lexi, and Kurt hung back.

The lead outrider fixed on them with her reddish eyes. "You three as well, *zaj*."

"You want us to ride?" Billy asked, surprised. "We're prisoners. They're going to . . ." Billy trailed off. *Execute us.* He couldn't say it.

"*Bosh*," the outrider scoffed. "I know who you are. And *zajnai* Starcaller'll order your deaths, but most likely *nai* today. So, until then, you're living here. And you're of age. So you draw your stones like the rest."

"Why not?" Kurt said and got in line.

After a moment's thought, Billy joined the line as well. Lexi followed.

"What are you doing?" Kurt said. "You two are too young."

Billy didn't like the superiority in Kurt's voice. "Hey, I've got hair on my—"

"Dude, too much information," Kurt interrupted.

"They said all of us," Lexi pointed out. "Better not to argue when you're under a death sentence."

Kurt gave in. Billy knew he couldn't argue with that.

One by one, the waiting Celestials drew stones, while Billy, Lexi, and Kurt watched from the back of the line. The first human to draw a numbered stone was a boy named Azam, a big burly carpenter's son who sometimes practiced fire-spinning with Kurt. He looked pleased with himself.

Alyseer drew next. A blank stone. She smiled sheepishly. "That's a relief."

As the bag worked its down the line, Billy could see Kurt's expression darken. "This was all a big mistake," he said quietly.

Billy shrugged. "We probably won't get picked."

"No, coming here. Staying. Everything since we followed Hop into that crazy city. We should have kept looking for a way home and never gotten mixed up in all this goblin stuff."

"We didn't have much of a choice."

"I should have figured something out. I mean, I'm the oldest. I'm supposed to be a leader. But I screwed it up. The whole time we've been here, I've screwed up. Or we wouldn't be in this mess."

Billy studied the perfect quarterback in his perfect despair and smiled a little, despite himself. "It doesn't always work that way. You can't control everything in your life. And beating yourself up when things go wrong is just another way of pretending you're the center of the universe. The Celestials, they've got it right. Sometimes things just fly at you. Unexplainable, crazy things. Like this entire place. And when that happens, you can try to juggle, or walk the tightrope, but that's all you can do. Try."

"Do you really believe all that?" Lexi asked.

"I'm working on it."

Kurt looked at Billy, surprised. "When did you get so philosophical?"

Since I figured out I had to stop blaming myself for everything or go nuts, Billy thought. Which was not an admission he was ready to make to Kurt and Lexi. "I guess Donegan's sermons must be sinking in."

Lexi got a thoughtful look on her face. "You know, what if Kurt wasn't the reason we showed up here—"

Luckily for Billy, before Lexi could pursue her question, they were interrupted by a commotion in the crowd. As the outriders passed the bag around, another numbered stone came up, this time pulled by a delicate girl a bit younger than Billy. She immediately burst into tears and ran to her mother. The Celestials didn't look happy about the idea of the girl participating in the potentially deadly race.

"*Nai* to worry," the lead outrider reassured the crowd. "We'll have her pick one of the older *vargaren* and strap her to the saddle. It'll walk her up and down the mountain nice and gentle like."

That seemed to calm things down. The draws continued, but no more numbered stones appeared. Finally, the outriders stood in front of Billy, Kurt, and Lexi, the last three in line.

"Three of you, and three stones left, one marked." The female rider grinned, showing her fangs. "Counted it out just right. So who're gonna get lucky?"

The goblin shook the bag and held it out to Kurt. He stuck his hand in, confident. "Don't sweat it, rugrats. It's gonna be me." But it wasn't. He pulled out a blank. "Man, this destiny stuff is overrated."

"Two stones left. And two of you."

Lexi reached for the bag, but Billy quickly stepped forward. "I'll go next."

Billy could tell Lexi's training had her pretty frazzled. He was determined not to let her race in her current condition. He reached into the bag and felt around. Sure enough, there were two stones left. Both were extremely smooth, like river rocks, so Billy couldn't tell if there was paint on one and not the other. One rock was slightly larger than the other with a more pronounced bulge in the middle. Billy felt the rocks again, trying to remember if there was anything distinctive about the winning stones.

Then he felt the air getting warm around him. He looked back at Lexi.

"Hey. No cheating."

Lexi looked sheepish; the air cooled. "I just thought with my magic I could probably do better than—"

Billy cut her off. "I don't need you to protect me. Besides, that's exactly the kind of thing you're *not* supposed to be doing."

Then Billy remembered. The two winning rocks had both been very flat, the better to provide a good surface for the painted numbers. His hand clenched around the smaller, flatter rock.

"Got you!" Sure enough, Billy pulled a rock painted with the goblin symbol for the number five. He held up the winning stone for all to see. The crowd cheered, Kurt included. But Lexi looked worried.

The goblin with the bag clapped Billy on the shoulder enthusiastically. "*Yob'rikit!* Now you, we'll give a *maja* big strong *vargar, zaj*?"

"*Zaj,*" Billy sputtered as he joined the two other Sunchasers, the jubilant Azam and the crying girl. Billy had to wonder. Maybe he should have let Lexi win. He'd never ridden in his life, not a horse, and certainly not a giant horned wolf.

Billy pictured himself falling from the saddle and plunging off a cliff to his death.

No, he told himself, *that's fear talking.* Somewhere past his worries, he knew that he'd done the right thing. He'd brought Lexi and Kurt here, he'd gotten them into this, and for once, he'd be the only one risking his life, he'd be the one facing the consequences.

Hopefully he wouldn't get killed for his efforts.

CHAPTER ELEVEN
To Chase the Sun

N*ai* half bad," Flyrat told Hop as they finished another day's training.

The old aeronaut had taken a liking to Hop, probably because he was the only goblin in the squad old enough to take a mate but still young enough that he didn't have hair growing on his ears. "Another few moons and I'll make a full-fledged flyer out of you. Then you can wear that pilot's cap you stole with pride. Assuming you do *nai* crash and die, mind you."

Unfortunately, they didn't get a few more moons. They didn't even get another week.

Two days later, Hop received his first official mission, a scouting sortie, supposedly a chance for him to test-fly his new warbat, Daffodil, a gentle, reliable female. Flyrat ordered the bat's eight *goben* crew stripped down for speed to just Snails, a sharp-eyed young *drogob* who was Daffodil's spotter, and Flutter, the warbat's flash-goblin, responsible for communicating with the Warhorde and the other bat-riders by signal flag and lantern flash. Struggling to get Daffodil to obey his inexpert whistles, Hop piloted her to her assigned position as the final bat in the formation. From there, all he and his crew had to do was follow the other warbats and relay their scouting reports back to Sawtooth's base camp. "A moon-view," Flyrat called it. An easy job. Snails and Flutter seemed relaxed and confident. Snails sang a flyer's ditty as he scanned the ground below them. Flutter joined in:

Waaaaaaazeeeeeer . . .
Every day above ground are a lesson
But to fly through the sky are a blessing
From the back of a bat
Can nai *gripe about that*
Though it scare me to death, I're confessing

Ah, the view it're fine
From the back of a bat
But you slip, then you're dying
So it go, that are that

Ahka, the groundhogs are all a shaking
At the risks that us flyers are taking
How the light wizards' magic
Bring us death, oh so tragic
But at least up so high we're nai *baking*

'Cause way up here it are nice and breezy
There are nai *dust to make you all sneezy*
And if we fall down
Then the nice rocky ground
Will make the end quick and easy

Ah, the view it're fine
From the back of a bat
If you slip, then you're dying
So it go, that are that

So if you must come put on your war hat,
Take me advice and soar high like Flyrat
True you put one foot wrong
Then you will nai *live long*
But at least you'll make a memorable splat
When you fall from the sky
From the back of your bat

Oh one day, we'll all die
Ev'ry gob, thin or fat
But 'til then, we'll fly high
And that? That are that!

At first everything went as planned. The warbats zigzagged over the hills and valleys around the Warhorde's camp, reporting on geographical features, natural hazards, and the occasional human patrol. Then, at dusk, as Flutter was switching her rig from flags to lanterns, the flashgob on the lead bat let loose with a stream of signals.

"That look important," Hop called back to Flutter, shouting over the wind. "What're the news?" Hop had been meaning to memorize Flutter's signals so he could read them himself, but learning to pilot Daffodil was taking all his time.

Flutter's brow furrowed in concentration as she passed the signal back to the Warhorde. She either hadn't heard Hop, or she'd chosen to ignore him.

Instead, Snails answered for her. "Redsight that next valley, Cap."

"Cap" was Hop's new nom de guerre, short for "Borrowedcap," the calling-name Flyrat had bestowed on him.

Hop squinted slightly, shifting his vision to redsight. In the failing light, he could barely see the next valley with his normal vision. But with redsight, the entire valley blazed red. Red meant heat, which meant fire or life, or both. Hop watched the red glow shift and surge, like a rippling tide. He focused, trying to distinguish the countless individual heat sources. There were hundreds of bright, stationary blobs that could only be bonfires, a cluster of bulky, quadruped glows that Hop recognized as picketed horses, and thousands and thousands of dull orange-red heat sources, gathered around the bonfires or moving purposefully through the valley. Only one thing glowed that particular shade in Hop's experience. Humans. The warbats had found the Army of Light.

"That're a *maja* big load of humans," Snails said, his voice squeaking a little from fear and excitement. It reminded Hop how young Snails was. Just a kid, like most of the soldiers in Sawtooth's army. Everyone fighting this war was either too damn young or too damn old in Hop's opinion.

"Too *maja* by far," Hop agreed as the scouting warbats broke off and wheeled back toward Sawtooth's camp. Time to report what they'd found. Whether Sawtooth wanted to hear it or not.

In his command tent, Sawtooth listened impatiently to his scouts droning on about the human encampment they'd located. How the humans outnumbered Sawtooth's army by at least five to one. How they'd fortified the hills around their camp, controlled the higher ground, and had several thousand cavalry to supplement their vast infantry.

One of the aeronauts, a lean, sharp-toothed goblin who struck Sawtooth as vaguely familiar, went on and on about the foolishness of a direct attack on the Hanorians. The annoying bat-rider, Borrowedcap, tried to convince Sawtooth to fall back into the mountains, break the Warhorde into smaller units, and continue the fight through ambush and night attack. Harass the humans' supply lines, snipe at their patrols, slow their progress, confuse their lines of communication, anything but a straight-up fight.

As if he were a general. As if he knew more about war than Sawtooth!

In any case, the numbers his scouts were reporting couldn't be accurate. Sawtooth's enforcers had rounded up nearly all the adult males in Kiranok. Many of the females too. So his new Warhorde was twice the size of the army he'd lost at Solace Ridge. There was no possible way the humans could have matched that, not here, so far from their coastal homelands.

And even if they have more troops than we do, it'll nai *matter. Humans are cowards,* Sawtooth thought contemptuously. *Them* skerboen *are afeared of their own shadows. Take 'em by surprise, throw 'em off guard, put the fright in 'em, and they'll always run.*

The more rational part of Sawtooth, the part not blinded by hate, knew the falsehood in that logic. When the Warhorde had attacked Bastinge and Fellentor, human defenders had fought to the last man. At Pollard, their garrison had held out for days, lasting until reinforcements arrived to drive Sawtooth's army away. In those battles, humans had proven every bit as brave as any goblin. But Sawtooth dismissed his doubts as quickly as they arose. He wasn't a goblin to bother with inconvenient facts when they conflicted with his hard-earned prejudices. For Sawtooth, there was only one way to handle the current crisis. One clear solution.

"Enough," he interrupted the blathering aeronauts. Then he turned to his sub generals and war-wizards. "We attack."

Hop left the meeting despondent. He'd risked his life to convince Sawtooth to retreat. And though the irascible general hadn't recognized him, in the end, it hadn't mattered. Sawtooth had listened to the scouting reports, then dismissed him and his fellow aeronauts and ordered an all-out attack on the human camp.

Hop reflected that Sawtooth had his faults, but a lack of courage wasn't one of them. Unlike most officers, the general led from the front, wading into combat with no thought for his personal safety. Hop couldn't even question the way Sawtooth treated his troops. He kept the Warhorde well fed, he was evenhanded in his discipline, and he never overworked his soldiers without good reason. When there was a tough job to do, Sawtooth was right there with them, marching instead of riding, eating the same grub they ate, and swinging a sword or an entrenching tool with equal gusto. The general would have been a good, solid mid-ranking officer. He would have made an even better sergeant, as good as Hop, maybe better.

Unfortunately, Sawtooth wasn't a sergeant. He was the

leader of the entire Warhorde. Which, in Hop's opinion, made his courage, confidence, and determination into serious liabilities. General Sawtooth had never met a battle he didn't like. He didn't retreat. He didn't maneuver. He just charged his army right at the enemy. The upcoming engagement against the humans promised to be no exception. As far as Hop could tell, the battle plan was typical Sawtooth—bold, bloody, and uncompromising.

Hop looked at Snails and Flutter and the other members of his crew, the too-young and too-old faces of the Warhorde. He could sense their unease. They knew the odds were against them, that Sawtooth was acting irrationally. Still, they were good soldiers, and they were defending their homeland. So they would fight.

It broke Hop's heart. Watching his crew prepare Daffodil for battle, he swore to himself that if Sawtooth's attack turned into another slaughter, he'd do everything in his power to save as many of his fellow goblins as he could . . . and maybe even save himself, just for good measure.

On the Fastness's parade ground, Billy and the other Sunchasers, almost fifty in all, lined up to choose their *vargaren*. The crying girl, Jesserel, stood just ahead of Billy, third in line. Billy was fifth. The final human, Azam, was near the back. The remaining contestants were all goblins in their teens or early twenties. Most were strangers, but Billy recognized Turner, the young novice who'd guided him, Lexi, and Kurt through the Fastness, standing a dozen or so places behind him. She gave him a nervous wave. Then Billy noticed Kettle, the belligerent goblin from the batreme, between him and Turner. When

Billy looked his way, the young goblin's face flashed with anger.

Outriders arranged the *vargaren* in a row at the far end of the grounds. They came in all shapes and sizes, from excited-looking adolescents bouncing around like gigantic puppies, to heavily muscled, snarling adults, to fat, gentle seniors, their coats dappled with gray and their eyes dulled by age. The Sunchasers studied the *vargaren* with care, trying to measure each one's potential without betraying their assessments to their new rivals.

Billy found himself watching an old female with a blunted horn, rounded teeth, and a happy, lolling tongue. She seemed amiable enough, the kind of *vargar* that would amble up and down the mountain without hurry, secure in the knowledge that, having whelped dozens of pups and raised them to adulthood, she had nothing left to prove and certainly didn't have to strain herself or risk her rider to win some silly race. Just the *vargar* for him. Billy felt a surge of relief. With his fifth pick, mama-*vargar* seemed like a lock. He might survive the race after all.

Billy looked around the parade grounds. Thousands of bystanders filled the field, eager to see which rider got what mount. He spotted a cluster of goblins handing coins to an old, blind *jintagob* wedged between a pair of towering *kijakgoben*. Bets, he guessed, certain that no one was stupid enough to wager on him.

After a moment, he spotted a friendly face. Two, actually. Frost and his brother, Leadpipe, stood apart from the crowd with the rest of the goblin prisoners. Billy was relieved to see that they both looked healthy. Frost gave Billy a discreet nod, but Leadpipe waved enthusiastically, accidentally splashing beer from a huge goblet onto his brother's head. Frost wiped away the spilled beer, looking more worried than angry. Though whether Frost was concerned for Billy or for himself, Billy couldn't guess.

Finally, Sawtooth's daughter, Shadow, strode to the front of the crowd, looking as controlled and impressive as ever.

"*Ahka*, you," she called out, easily making herself heard throughout the parade grounds. "I're here to tell you the rules of this here race. And they're this . . . We are *goben*! There are *nai* rules!"

This pronouncement was met by a cheer of approval from the crowd.

"On the second taste, though, there are consequences. Consequences are what happen if you do something you should *nai* and you get catched, *zaj*? So here they are. You're to be searched afore the race. We find you carrying a weapon, you're out of the Chase. If you actually *try* to kill anyone on the course, and you get spotted by one of our batty fellows here"—she gestured to a trio of bat-riders dressed in bright orange silks and armed with bows—"they *will* shoot you. But accidents happen and *goben* are *goben*, so if they do *nai* spot it, it never happened, *zaj*?"

Another cheer.

"Other than that," Shadow continued after the cheers subsided, "the sun rise, you ride up one side of the mountain. You grab a flag up top. You ride down the other side. First one that make it back here with a flag win. Simple."

Then Shadow looked out at the Sunchasers, meeting eyes with each one. "And now come the best part." Shadow scraped a line in the dirt with her boot. "If the winning *gob* reach this line afore the sun set, *nai* only will that *gob* get the traditional gold and ale and eggs, the winner will also get one wish, one request, any one thing what the Great Priestess Starcaller have it in her power to give. If you're first across this line by sunset, mountain-top flag in your hands, that wish are yours."

Shadow paused to let her words sink in, then smiled. "So who want to chase the sun?"

With that all the riders, even little Jesserel, shouted and whooped and cheered.

All except Billy. He was too busy thinking.

If the winner crossed the line before sundown, he or she would get anything within Starcaller's power? Starcaller was the judge who'd sentenced Lexi, Billy, and Kurt to death, along with Frost and his brother. And despite the surprising comfort of their captivity, the threat of execution still hung over their heads. Then there were the dozens of goblins who'd been exiled to the Fastness for helping them. If Billy won, could he ask for a pardon? For all of them?

He spotted the exile Kettle, who was studying the *vargaren* intently, oblivious to everything but his potential mount. Billy knew what Kettle was racing for. His freedom. Except if Kettle won, Billy doubted he'd include the humans in his wish.

"First rider," Shadow announced, "choose your mount."

A young male goblin stepped forward and nervously surveyed the *vargaren*. After a minute or two, he pointed to an adolescent female with a good-natured expression and an especially short horn.

"Tasty choice," Shadow said. "Steady. Reliable but with good speed."

The next goblin in line, a tall broad-shouldered female *kijakgob*, picked the biggest *vargar* she could find, a burly male whose fanged mouth foamed with drool.

Shadow nodded her approval. "That're one ill-tempered brute. *Nai* the fastest. But he'll carry you. And take the arm off anyone what mess with you."

Now it was Jesserel's turn. The Celestial girl stood

there, looking confused and intimidated.

"Need some help, *derijinta*?" Shadow said, looking at Jesserel with a surprisingly kind expression.

"I don't know which one to choose," Jesserel sputtered.

"Try this one." Shadow pointed . . .

. . . At Billy's *vargar*. The big, lazy, gentle female he'd chosen as the one most likely to get him up and down the mountain safely.

"She're the sweetest, slowest *vargar* we have. Mother to half the pack so *nai* will nip at her or her rider. Dewdrop are as safe as it come."

Jesserel smiled shyly and approached the old female. "Hi, Dewdrop. I'm Jesserel." The *vargar* snuffled at the girl, then gave her face a gentle nuzzle. In return, Jesserel hugged the *vargar*'s massive neck. "We're going to be best friends."

That sealed it for Billy. He was already having second thoughts about the mother *vargar*. Once Shadow announced the reward for crossing the line before sunset, he knew he couldn't just play it safe. If he wanted to live and save his friends, Billy was going to have to *race*.

His gaze fell on a pitch-black *vargar* with a sharp, glossy horn and intense, orange eyes. The beast was male, muscular but not bulky. His mane was the color of coal, but it wasn't large or particularly bushy. So he was young, Billy guessed, just out of adolescence, the age when you've got everything to fight for, everything to prove. The black *vargar* looked energetic, agile, and strong. He also looked vicious. Even as Billy studied him, the beast growled and snapped at one of his pack mates. The offending *vargar*, though older and larger than the young male, whined and backed away. The black *vargar* definitely had spirit. Billy got the feeling he wanted to win the race almost as much as Billy did.

But it wasn't Billy's turn to choose. There was one goblin ahead of him, a tough-looking adolescent with a scar across his face that twisted his expression into a permanent sneer. And he was watching Billy watch the black *vargar*.

"You've a good eye," he said to Billy with a wide grin. "Too bad I go next." With that, the disfigured goblin ambled up to the black *vargar* and clapped the beast on the shoulder. "*Ahka*, you *pizkret*. You're working for me now."

It happened so fast, Billy barely saw it. One second the scarred goblin was patting the *vargar* on the shoulder, the next he was on the ground, and the *vargar* was holding him down with one giant paw, huge jaws inches away from the goblin's face.

"Back, Torrent! Back!" Handlers rushed the black *vargar*, shouting and waving. The beast gave a low growl, then backed away, letting his would-be rider loose.

The handlers herded Torrent away from the rest of the *vargaren*. The disfigured goblin approached the handlers, looking confused. "So what do I—"

Before he could finish his question, Torrent started snarling, growing, and snapping again.

"Pick another one!" shouted a handler.

It took the handlers several minutes to calm Torrent, stroking his fur and whispering quietly in his ears. The scarred young goblin seemed cowed by his experience. Once order was restored, he quickly chose a different *vargar*, a graceful but gentle female.

Then it was Billy's turn. He looked at the remaining *vargaren*, trying not to panic. There was no time to get a feel for them now. Not with everyone watching.

"Pick a nice slow one, sprout," Kurt called out to him.

The spectators laughed at that. Billy did his best to tune out Kurt, the crowd, and his own nervousness. He had no intention of picking a slow one. He needed a mount that was fast, smart, and aggressive. But which one? As he studied the available *vargaren*, Billy realized he'd already made his choice. He walked forward. A murmur went through the crowd when they realized which *vargar* he intended to ride.

"Torrent," he said. "I want the black one."

"Billy, get away from that thing," Lexi warned him, obviously concerned.

"Seriously," Kurt added. "You don't want a piece of that."

Torrent glowered at Billy suspiciously as handlers held back the temperamental beast. Ignoring his friends' warnings, Billy stepped closer.

"I'll take him," Billy said quietly. "If he'll have me. Let him go please."

Reluctantly, the handlers eased their grip on the black *vargar*. Torrent snapped at them, and they backed away. The black *vargar* shook himself violently, as if checking to make sure he really was free. Satisfied, he turned his attention back to Billy.

Billy slowly extended his hand. "What about it, boy? You want to be friends?"

The crowd gasped as Torrent lunged forward. But to Billy's relief, the *vargar* didn't bite his arm off. Instead, he snuffled at Billy's outstretched hand. Ever so gently, Billy reached up to the *vargar*'s giant horned snout. Ignoring the drool dripping from Torrent's fangs, he stroked the side of the beast's face. The *vargar* tolerated his touch. Carefully, he moved his hand behind the *vargar*'s ear and scratched.

Torrent's tongue lolled. Billy had never met a dog that

didn't love getting scratched behind the ears. The beast licked Billy's face, his massive tongue leaving a trail of slime across the boy's cheek.

"Billy," Lexi said, worried, "what do you think you're doing?"

"Me?" Billy replied in a calm, measured voice that he hoped wouldn't agitate the black *vargar*. "I'm racing to win."

CHAPTER TWELVE
The Race

Below Daffodil's outstretched wings, Hop could see the goblin Warhorde fighting desperately in the early-morning mist, trying to repel a relentless human attack. As he piloted Daffodil over the battle, a cold certainty settled into Hop's bones.

This was Solace Ridge all over again.

Before dawn, the entire Warhorde had formed up and marched out to battle. Just getting Daffodil off the ground with her full complement of nine crew members (Hop, his signaler Flutter, his spotter Snails, and six archers) had taken every bit of Hop's limited skills. Still, sooner than Hop would've liked, they were soaring above the front lines, watching the Warhorde's thunderous charge from a hundred spans up.

Sawtooth's initial attack had caught the humans off guard. The violence of the goblins' unexpected assault had overwhelmed the humans, neutralizing their wizards and archers. Hop and his crew had been able to sail over the battle unmolested, firing down on the humans without reprisal.

But good things never last. The humans had rallied, their superior numbers absorbing the goblin attack. The Army of Light had bent, but it refused to break. Now the humans were counterattacking with enthusiasm.

"Incoming!" shouted Snails, interrupting Hop's musings. "Fire bolts. Belly-left!"

Hop whistled and lightly pricked Daffodil's neck with his goad. The warbat banked sharply right, avoiding a volley of flames coming up from the human army.

"This are the dumbest thing I ever do," Hop muttered.

"Do *nai* let Flyrat hear that," Flutter said with a smile.

"Ballista right!" Snails warned.

Hop leaned left, whistled, and used the goad. Daffodil responded with agonizing slowness. A huge iron arrow whirred past Hop's head. Hop heard a horrible gurgling scream behind him. Out of the corner of his eye, he saw someone tumbling off the bat.

"*Gob* down," Snails said, his voice choked with emotion. "Keenest."

Keenest was a willing lad from the Bowlus Plateau, eager and honest, though plagued with a perpetual snuffle. He'd been born only a few miles from Hop's own hometown. There was even a slight resemblance. Privately, Hop had speculated they might be distant cousins. Now Keenest's village would be missing yet another brave young goblin. And for what? Not to save all of goblinkind, not at this rate. No, Keenest and countless others were dying because of Sawtooth's monumental ego, his incompetent planning, and his suicidal recklessness.

"New orders!" squeaked Flutter, her signal flags whipping in the wind.

Praise the Night, Hop thought, hoping that, for once, Sawtooth might actually order the Warhorde to withdraw. But as Hop watched Flutter snap her flags back and forth, his hopes died. He'd finally learned a few of her signals, including the one for "retreat."

Flutter wasn't signaling retreat.

"No surrender," Flutter said grimly, relaying Sawtooth's orders and confirming Hop's worst fears. "Fight to the death."

General Sawtooth stood at the crest of a hill, surveying his handiwork. He'd participated in the initial charge, personally hacking down dozens of humans. Then he and his bodyguards had climbed this small rise to evaluate the progress of the battle. Nearby, signalers relayed Sawtooth's latest orders to the warbats and the forward commanders.

Rumblejaw, his *kijakgob* bodyguard, stood at his side. "Boss," the giant said cautiously, "this do *nai* look too good. *Zajnai* we should . . . regroup?"

"Retreat, you mean?" Sawtooth snapped. He had no intention of retreating. "The *skerboen* are cowards. They'll break. Long as we keep pressing, they'll break."

Sawtooth wasn't sure he believed that, but he'd bet everything on this play. And by the Goddess, he wasn't going to turn tail now. No. Despite the carnage, despite the overwhelming odds, Sawtooth would make sure his soldiers continued to throw themselves frantically against the human lines.

Victory. Or death.

"Bank right, bank right!" Snails yelled.

Hop put Daffodil into a steep right turn, narrowly avoiding a gigantic boulder flung from a human siege machine. Down below, he could see goblins and humans dying by the hundreds. Determined to make sure he and his crew weren't more victims, Hop goaded Daffodil into another series of twisting turns and rolls.

"We're supposed to provide suppression fire," Snails reminded him. "The archers can *nai* shoot if you're throwing 'em back and forth like younglings on a swing."

"They can *nai* fire if they're dead neither," Hop said. "Flutter," he barked to his flashgob, "signal Command. Tell 'em the charge are failed. Tell 'em to sound the retreat."

Flutter didn't respond. Hop glanced back and saw the signaler staring up at the sky, mouth open wide in horror.

"Flutter?"

"What . . . are that?" Flutter stammered, pointing to the clouds above them.

Hop, Snails, and the five remaining archers looked up, squinting into the hazy sunlight. In the glare, they could just make out a vast shape moving toward them, glowing with its own magical light. A flying ship.

"Are it a batreme?" Hop asked.

"If it're a batreme, where are the bleedy bats?" Snails replied.

As the ship flew closer, Hop spied masts along the thing's hull supporting an array of giant mirrors. The mirrors sparkled as they caught and focused the sunlight, creating two huge light beams that shone down from the vehicle's wings, keeping it aloft. Three more beams streamed out from the stern, driving it forward. As Hop watched, a warbat dove down at the lightship, its goblin crew peppering the strange vehicle with arrows.

"That're Flyrat," Snails said. "On Thistle."

Hop watched in admiration as Flyrat expertly guided Thistle on a close approach, then, as soon as his archers finished their volley, pulled up and turned sharply to avoid any return fire from the enemy vessel. It was a perfect pass. Flawless.

But as Thistle soared out of arrow range and leveled off, the crew of the lightship adjusted one of the mirrors—

And a blinding ray of light lashed out from the ship, washing over Thistle, Flyrat, and their crew. Thistle caught fire. The warbat let out a shrill cry that set Hop's teeth on edge, even several hundred yards away. Flyrat and his goblins went up like dry tinder. The warbat spiraled to the ground, trailing smoke and flame.

Hop could hear Flutter crying quietly behind him.

"They're more of 'em," Snails said.

Hop tore his eyes away from the horrific destruction of Thistle and his crew and saw four more human lightships sailing out of the clouds, blasting warbats and goblin troops on the ground alike with their fiery mirror weapons. Down below, the Warhorde's lines shattered completely. Facing certain death, the goblin soldiers broke formation and fled for their lives.

"More orders coming," Flutter said, blinking back tears as she decoded the flag signals from Sawtooth's command post. "Relay to all warbats: *Nai* surrender. Fight on. Fight to the death."

Hop saw the lightship that had killed Flyrat and his crew soaring toward him, moving fast. Another few seconds and Daffodil would be within range of the humans' devastating new weapons. And for what? The warbats' job was to support the Warhorde's ground forces, but the battle was over; there was no chance of victory. Fighting on now would be suicide, pure and simple.

"Acknowledge. Then relay the following to the other warbats," Hop ordered deliberately. "Retreat. Retreat. Preserve your bats and crews. Retreat. Retreat."

Flutter froze.

"Do as you're told, *gob*," Hop growled in his best sergeant's voice. "Or I'll toss you off this bleedy bat!"

It was a bluff, of course. If Flutter decided to disobey him, it wasn't like Hop would actually throw her overboard. He turned away, hoping the gesture would end the conversation. Besides, he had to keep Daffodil steady. Maneuver now and Flutter wouldn't be able to signal at all. So he had to trust that right now Flutter was more frightened of him than of Sawtooth.

The lightship was closing fast. In its rigging, humans wrestled their killing mirrors toward Hop and his warbat. If Flutter was going to relay Hop's false orders, or even Sawtooth's real ones, she needed to do it soon.

Then Hop heard the signal flags snapping in the wind behind him as Flutter went into action. "Snails?" Hop said.

"She're signaling it," Snails said, his voice shaky. "Your message, Cap. Retreat."

"Finished!" Flutter yelled.

The humans had their killing mirrors pointed straight at Hop and his crew.

"Hold on!" Hop whistled shrilly and leaned left. Daffodil banked sharply as a beam of light lashed out at them from the human ship.

The air tasted like fire, burning at Hop's throat and lungs. Blinking to clear the spots from his vision, Hop saw a long column of smoke in the air where the light beam had passed. It had missed Hop's warbat by less than a half dozen spans.

"The other bats?" Hop asked, his voice harsh from the heat.

"Running for it," Snails said, "like you wanted."

"Us too." Hop turned Daffodil toward the mountains and goaded her to her top speed. But the bat wasn't his only worry. With his years of experience as a sergeant, Hop knew that his crew was teetering on the edge of rebellion. They didn't like disobeying orders from their general, no matter how incompetent he might be. And they especially didn't like running and telling others to run. Hop knew he had to get them on his side now, or they'd all be doomed.

"Listen close you," he said above the rushing wind. "Sawtooth ordered us to throw our lives away. To die for nothing. But right now the last thing our folk need are more corpses. That're why I ordered the retreat. Daffodil and the rest of the warbats and their crews have to survive this. So we can try to make sure there're still *goben* left when this war are through. Now, you can come with me, or I can drop you off on the next clear mountainside. To be honest, smart thing are to take the mountain. 'Cause if you stay with me, they'll call you traitors, most like. And you can expect hard times and fighting and death afore this're over. But I have to try. Much as I want to find me some hole to hide in, I have to try to set things right." Hop paused for a moment to let his words sink in, then added, "Time to choose. You with me? Or do you want out?"

Behind him, he could hear the crew whispering, discussing their options. It was Bead who finally answered for them all. Bead was Daffodil's chief archer, older, quiet, and intense. "We're with you." Then he added, pointedly, "Hoprock."

Hop snapped his head around in surprise. "You know me?"

"Hoprock One-Ear. The rebel Copperplate. *Zaj*, we know you. We're *nai* idiots. Flyrat knowed from the start,

I think. The rest of us guessed."

"And you *nai* turn me in?"

"*Drak*, you're an aeronaut, brother. And aeronauts stick tight."

Hop nodded, shocked and grateful all at once.

"Asides," Snails said, "you're right. If we let him, Sawtooth'll general us all to death."

Grateful for his crew's show of support, Hop turned his attention back to his piloting. "Stow weapons and flags. Hunker down. Brace for fast running."

"Err, Cap? I mean, Hop?" It was Flutter, her voice nervous.

"Spit it out, Flutter."

"Afore I stow me gear, you want me to give any more orders to the rest of the formation?"

"Formation?" Hop was confused. "What bleedy formation are that?"

"They're following you, sir. Every surviving warbat are forming up aback of us."

Hop glanced back. Sure enough, six other warbats were taking up flight positions in Daffodil's wake.

And behind them came the lightships, determined to wipe the warbats out of the sky.

"They're supposed to scatter," Hop said.

"Guess they think otherwise" Flutter said with a cock-eyed grin.

Hop suppressed a groan. He'd never liked responsibility, but somehow folk kept treating him like a leader, as if he knew what he was doing. When in the truth he was at least as confused and panicked as everyone else. Usually more so.

Nai *time for doubt or fear,* he chided himself. Nai *time for second thoughts. Too much are depending on you.*

"Them lightships are slower than us," Hop said. "Barely. We can *nai* outfight 'em. But we can outrun 'em." He tried to sound confident. That was important right now. "Tell the other crews we're heading west, top speed."

As Flutter relayed his orders, Hop tried to calculate the odds. The bats were faster than the lightships, but the bats would tire eventually. Four or five hours flying. An hour of rest. Then another four or five hours until the bats would have to sleep. Could the lightships operate at night? If they could, the warbats and their crews were doomed.

If not . . . well, it'd be tight. They'd sleep when the lightships anchored. Take off before dawn, then back to fly-rest-fly-sleep. And pray that their pursuers would give up, eventually. Either that or hope that the warbats could build enough of a lead that when they got to their destination, they'd actually be able to do some good.

Daffodil soared toward the mountains, the other warbats sailing in formation behind her, the pursuing lightships following slowly, but relentlessly.

The race was on.

The days after Billy chose his mount flew by in a blur. Billy spent every waking hour learning to ride a *vargar*. How to secure the saddle, how to arrange the stirrups, how to get Torrent to turn, to go faster or slower, to jump, to stop. *Vargaren* wouldn't tolerate a bit or a bridle. Billy had to deliver all the commands by leg pressure and voice. A tap here. A click or a whistle there. Luckily, Torrent mostly listened to him, though the *vargar* acted as if he only did what Billy suggested because it amused him. Torrent seemed to think that Billy was his pet, instead of the other way around.

But Billy wasn't picky. No matter how bad Torrent's attitude was, if the *vargar* turned left when Billy clicked left and turned right when he whistled right, Billy was happy.

Finally, the day of the race arrived.

As Billy edged Torrent past hordes of spectators to the Sunchase's starting line, he obsessed about everything that might go wrong. He could get lost. He could fall off Torrent's back. He could get attacked by the other Sunchasers. He could even die. Or worse, he could lose. Probably he *would* lose. Then all his efforts would be for nothing and he, Lexi, Kurt, Leadpipe, and Frost would be executed.

Torrent strode forward in response to his signals and joined the other *vargaren* at the starting line. Billy looked down at his fellow Sunchasers, squinting to make out their faces by the light of the setting moon. Most of them seemed just as nervous as he was. A few, like Jesserel, were plain terrified. Their mounts reflected their fear and confusion, shifting back and forth, growling, whining, even snapping at each other. But a dozen or so of the riders sat at ease in their saddles, their expressions determined, their *vargaren* attentive and responsive. They were mostly goblins Billy's age or older, including Turner and Kettle, and they were definitely in this race to win it.

To Billy's amazement, Torrent settled in at the starting line with a strange, intense calm. It was as if the black *vargar* sensed what was about to happen and was readying himself for the contest to come.

Nearby, the three referees mounted their riding bats and lifted off. They hovered over the Sunchasers, pointedly readying their bows to remind everyone of the penalty for overt cheating. Their bats were just large enough to carry a single rider each, and they looked fast and nimble. *Good luck trying to outrun them*, Billy thought.

Shadow strode up a small hillock overlooking the racers.

"Ears to me," she said in a slow, measured tone. "When the first bit of sun poke over the horizon yonder, I'll say go. When I do, you ride for all you're worth, *zaj*?"

Murmurs of "*zaj*" and "*yob'rikit*" rippled through the line. Billy whistled quietly to Torrent. His mount snorted and leaned back on his haunches into a powerful crouch, like a coiled spring. Shadow smiled. "*Nai* more words. If you're *nai* ready now, will *nai* matter what I say."

With that, Shadow went silent, standing like a statue in the predawn light. As the riders followed her example, an expectant hush fell over the crowd. Billy glanced at the spectators. He could just make out Lexi and Kurt standing with the humans from the Court of the Orbs. He knew Lexi was worried for him. While he'd been training for the race, Lexi had repeatedly offered to cast spells on Billy and Torrent to make them faster, stronger, more nimble. Billy had refused. Frost's story about the wizard who went crazy from overusing her powers had stuck with him. He didn't want Lexi to turn herself into some kind of magical zombie on his account.

To his surprise, after some initial resistance, Kurt finally got behind Billy's plan. He'd taken Billy aside the night before the race so they could talk in private.

"Listen, runt," Kurt had said. "I know what you're going through. The butterflies. The pregame jitters. Can I give you some advice?"

"If you want," Billy replied, guarded.

"Forget the finish line. The cheerleaders, all that junk. Just be in the moment. The right now. When you see the open man, you throw. No hesitation. Don't worry about the interceptions. Just throw. You know what I mean?"

"Is that what your dad used to tell you?" Billy couldn't help but ask.

"No. But I bet it's what *your* dad would say." Kurt smiled and clapped Billy on the shoulder. "You'll get it. When you're in the middle of everything, when the world is moving so fast that your eyes can't take it all in, it'll click. Then everything will slow down. That's the zone. When you get into the zone, go with it. Stay in the zone, and everything will be shiny."

At the time, Billy had hoped everything really would be "shiny," whatever that meant. But now, at the starting line, he didn't feel so confident. The calm, centered zone the quarterback had described seemed miles away. Still, Kurt flashed Billy a thumbs-up when they caught each other's eyes. At least someone thought he could win this thing.

"Go!" Shadow shouted as a tiny sliver of light appeared in the east. "Go! Go! Go!"

The other *vargaren* surged ahead as Billy snapped out of his reverie. Shadow had made the call, and Billy had missed it. The race had barely started, and he was already behind.

"Torrent, run!" Billy cried.

The powerful *vargar* leapt forward, his muscles rippling. Torrent took one bound, two, three, and he and Billy sailed past the slower riders into the middle of the pack. Two more bounds and they were right behind the leaders.

The race was on.

CHAPTER THIRTEEN
Easy Way, Hard Way, Any Way at All

S awtooth walked through the smoldering wreckage of his old home, bones crunching under his feet. He tried to get his bearings, confused. How did he get here? He hadn't been back to the little house in the Fastness since Cutty died. He looked around the main room. The couch where his wife had slowly wasted away lay in ruins by the window. As he stepped toward it, rats nesting inside the padding scampered away, squeaking in alarm as they sought new hiding places.

"You tryed, Saw. You doed your best, but it're fate. And you can *nai* dodge fate."

Sawtooth spun and saw his dead wife descending the stairs that led to their bedroom, stairs she'd been too weak to climb in the final months of her illness. Cutty looked healthy, young, and as vibrant as the day they'd met. Her dark hair cascaded down her shoulders. She'd always been proud of her long hair; combined with her small, delicate ears, it made her look striking and a little exotic.

"Fate are what we make it," Sawtooth shot back, angrier than he'd intended.

"Sometimes, *zaj*," Cutty answered with uncharacteristic calm. "But there're some things you can *nai* change *nai* matter how much you want to. What happened to me for one. The wasting stealed me away from you, and there were *nai* you could do about it."

A cold breeze kicked up, rustling through the ruins.

"I are never giving up on you," Sawtooth said, watching the wind whip Cutty's hair around her face.

Cutty smiled gently. "That were always your problem, Saw. You never knowed when to retreat. When to think about another way."

"What're you talking about?" Sawtooth replied, genuinely confused.

"All them dead lads. All that blood. And you do *nai* remember?"

Suddenly Sawtooth could smell burning flesh. He heard the sound of clashing steel and his own voice yelling above the din. "Attack! Attack! Attack!"

"The battle," he whispered, his voice choking as memories of the final desperate fight against the Army of Light flooded back to him.

"You killed them, Saw." The wind seemed to blow Cutty back up the stairs. She flew away from him, lighter than air. "You murdered them all."

"Do *nai* go!" Sawtooth rushed after his wife.

"What you do, you can *nai* undo." Then the disease took her. In an instant, Cutty went from being healthy and vibrant to sick and dying. Dark shadows appeared under her eyes. Lesions opened on her skin. Her long hair fell out and turned to ash. "There are *nai* victory in death."

Sawtooth woke with a shout of protest.

He was back in his office in Kiranok, lying on a pallet under arrow-slit windows, far from the bloody battlefield and even farther from his old home in the Fastness.

"It're a dream," he realized. "A nightmare."

Or at least, Cutty had been a dream. Sawtooth's recent, bitter defeat against the human Army of Light—*that* had happened, as much as he wished it hadn't. He remembered the final attack. With his lines shredded and his warbats driven away, Sawtooth had ordered one last mad charge. He remembered how he and his bodyguards had run screaming into the human lines, hacking and slashing, kicking and biting, leaving a wake of broken bodies and bloodied earth.

Miraculously, he'd fought his way through the Army of Light, battling past countless human fighters. He, his bodyguard Rumblejaw, and a half dozen or so other goblins had reached the far side of the Hanorian army just as the sun finally set over the bloody battlefield.

"Time to run, boss," Rumblejaw had said.

"*Nai* retreat. Attack. Keep attacking," Sawtooth had answered.

Or he'd tried to answer. But all that had come out was a rasping groan. Blood filled his mouth, and air hissed out of a wound in his chest, bubbling red. That was the last thing Sawtooth remembered.

"Fifty percent casualties," said a familiar bass voice, startling Sawtooth from his hazy reverie. Rumblejaw stood over him, bandaged and battered, but still alive. The giant goblin must have carried him back here, through the mountains to safety. But Sawtooth didn't want to be safe. He didn't want to be anywhere. He wanted to die.

"A wizard patched up your lung," Rumblejaw continued, anticipating Sawtooth's questions. "A near thing, but you're a tough one."

"We still control the city?"

"*Zaj*," Rumblejaw nodded. "And we hurt the human army *maja* bad."

"They run home?" Sawtooth asked. If the humans had retreated, the battle would've been worth it, no matter the cost.

Rumblejaw shook his massive head. "They're regrouping, resupplying, bringing in new recruits."

Sawtooth's heart sank. "How long?"

The giant goblin shrugged. "*Nai* way to tell. But they're still coming."

Sawtooth stood up, decisive, his old stubbornness returning even as his dream of Cutty faded from his memory. "Then we have to get ready for 'em."

Rumblejaw nodded, not surprised. Still, something was bothering him. "Boss, there're one other thing."

"Spit it."

"It're the Heir. Our spies, they say they been watching the Heir to the King. At the Fastness."

"The Heir?" Sawtooth felt his temper rising. "That ridiculous *skerbo* boy with the yellow hair? He failed. He're *nai* the King."

"*Zaj*. But some of us started thinking . . . there're more than one boy."

Torrent snarled at a rival *vargar* as he muscled his way down a narrow path. Billy struggled to stay in the saddle as the two wolf-like beasts banged against each other, each striving to win the high ground and nose ahead.

Every part of Billy's body ached. Torrent had been running for hours, dodging trees, leaping fallen logs, weaving around rocks, and charging uphill, always uphill. At first the *vargaren* and their riders had been packed close. Now the slower mounts had fallen behind, leaving only a few racers to fight for the lead.

Billy and Torrent were right there with them.

The path widened, and Billy relaxed a little. Hopefully with a bit more room Torrent and the *vargar* at his side could avoid bumping into each other.

"Eat dirt, Curlyhead!" shouted the rider of the other *vargar*, a young goblin with a towering Mohawk haircut. He kicked at Billy, trying to knock him off Torrent.

Pain shot through Billy's leg as the kick connected. He gripped his saddle horn with both hands, hanging on for all he was worth. Sensing his rider's pain, Torrent snapped and growled, eager to counterattack, but Billy guided Torrent away from the other racer, trying to avoid another confrontation.

"What? You can't beat a human without cheating?" Billy shouted back, determined not to be intimidated.

"This're how we play, *skerbo*. You *nai* like it, stop racing." The mohawked goblin steered his *vargar* closer and kicked at Billy again.

This time Billy was ready.

"Ha!" he shouted, squeezing his knees tightly into Torrent's side, praying his *vargar* would respond. It was the signal to stop. Torrent dug his paws into the dirt, skidding to a halt. The mohawked goblin kicked at empty air, throwing himself off balance. He teetered in his saddle.

"Ya!" Billy yelled, and Torrent surged forward, his

massive horned head ramming into the kicking goblin's extended leg. The impact sent the mohawked rider spinning from his *vargar*, crashing into deep brush off the side of the trail.

"Don't call me *skerbo*," Billy shouted as Torrent raced ahead, leaving the dismounted goblin sputtering and flailing in the bushes.

Serves him right, Billy thought, setting his sights on the next Sunchaser in line.

Serve me right, Hop thought. *I shoulda deserted. But* nai, *I haved to stay and fight. And look what that getted me.*

The chase was wearing on Hop and the rest of Daffodil's crew, and the goblins from the five other warbats weren't holding up any better.

There'd been seven bats in total when they'd started. But this morning, exhausted and overworked from successive days of long flying, the warbats had been too slow getting off the ground. Ninebark had been the last bat to lift off. The lightships had attacked just as he was launching. Ninebark's crew, cut off from the rest of the formation and hopelessly outmatched, had selflessly piloted their warbat straight at the enemy ships. The humans' mirror weapons had set Ninebark and his crew on fire. But their sacrifice allowed Daffodil and the five other bats to escape.

For a while, anyway.

It was midday, when the blazing sun powered the lightships to their top speed. The lightships were gaining on them. Hop knew they had to escape the enemy once and for all or they might never reach their final destination. He surveyed the area. Finally, he saw what he was searching for—a valley choked with towering red-barked trees and cut in half by a mountain stream.

"Signal the others," Hop called back to Flutter. "Rig for maneuvering and prepare to dive."

"Dive?" Flutter asked, clearly worried. "Are *nai* much room below us for a dive."

"What're this, a town meeting?" Hop snapped.

"Are *nai* the army *nai* more, that're sure," Snails said with a tired smile.

Hop resisted the temptation to chew out his spotter. What did he expect? A leader set an example, even when he didn't mean to. After seeing how Hop had defied Sawtooth, he doubted any of Daffodil's crew would mindlessly obey orders ever again. So instead of trying to sergeant his crew, Hop explained what he was planning.

"That're the craziest thing I ever heared," Bead, the lead archer, responded once Hop finished.

"What're the worst what can happen?" Hop asked.

"We could die," Flutter said accurately.

"They catch us, we die sure. My way, we only probably die. And *zajnai* we take some with us."

No one had any objection to that. Sensing consensus, Flutter grabbed her flags. "Signaling. Rig for maneuver. Prepare to dive."

"That're me *gob*," Hop said, relieved. Explaining himself to his crew might take longer, but at least he didn't feel quite so guilty when they risked their lives on his mad plans.

"Hold on tight!" Hop sent Daffodil into a precipitous descent.

Hold on, Billy, Lexi thought as she watched him ride up the mountain astride Torrent. She'd carefully cast a spell

Sarlia had taught her that compressed and shaped the air before her eyes to create a kind of magnifying lens. So even miles away she could watch Billy riding higher and higher. The trail up the mountain grew progressively steeper, until Billy was riding right along a cliff face. The path itself was rutted, crumbling, and barely wide enough for Torrent's huge paws to find purchase. One false step and Torrent and Billy would plunge straight off the mountain.

Lexi wished again that Billy had accepted her offer of magical help. Though she had to admit, it was taking all her concentration to keep the telescope spell from literally burning her eyes out.

She watched as the Sunchasers and their mounts strung out into a single file along the narrow trail. There were only three opponents ahead of Billy now—Turner, Kettle, and a quiet, intense little goblin that Lexi didn't know. From the cries of the crowd, he seemed to be named Cornstalk. Turner was in the lead. A nimble rider, graceful and quick, she'd gotten out to a fast start. But her *vargar* wasn't the strongest climber, and Torrent and several other *vargaren* had closed on her once they'd reached the steeper slopes. Now Cornstalk was fighting to pass Turner, with Kettle in third, just a few yards ahead of Billy. Lexi thought that if the trail opened up, Billy could easily surge by his three rivals and take the lead.

Unfortunately, if anything, the path looked like it was getting worse. The trail was so narrow and treacherous that all Kettle had to do to keep Billy from passing was ride directly down the center of the path. Lexi could see Kettle shouting at Billy. She knew the young goblin blamed her, Billy, and Kurt for his exile . . . and she couldn't say she disagreed with him.

Then, as Lexi watched in horror, Kettle's *vargar* dug its paws into the dirt, skidding to a halt. Neither Billy nor Torrent could react fast enough. Torrent slammed into the back of Kettle's mount. The crash made Torrent's paws slip out from under him, and suddenly Billy's *vargar* was flailing at the air, leaning dangerously toward the cliff's edge.

Lexi gasped as Torrent scrabbled at the loose rock of the path. In a rush of panic and fear, she shouted toward Billy, far in the distance. "Don't fall!"

The air filled with thunder and fire.

Billy's stomach fell out from under him. Fear pulled at him as Torrent slipped farther and farther toward the cliff on their left. Billy leaned right as hard as he could, willing Torrent back onto the path. But it wasn't enough. He and Torrent were going to fall. They were going to die.

Suddenly a gust of fiery hot wind slammed into them, shoving them back on the path. Billy could feel the little hairs burning off his arm. Torrent's fur began to smolder, and tiny fires sprung up in the dry mountain brush around them.

Lexi. It had to be her. Billy looked down the mountain. He could just barely make out the crowd of spectators far below. He couldn't pick out his hot-tempered friend, but he knew she'd saved him.

He hoped it hadn't cost her. He imagined her lying unconscious on the ground, heat steaming from her, her body drained from the force of the spell.

Whatever was happening far down the mountain, Billy knew Lexi would pay a price for helping him. He needed to make sure what she'd done mattered.

Kettle called back to Billy as he and his mount pulled ahead. *"Prenir y'biben, skerbo!"* Billy knew if he raced up on the belligerent goblin, he'd probably just try to knock Billy and Torrent off the cliff again. Time to get past Kettle, once and for all.

"Ya!" Billy dug his heels into Torrent's side. The black *vargar* growled and shot forward, straight toward Kettle and his mount. "Ya ya ya!" Billy encouraged his *vargar* to greater and greater speed. Torrent let out a hair-raising howl that grew louder with each giant, loping bound. His claws tore up the trail as he accelerated, flipping stones into the air. Billy's world became a blur of speed and wind and flying dirt.

Ahead of them, Kettle's eyes went wide with fear. "Stop! Stop, you crazy *skerbo*!"

But there was no stopping Torrent now. There was only one way to go.

"Up, Torrent! Up!" Billy shouted, steering Torrent toward the cliff face and signaling a leap. Torrent gathered himself like a spring . . .

And jumped.

Billy crouched tight against Torrent's mane as the *vargar* leapt upward, toward a switchback in the trail far above their heads. Five feet. Six, seven. They sailed clear over Kettle and his mount. Then Torrent's feet hit the mountainside in a spray of rocks and dirt. The black *vargar* scrambled to find purchase on the rocky surface, to leverage himself even higher. Billy could feel his mount's powerful muscles straining, ripping at the stones as he clawed his way up the face of the mountain. Eight feet. Nine. Billy could see the switchback just ahead of them, tantalizingly close. Another few feet. They were almost there.

Torrent began to slip. His front paws lost their grip. His back paws scrambled in the air. They were falling backward.

"No, Torrent! Up! Push!" Billy shouted, gripping

Torrent's mane, trying to keep his body forward, knowing that if he threw the *vargar* off balance they were both dead.

Just then Torrent's hind paws slammed back into a small ledge. Using the tiny outcropping as a launching pad, his body coiled again. He leapt.

Billy shouted with joy as Torrent's second jump carried them onto the switchback. Torrent let loose a triumphant roar.

"*Prenir y'biben* to you too!" Billy yelled to a stunned Kettle. The hostile goblin's mouth hung open in shock as dirt and rocks dislodged by Torrent's leap rained down on him.

"Ya!" Billy shouted again, and Torrent pivoted and sped up the trail, leaving Kettle, quite literally, in his dust.

"This're the tricky part," Hop said as he guided Daffodil up a narrow creek bed, cutting through towering redwoods all around them.

"What?" the sharp-eared Snails chimed in. "So all that diving and swooping were the easy bit? Wish I knowed. I woulda relaxed and enjoyed meself."

"You want to sergeant instead of me, Snails?" Hop sighed wearily.

"*Drak, nai.* It're more fun to grumble than to shout."

"Too bad *nai* one told me that," Hop said.

The five other surviving warbats followed, single file, behind Daffodil. It was a tight fit. Daffodil's belly skimmed the surface of the creek, and her wingtips sent leaves flying from the surrounding brush.

The Hanorian lightships flew high above them, their hulls scrapping the treetops, unable to descend any lower for fear of tangling their riggings. At least, Hop hoped

they wouldn't. That was the whole reason for his precipitous dive into the forest. To go somewhere the lightships
couldn't follow.

Suddenly the lightships opened fire. The trees were
supposed to prevent them from getting clear shots, but
Hop heard a sick sizzling sound, accompanied by screams
and smelled burning flesh. A blast of flame had raked one
of the warbats.

"Lily," Snails said. "She're still flying, but it do *nai*
look good. Her wings are crisped and three of her crew,
they're just . . . gone."

Hop knew he had to get the warbats out of the streambed.
Finally, the former Copperplate saw what he'd been looking
for. Up ahead, a massive redwood had fallen across the
gully, opening up a gap in the dense brush lining the creek
bed. Daffodil was approaching the gap. Fast.

"Prepare for wingovers!" Hop shouted.

"Wingovers!" Flutter repeated, whipping her flags to
relay Hop's command to the other bats.

"Now!" Hop yelled, praying he'd timed it right.

Hop's crew grabbed their safety straps as Hop whistled
Daffodil into a sharp turn. With inches to spare on either
side, the warbat banked through the break in the scrub and
into the redwood forest beyond. Past the gap, the forest
opened up like a huge cavern. The redwoods stood like
columns, their high canopies blocking the light and choking
out the underbrush. The towering trees were spaced dozens
of yards apart, allowing just enough room for Daffodil and
the other warbats to maneuver.

One by one, the surviving bats turned sharply through
the gap and into the forest. They all made it . . . all but
Lily, who clipped a tree with one burnt wing. The bat went
down with a piercing shriek, followed by a crashing sound

and a grim silence. Hop knew he couldn't look back. He had to keep his attention on the trees ahead or Daffodil would suffer the same fate.

"Lily are down," Flutter said, grief-stricken.

"Her crew?" Hop asked, dreading the answer.

"Bailed out. Scattering through the woods."

"Luck to 'em, then," said Hop. "And to us."

With Hop guiding her, Daffodil swooped and dodged through the trees. Suddenly a blast of fire tore down through the canopy. Daffodil veered just in time. Ash and burning needles rained on Hop and his crew. More beams of light poured down from above as the lightships opened fire with everything they had.

"*Bosh!*" Snails shouted. "Them *pizkreten* are burning the whole forest."

Bosh *are right*, Hop thought. This wasn't part of the plan. Once the goblins disappeared under the redwood canopy, the humans were supposed to give up and go home. Not destroy the entire forest just to take out a few stray warbats and their crews.

"Why are it never easy?" he said, more to himself than his crew.

"'Cause we are *goben*," the normally taciturn Bead answered. "And *goben* always have to fight and scrape and sneak. It're the way of things."

This brought a chorus of agreement from the rest of the crew, including Hop. "*Yob'rikit*," Hop said. "We're *goben*. We're alive. Guess we do this the hard way."

He shouted new orders, and Flutter relayed them to the other crews, who were busy weaving their own bats through the redwoods, dodging the lightships' constant firebolts. Hop was determined to make sure the warbats and their crews survived. Easy way, hard way, any way at all.

Billy bent low in his saddle and reached for a flag as Torrent sprinted across the glacier, snow flying from his paws.

Several dozen banners flapped in the high winds atop the mountain, planted across an ice field on short sticks about a foot high. The flags were positioned so that a rider could either dismount and pick up a flag safely or try to grab one while riding and risk missing it or tumbling off his *vargar*. Billy took one look at the flags, their shadows growing long against the snow, and decided he couldn't afford to stop and dismount. The sun was already past its zenith and headed into the west, and Billy hadn't even started down the other side of the mountain yet. He had to grab his flag as quickly as possible if he was going to have any chance of crossing the finish line before sunset.

And he'd have to catch Turner.

Billy and Torrent had overtaken Kettle and Cornstalk on the upslope, but Turner and her quick-footed mount had reached the ice field a half second ahead. Now, on the flats, her faster *vargar* was opening up a lead again. Which meant Billy definitely needed to get his flag before she headed down the mountain or he might never pass her. A few *vargar*-lengths ahead, Turner flawlessly executed a riding grab on a flag of her own. That sealed it. Billy couldn't stop now.

Torrent charged. Billy reached down for a flag, leaning almost completely out of his saddle. *Just a little farther*, he told himself. *Now!* Billy's right hand clenched around his flag. He had it!

Then Billy's stomach lurched as he felt himself sliding off Torrent's back. He'd shifted his center of gravity too far. Now the only things keeping Billy mounted were his left hand, tentatively grasping his saddle horn, and his left foot, which was hooked over the saddle. Billy knew that wouldn't hold him for long. He was going to fall.

Desperate, he passed the flag to his mouth, gripping it with his teeth, and then lunged for his saddle horn to secure a two-handed grasp. But as he groped for the saddle with his right hand, his left leg lost purchase, and Billy slid completely off Torrent's back. Just like that, he found himself hanging by one hand off Torrent's side.

Torrent seemed to sense Billy's troubles and slowed enough that Billy was able to get his legs under him. Running alongside the *vargar*, Billy jumped and managed to get both hands on the saddle horn. Then using strength he didn't know he had, he hauled himself back onto Torrent.

Unfortunately, while Billy was struggling to remount his *vargar*, Cornstalk crested the summit at full gallop, bent down and skillfully grabbed a flag of his own, then rode down the mountain. Now Billy had two opponents to beat, and the sun was getting lower in the sky every second.

Pulling the flag from his mouth, Billy shouted, "Go, Torrent! Go!"

Torrent responded with a roar. Flinging snow high into the air, Torrent tore across the glaciated summit and plunged headlong down the mountainside. Billy fought back vertigo as Torrent ran straight down the slope. Billy guessed that being passed by Cornstalk and falling farther behind Turner had infuriated Torrent. The way the *vargar* was throwing himself down the mountain, oblivious to all danger, it felt like Torrent had decided to either win or die trying.

All Billy could think was *Yeah. That works for me.*

CHAPTER FOURTEEN
The Last Ray of Sunlight

I t was a small thing. Sawtooth didn't even voice the order. He merely nodded when his spies proposed the plan. That small nod triggered the entire plot, like a pebble setting off an avalanche. Sawtooth nodded, a wizard sent a silent message, and now there would be a murder. But Sawtooth felt no remorse. The humans were still coming. The last thing he needed now was a distraction.

So he nodded and went on to more important things.

The Hanorian lightships floated on a high mountain lake, their mirrors gently reflecting the moonlight. At rest, the lightships looked elegant rather than deadly, with swooping lines and carefully worked hardwood hulls.

The lake itself was calm, barely rippling from a gentle night breeze. Only a distant red glow from the raging forest fires ignited by the ships hinted at their true nature.

A handful of crewmen patrolled the decks, keeping a perfunctory watch while their comrades slept. Though Hop couldn't see their faces in redsight, he imagined they had the satisfied looks of men who'd accomplished their mission and were thinking about home and hearth.

It was a look Hop intended to wipe off their faces.

The surviving warbats flew close to the earth, in single file, hidden by darkness, soaring ever closer to the unsuspecting lightships. The bats' goblin crews clung to their riggings, faces stained with ash, lungs aching from hours of breathing hot choking air.

Hop and his companions had sheltered from the humans' inferno in a cave deep in the forest, watching as the trees outside exploded in flames. At one point a gigantic brown hawkbear, its feathers seared crisp, had staggered into their rocky shelter. It had eyed the goblins and their bats with an exhausted, desperate expression, let out a long, mournful cry, and then collapsed in the cave mouth. It shuddered and died, another victim of the humans' wanton destruction.

Delicate little Flutter had gone up to the dead hawkbear and yanked out a single, singed feather and tucked it in her smoke-stained hair.

"To remember" was all she'd said.

Hop and the other goblins had followed suit. They knew what Flutter wanted to remember. Flyrat and Thistle. Ninebark, Lily, and their crews. All the *goben* who'd died during Sawtooth's final battle and the warbats' long retreat.

Now it was time to taste revenge. A determined anger surged through Hop's veins, a murderous desire to punish the humans for their crimes. Part of him recoiled from his own rage. He knew this was what the humans had felt after the Warhorde's invasion of the Uplands, that a similar terrible anger had fueled the humans' own rampage after Solace Ridge.

Another part of Hop's mind justified what they were about to do. Slipping away from the lightships in the dead of night would've only allowed their enemies to work more evil. The goblins had to attack. However, truth be told, none of that really mattered to Hop. He just wanted to hurt the people who'd hurt him.

Hop signaled silently to Flutter, who relayed his commands to the other warbats using smoldering flashpots only visible with redsight. *Spread out. Prepare for battle.* The warbats responded with clockwork precision. The other pilots flew their bats with an ease that Hop couldn't help but envy. He was the least skilled bat-rider here, yet somehow he'd ended up their leader. Watching them, Hop felt a stab of concern. If his plan didn't work . . .

Hop shook his head dismissingly. If his plan didn't work, they were no worse off than if they'd followed Sawtooth's suicidal orders. At least this was a fight Hop could believe in.

The warbats shot toward the lightships. Daffodil soared over the deck of Hop's target, the largest of the enemy vessels.

"Drop 'em!" Hop yelled.

His crew shoved four huge boulders off Daffodil's side, the biggest rocks the warbat could carry and still get aloft. The stones came crashing down, smashing into the lightship's deck and breaking its masts. Then Hop heard the sound he'd been praying for. Shattering glass. A boulder had hit one of the magical mirrors that propelled the lightship and provided its weaponry.

"Fire!"

The warbat's surviving archers pelted the lightship with flaming arrows. Hop saw an arrow slam into a human watchman. The man screamed, reminding him of the dying hawkbear.

Hop and his fellow bat-riders rained destruction down on the shocked humans. In the feeble moonlight, without the power of the sun, the lightships and their crews were helpless. This time they were the ones dying without a chance. They were the ones that'd never go home to their families and their children. Hop's mouth tasted like ash. He circled Daffodil back over the lightships. His archers kept firing. Another circle. More firing.

Finally Bead spoke up. "We're outa arrows, Cap."

Hop looked around. The lightships were broken and burning. There were arrows everywhere. On one blood-slicked deck, Hop saw a corpse with a dozen shafts sticking out of his back, like a fresh-killed porcupine. Hop and his companions had won.

So why didn't he feel like celebrating?

"Time to go," he said.

Flutter signaled the other bats, and together they flew away into the darkness.

"*Wazzer*. You're crazy!" Turner yelled to Billy as he and Torrent crashed past her through the brush, half falling, half charging down the mountainside.

Billy couldn't argue with that. He and Torrent were covered in scratches and bruises from their headlong plunge. Torrent had fallen twice, once spilling both himself and Billy fifty feet down a scree of loose stones. But both times, the *vargar* and Billy had bounced right back up and resumed their mad descent.

Cornstalk had been carefully picking his way along a series of switchbacks when Billy and Torrent had ripped by him. Now they'd passed Turner as well, and there were no Sunchasers left between Billy and the finish line. Behind him, Billy heard Turner cursing to herself. "*Drak*. Mad as a *duenshee*." He risked a glance back just as she signaled her own *vargar* to turn straight down the mountainside, imitating Billy in his pell-mell ride for victory. Billy smiled. It was good to know he wasn't the only crazy person in this race.

As he and Torrent charged recklessly for the finish, Billy heard a slow flapping sound above him. It was a riding bat. He glimpsed a bright orange shirt, confirming that the rider was one of the referees who were supposed to watch for cheaters. Now a race monitor showed up? Where were the referees when Kettle or the mohawked goblin had attacked Billy? As far as Billy could tell, the referees had been basically useless.

Suddenly Billy felt a slam of impact in his left shoulder, coupled with a sharp stabbing pain. Despite his determination to watch the path ahead, his eyes flicked back and he saw there was an arrow sticking out of his back. The referee had shot him!

It was the most intense pain Billy had ever experienced. It felt like the arrowhead had sunk in almost a full inch. And every jarring bound Torrent took made his agony even worse.

But Billy hadn't done anything wrong! He'd obeyed all the rules. He hadn't attacked anyone. So why had the referee shot him? Maybe it was some kind of mistake?

Confused, Billy looked behind him and saw Turner signal her mount to a halt as she stared up at the referee in confusion. "What are he doing?" she shouted.

But Billy had no time to answer. He heard a twang and a hiss as another arrow shot down at him from the riding bat. Then another. And another. Arrows peppered the ground around him. Fighting the pain from his shoulder wound, he guided Torrent into a series of quick zigzags, hoping to throw off the archer. But just when he thought he might be able to avoid his airborne attacker, he saw another riding bat looming ahead . . . and its rider was firing at him too. An arrow sliced the air only inches from Billy's face.

Billy's heart pounded. His breath came in gasps. It was like he was back in the lunchroom or the storm drain again. Only this time the world wasn't changing around him. He was stuck here. This time there was no escape.

"For Sawtooth!" Billy heard a referee shout as more arrows whizzed by.

Sawtooth? he thought. *The snipers are working for the goblin general?* That meant Sawtooth knew that the real threat to his power wasn't Kurt. It was Billy.

As this horrifying realization struck, a strange thing happened. All Billy's panic, pain, and fear drained away, as if his overloaded nervous system had decided there was no point in sounding any more alarms. A strange calm settled over him. He leaned to one side as another arrow flew by, dodging it as if it were moving in slow motion.

Adrenaline, he thought. His mother, the emergency room nurse, had told him about this. How adrenaline suppresses pain, calms the mind, and makes everything seem like it's moving in slow motion. *This is all perfectly normal. A perfectly normal reaction to having a bat-riding goblin shoot an arrow into your shoulder while you're racing down a mountain on a giant horned wolf.*

Unfortunately, Billy knew the next normal, logical thing that was going to happen. Sooner or later, another arrow or two or ten would hit him. Or worse, hit Torrent, who was continuing his headlong plunge down the mountain, easily outpacing Turner and the other riders, but not the referees and their bows. If the *vargar* crashed now, it'd be over for both of them. Even if they somehow miraculously dodged the archers, the slow seep of blood coming out of Billy's shoulder would eventually turn into a trickle, then a stream, then a rush, until there was no blood left.

One way or another, Billy was going to die.

For once, things were going Hop's way. The attack on the lightships had gone flawlessly. Despite the hollow feeling in his heart when he thought back to the battle, Hop was glad to be away from the humans at long last. One more ridge, one last mountain to crest, and this desperate flight would be over.

Flutter broke Hop's reverie. In a strained voice, Flutter choked out three broken words, "They're still coming."

Hop looked back, knowing what he would see but wishing with all his might that he'd be wrong.

He wasn't. It was there. A few miles back and gaining quickly. A single remnant of the squad of flying ships, blazing with light from a half dozen of the human's magic mirrors. "They musta loaded that one up with every unbroked mirror they haved," Hop said.

"*Drak*, that thing are *vershakorz*," Snails said. *Vershakorz* was a goblin idiom for something very fast indeed, and its literal meaning seemed particularly apt at the moment.

"*Vershakorz*," Hop agreed. "Fast as death."

Billy's world grew foggy and dull and strangely quiet. He knew that meant his adrenaline rush was fading, that his body was going into shock. But he didn't care anymore. He was tired and hurt, with an arrowhead stuck in his shoulder blade. He just wanted to lie down and sleep.

Fortunately, Torrent had other ideas. The *vargar* kept leaping and weaving his way down the mountain, spurred to even greater speed by the constant stream of arrows from the bat-riders above. Trees and bushes flew by Billy in a green blur as the shadows grew steadily longer and the fading light turned red. Sunset. Billy knew that was important, but he couldn't remember exactly why.

Then a low-hanging branch slapped him in the face, nearly knocking him off Torrent's back. The sharp sting of impact jolted Billy out of his haze.

Sunset! He had to cross the finish line now or all his efforts would be for nothing. *Forget the pain*, he told himself. *Forget Sawtooth's assassins and the arrows and the blood. Just go! Go! Go!*

"Go!" Billy shouted with newfound strength, and Torrent muscled himself into an even faster gallop, plunging through bushes, leaping fallen trunks, and dodging around trees with abandon.

Suddenly Torrent broke into a clearing. For just a second, Billy caught site of the finish line. It was close. A mile, maybe two. Thousands of goblins had gathered at the bottom of the slope, and a huge cheer went up as they spotted Billy.

Then he heard Lexi yelling above the crowd, her voice charged with surprise and unexpected hope. "Billy! Go, Billy! Go!" Kurt, Leadpipe, and Frost joined in: "Go, Billy, go! Go, Billy, go!"

Billy's heart swelled. They were cheering. Cheering for him.

But his excitement didn't last long. A riding bat flared

up over the trees ahead of him, blocking his route to the finish line. The orange-shirted rider took aim with his bow. Behind him, Billy could hear the flapping of a second bat, no doubt piloted by another of the murderous referees.

Billy felt a sudden rush of anger. He could almost accept the fact that he was going to die. Death had been hovering around him practically since his arrival in this strange, magical world. It wasn't the prospect of dying that infuriated Billy. What really made him mad was the idea that he might lose the race.

Billy gritted his teeth and whistled encouragement to Torrent as the black *vargar* galloped ahead. One way or another, he was crossing that finish line before sunset. He might die doing it, but he was going to win.

The bat-riders let their arrows fly.

Goblins have an expression: "*Zeesnikken eger zapergritten.*" It means "Bee stings on top of mosquito bites." Which is just their way of saying, "If it isn't one thing, it's another."

Right now, Hop felt more than a little stung. The last surviving human lightship was hot on his tail and gaining. And now this . . .

Only a few miles from the Fastness, the goblin fortress city that had been his destination all along, Hop could see a pair of riding bats circling a clearing, their orange-shirted riders firing at something down below. Had the humans already gotten this far? If the Fastness was under attack, all his plans, all the sacrifices of the warbats and their crews, would be for nothing. If the Fastness fell, there was no refuge, no safe place, nowhere to run.

"The Sunchase," Flutter said. "Them're referees. It're *Genzirjad*. The race are today."

"But why are they shooting?" Snails asked.

"Cheaters," said Bead. "They shoot cheaters. Sometime."

Hop felt a surge of relief. He knew about the Sunchase, of course, with its racing *vargaren* and its bat-riding monitors, but he'd never witnessed it. He'd always meant to come to the Fastness on *Genzirjad*, but he'd never gotten around to it. *Next year*, he'd always told himself. *I'll go next year*. But next year never came. Now here he was, at the Fastness on Balance Day, and the race was being run right beneath him. Even better, because of the Sunchase, the Fastness already had fighting bats in the air. So all Hop and his crews had to do was call for help, and they were home free.

"Flutter, signal the Fastness. Tell 'em what are what," Hop ordered as he dove Daffodil toward the riding bats below.

Then Hop saw something that made him swear. He recognized the Sunchaser the referees were shooting at. "*Bosh!*" Hop cursed, venting his frustration. "*Zeesnikken eger zapergritten!*"

Just when Hop thought he was safe, a final bee sting. If it wasn't one thing, it was another.

Horrified, Lexi watched the huge warbat swoop down between Billy and the snipers. By some miracle, Billy had been able to dodge most of the arrows from the malevolent referees, but the new arrival was much larger than the other bats and crewed by several riders, including at least four with bows. Lexi knew once they opened fire, Billy didn't stand a chance.

She focused her telescoped vision on Billy. She could

see his expression as he noticed the giant bat, then lowered his head and urged Torrent on, ignoring the certain death hovering above him. She could tell he was determined to ride to the finish. No matter what.

With her attention focused on Billy, at first Lexi didn't completely understand what was happening around her. Why the arrows weren't landing near Billy anymore. Why goblins were shouting, both above him and ahead, at the finish line. Why their yells had turned from cheers to chaotic, cacophonous shouts of anger. Inexplicably, she could hear soldiers bellowing commands. Goblins running.

Lexi released her spell so she could see her immediate surroundings. In the sunset-painted sky, she saw three bats, one slow-moving giant and two darting streaks. Though the riders of the smaller bats seemed determined to kill Billy, the crew of the larger bat was doing its best to defend him. Magnifying her vision again for a closer look, Lexi spotted Hop standing behind the head of the giant warbat. She couldn't believe it. Somehow the one-eared goblin had arrived to save Billy. As she watched, archers on Hop's warbat fired at the two bat-riding referees. Though the arrows missed, it was clear that the snipers were no match for the giant bat and its crew. And Lexi could see four more giant warbats on the way. Outnumbered, the assassins turned and flew away as fast as they could.

"They saved him. Hop saved Billy," Lexi gasped, overwhelmed with relief.

Then she heard Frost, standing at her side, using his own magic to watch the riders hurtling down the mountain. "It're *nai* over. The worst are still coming."

That's when Lexi saw Hop's warbat dodging fire from a giant flying ship. The attacking ship was using some sort of magical mirrors to redirect the sunlight and turn it into a weapon. Hop avoided the attack, but as Lexi watched helplessly, a stray beam from the lightship hit the crowd of onlookers. A cluster of goblins cried out in pain as the flames consumed them.

That was the last straw for Lexi. That's when her own fire broke loose.

The sight of Hop at the reins of the giant warbat almost made Billy stop Torrent's mad run. Almost made him forget the grinding pain from the arrow in his shoulder, forget the finish line and the race. Almost.

But Hop helped him focus. "Keep riding!" he shouted down to Billy. "The worst part are still coming!"

And, indeed, something else was heading their way. A flying sailing ship with sparkling mirrors on the end of its masts. Mirrors that blasted away at Billy's rescuers with fire.

Out of the corner of his eye, Billy saw Lexi shoot back at the attacking ship, sending bolts of flame roaring up at it, trying to help Hop and his warbat. Goblins rushed from the Fastness. Warriors and archers and *vargar*-riders.

Somewhere an alarm bell was ringing.

Somewhere a war drum was beating.

And somewhere, ever so faintly, Billy could hear a female goblin singing with a clear, strong voice. Between the sounds of battle, the blood pounding in his ears, the thumping of drums, the shouts in *Gobayabber*, and the clanging alarm bells, Billy could just barely hear her song, a word here, a snippet of melody there:

See the crescent rise

In the darkened skies
Let the goben *roam far and wide*

It was the Nightsong. Which meant Billy was almost out of time. The sun was a fading sliver, rapidly disappearing behind the western horizon. It would soon vanish, along with any hope for him and his friends.

But Billy was so weak, so tired. His back was sticky with blood; his hands felt cold; he couldn't move his left arm. If he fell now, no one would blame him. "It was a good try," they'd say. "It was just too hard." Easier to just let go. End the pain. End the trying.

Come the darkness
Come the night
End the day
Douse the light

The ground in front of Billy erupted in flames. A beam of fire from the flying ship lashed at the goblin soldiers pouring out from the Fastness, striking right in Torrent's path. The flash overwhelmed Billy's vision. He clenched his eyelids shut in pain . . .

And found himself remembering everything that had brought him to this place . . . the incident in the cafeteria, the run through the culvert, the awful wet sharp feel of Lexi's broken bone sticking out of her leg, the bizarre journey through the caves. Hop, Frost, and Leadpipe. The battle to make Kurt king. The trial. The incredible batreme flight. Little Turner and the hospitality of the Celestials in the Court of the Orbs. As much as he wanted to give in to his pain and exhaustion, Billy realized he couldn't. He had to fight, to keep riding, to justify all the trials that he, Lexi, and Kurt had been through together. To make it all mean something.

'Cause the debt we are owed
We'll collect, heads unbowed
And that what we take we are keeping

Billy pried his eyes open. The song was almost done, the last ray of sunlight almost gone. Up ahead, a wall of smoke and fire blocked Billy and Torrent's path to the finish line. But there was no time to slow down. No time to try to find a safe way around the flames. Billy had only one choice.

"JUMP! Jump, Torrent! UP!" Billy yelled.

Come the darkness
Come the night

Searing heat washed over Billy as Torrent leapt through the flames. The brave *vargar*, his energy finally spent, landed awkwardly and began to fall. Billy lost his tentative grip on Torrent's mane and flew out of his saddle, slamming into the dirt with a thud that sent the air rushing from his lungs.

End the day
Douse the light

The Nightsong ended. Stunned, Billy tried to rise to his feet, but his legs refused to support his weight. It was all he could do to crawl to Torrent, who lay panting on the ground a few yards away. The great black *vargar* whined. His fur was scorched and streaked with blood. It was only then that Billy realized Torrent had an arrow wound of his own, a long gash down his left flank. The black beast's breath came ragged, and his muzzle was flecked with foam.

Ignoring his own pain, Billy wrapped his arms around Torrent's giant neck and whispered, "Good boy, Torrent. Good boy."

The race was over. The sun was gone. Billy and Torrent had done their best. The two of them lay there, spent, in a landscape from a nightmare. Fires burned out of control all around them. Up above, the flying ship was still blasting away with its fiery mirrors, both at the goblins on the ground and the ones fighting from the back of the giant warbat. No, make that five warbats, buzzing the enemy vessel like fighter planes. Frost, surrounded by a personal snowstorm, sent a volley of hailstones up at the mirror ship. Nearby, Lexi floated ten feet off the ground, beams of light shooting from her eyes, looking like something out of a video game.

And in the middle of the chaos, exhausted but alive, Billy realized that he and Torrent were lying just across the finish line of the Sunchase, the sun only now vanishing behind the horizon.

They'd done it. They'd won.

Billy heard a familiar goblin voice chanting. It was Starcaller, the old goblin priestess. "*Chom-chom-chom. Chom-chom-chom.*" More goblins joined in. "*Chom-chom-chom! CHOM-CHOM-CHOM!*"

Starcaller knelt in front of Billy, blocking his view of the fighting. "Bravely raced, *derijinta.* Bravely raced."

"I won?" Billy managed, "I really won?"

"*Zaj.* That you have. And in heroic fashion."

"My reward . . ." Billy could barely get the words out.

"Time for that later. For now, sleep." Starcaller placed

one gnarled hand on Billy's brow. He felt an icy chill radiate from her palm.

Billy somehow found the energy to reach up and push Starcaller's palm away. "No." After all he'd been through, all Torrent's heroism, he couldn't just let her magic him to sleep before he'd had a chance to say it. Out loud. "Let me put on the Crown," Billy said as slowly and clearly as he could manage. "It will show you. I'm the Wheelwright's Heir. It was me all along. I want you to make me the Goblin King."

"You want to wear the Crown? Then wear it you will."

Starcaller smiled gently, like she'd known exactly what Billy was going to say, then pressed her palm to Billy's forehead. This time he didn't resist. Before he knew it, despite the pain, despite the battle raging around him, Billy fell into a deep, healing sleep.

CHAPTER FIFTEEN
Careful What You Wish For

The next few days passed in a haze. Billy spent most of his time asleep, his dreams interspersed with vague impressions of visitors. Frost and Leadpipe, Hop, Shadow and Starcaller all came to see him. So did Kurt and some of the Celestials. Turner even brought Torrent into Billy's room. The big black *vargar*, healing from wounds of his own, snuffled Billy and licked his face. It made Billy laugh, which hurt his shoulder. But it was worth it.

Mostly, though, Billy remembered Lexi. His schoolmate was a constant companion, feeding him soup, reading him stories from a thick book of goblin history, and making sure the little room where he was convalescing was never too hot or too cold.

One morning Billy finally woke up without feeling pained or sleepy. His head was clear. His shoulder no longer burned. His various scrapes and bruises had stopped itching.

Starcaller looked down at him with approval. "All better."

The goblin priestess patted Billy on the forehead and headed for the door.

"Wait," Billy said, louder than he'd intended. "What about my reward?"

Starcaller lingered in the doorway. "Us *goben* say, 'Pray for light, the sun'll rise. Hope for darkness, the night'll come.'"

"In other words, be patient?"

"In other words, careful what you wish for."

Then she was gone.

The boy lived. Another failure. In Sawtooth's dreams, half-glimpsed visions of Cutty and the Dark Lady haunted him, often merging one into the other, laughing at him, surrounded by images of death, defeat, and disaster.

Sawtooth's waking hours were no better, swallowed up by ceaseless scouting reports warning of the encroaching human army and hastily drawn maps showing his rapidly shrinking area of authority. He still had control of the city . . . barely. When he'd marched off to war, Sawtooth had left his enforcers, the Teeth, behind in Kiranok, and they'd maintained his iron grip over the populace. However, most of his veteran soldiers had died in the Warhorde's final battle, or deserted. So Sawtooth's men were spread thin, and if they lost control, he knew the people of Kiranok, the widows, the orphans, the wounded soldiers, the sonless mothers, would rise up and come for his blood. It was like there was a noose around his neck, drawing tighter every day.

More and more Sawtooth felt like he should just surrender to the inevitable. The human army would arrive, storm the city, and slaughter everyone, and he would stand in Rockbottom as the pooling blood rose high enough to drown him.

In the end, though, Sawtooth's anger always overrode his despair. He knew that when the enemy came, like a cornered *vargar*, he would lower his horn and charge.

And he'd make sure every last goblin in Kiranok did the same. Even if he had to slaughter half of them to do it.

Lexi sat in the sun, letting the heat wash over her, trying to find the calm center Sarlia was constantly describing. Since she'd helped fight off the lightship, that had proven harder than ever. Whenever Lexi closed her eyes, she could feel the flames rushing through her body, lashing out at the strange mirror-masted vessel, setting everything she looked at on fire. She knew she should be horrified at the memories, but the truth was, she'd never felt as powerful or alive as she had in the middle of the battle. She wanted desperately to feel that way again, to blast away at anything and anyone that opposed her.

Empty glass, she thought to herself. *Don't go that way.*

Unfortunately, Lexi was starting to wonder if becoming an empty glass might be an improvement. The peace Sarlia preached never seemed real. Happiness was for other people. So why not let the magic take over? Give in to the rush and the fire? At least she wouldn't feel so frustrated all the time.

Yeah, destroy everyone around you. That's an awesome life plan.

Lexi sighed and tried to meditate some more. Even though all she really wanted to do was make something explode.

"Lexi? You okay?"

Lexi opened her eyes and saw Billy stepping outside of the small house where he'd been recuperating. She'd been using the house's courtyard as a retreat. It was one of the only quiet places left in the Fastness. The rest of the fortress-town was bursting with activity. Lately, it seemed like there were goblins everywhere. Goblins marching. Goblins riding *vargaren* and driving wagons pulled by giant rams. Goblins carrying packs. Goblins rolling barrels. The only place they steered clear of was the little house at the edge of town where their new hero was recovering from near death.

"Billy!" Lexi leaped up and grabbed him in a tight hug.

"Ouch!"

Lexi let go, realizing she'd grabbed Billy's injured shoulder. "Sorry."

"It's okay." Billy looked a lot better, but seeing him healthy just reminded Lexi of how he'd gotten hurt in the first place. And what he'd earned as his reward. "You dork. Do you have any idea what you put us through?"

"Uh . . . I was trying to make things right."

"By telling the goblins to make you their king?" Lexi shook her head. "Remember how well that worked out for Kurt?"

"I . . ." Billy trailed off. But then his expression changed. Suddenly he looked stronger and more determined. "Look, you have to trust me. Becoming the Goblin King is the right thing to do. It's my responsibility. It always has been, ever since we all showed up in that cave."

"You don't know that."

"But I do," Billy confessed. "I've always known. Plus, I'm pretty sure until I do whatever it is I'm supposed to do here, none of us will be able to go home."

Lexi wanted to tell Billy he was crazy, to convince him that they could still get away from the goblins and find their way home, but somehow she knew he was right. Some kind of weird destiny had brought them here. Now they had to fulfill it. No matter what.

"I believe you."

"You do?"

"You being some kind of magical king? It's not the craziest thing I've had to deal with since we got here. I'll help. We all will. Whatever you need. And besides, like you said, it's the right thing to do."

Lexi could tell that Billy didn't know what to say to that. But as he fumbled for a reply, a group of goblins on some sort of errand entered the courtyard. As soon as they saw Billy, they stopped in their tracks. Lexi heard a goblin gasp, "It're the King!"

The goblins all looked at Billy, wide-eyed and hopeful. The first goblin started singing, low and alone. The other goblins soon picked up the song:

The fire are sweeping o'er the field
The breaking spear, the cracking shield
'Til all that are, are soot and dust
The sun it burn, the iron rust

But the sun will go
But the rains will come
And out of the ash
Spring the brightest bloom

When the water run red
When the last hope're dead
Then come the King!

Come the King, come the King
From the dark, from the gloom
Come the King, come the King
And make us live again

The Wheelwright sweared to hear our prayers
Of home walls teared and widow's cares
The Wheelwright sayed when he're nai *more*
He'd send us his sons from afar
To right our wrongs, mend what're breaked
Drive back fear, return what're taked

When all are dust
And skerbo *lust*
Bring bleedy war
To us once more
Then come the King!

Come the King, come the King
And vict'ry bring
Come the King, come the King
And then we'll sing
Come the King! Come the King! Come the King!

Even after the song ended, the goblins kept chanting, "Come the King! *Chom-chom!* Come the King! *Chom-CHOM!* Come the King! *CHOM-CHOM!*" The chant echoed through the Fastness, and more and more goblins joined in. "*CHOM-CHOM! CHOM-CHOM!*"

Billy turned to Lexi, his face filled with concern. "Good. 'Cause I'm gonna need all the help I can get."

Hop stood atop a watchtower overlooking the Fastness and Coaler's Break. From the parapets, the fortress town looked like a honey wasp hive ripped open by a hawkbear. The streets swarmed with activity. Goblins ran to and fro, readying weapons and packing bags. The Templars drilled on their parade ground with fervent intensity. And everywhere, the black-garbed clergy of the Night Goddess urged their followers on. All because one human boy had won a race and asked to be king.

Hop should've been happy. After all, that had been his plan all along, to crown a Goblin King and take power away from Sawtooth. But that was before Sawtooth committed all of the goblins' remaining resources to one final, futile battle against the humans. Now, after Sawtooth's defeat, would crowning Billy make any difference? Not far from Hop's perch atop the tower, the crumpled remains of the human lightship lay on the scorched hilltop where it had crashed with all hands. It had taken the combined efforts of the Fastness's Templars and Hop's warbat crews to bring down even this one human lightship. What chance did they have against an entire human army? By trying to crown Billy, was Hop just setting up an innocent boy for failure and death?

Hop wondered if he shouldn't just head for the hills. In the two weeks since the battle with the lightship, Daffodil had recovered from her injuries. The other warbats and their crews were flight ready. Hop could have them in the air at a moment's notice. If he told his crews to leave, he knew they'd listen. They could take off, and no one would stop them. Hop pictured the cave in the redwoods. It was isolated, safe. The fire had only burned a small portion of the primal forest. He could pilot Daffodil there, and he, Flutter, Snails, and the rest could hide and wait out the war.

"*Jegen* for your thoughts, Copperplate."

Hop turned and saw Shadow emerging from the trapdoor behind him. He considered lying to her, but her steady gaze made him certain she'd see through any deception. Since he'd arrived to save Billy, High Priestess Starcaller had forgiven Hop his earlier wrongdoings, and her Templars, including Shadow, had begrudgingly admitted that he'd been trying to help his fellow goblins all along. He and Shadow had been spending hours together planning their return to Kiranok. Hop found himself looking forward to their meetings more than anything since . . . Hop touched his copper band, as he always did when he thought of Cotton. But since meeting Shadow, those thoughts had hurt a little less. Now getting caught in a lie by the attractive *svagob* was the last thing he wanted.

"Thinking a running, to lay it out plain," Hop admitted.

"You do *nai* like the odds?" Shadow didn't seem angry or hurt, just curious.

"I do *nai* like the cost. Already seed too much dying for one lifetime."

"If we do *nai* stop me father, dying are all we'll get."

"Answer me a question?" Hop asked quietly. Shadow nodded. "Sawtooth are your father. So why do you want him replaced by a human boy?"

Shadow shook her head sadly. "My father were a good man, once. But when me mother died, I think part of him breaked. Soon enough, he falled under the spell of the Dark Lady. That *duenshee* witch . . . she fixed him up, but all crooked-like, you follow? Now all he do are destroy. We have to stop him. So long as he lead our people, we have *nai* hope."

Hop ran his tongue across his fangs in thought. "*Naizaj* . . . but what if we're doomed *nai* matter what? What if crowning the boy make *nai* difference? If he can *nai* make things better, why shed blood to put the Goblin Crown on his head? I do *nai* like the taste of it. Especially now. Them assassins comed after Billy for a reason. Sawtooth know the boy are the Heir. Last time we catched your father off guard, and me and the human children still failed. This time he are on guard. Mostlike, this time we will *nai* escape with our heads still attached."

"That're why we're bringing the entire garrison, the Templer, the Night Priests with their magic. Me father can fight. But he'll *nai* win."

"And how many dead *goben* at the end? Win or lose? How many'll die?"

"Some. But if Sawtooth do *nai* kill us, the humans will. So if that're how things lay, if we're all cursed and dead, why *nai* at least try to make things right? Pull at the thread of fate and weave it more to our liking."

Hop shifted uncomfortably, torn between his desire to impress Shadow and his own survival impulse. "I guess it come down to this . . . I do *nai* want to die, or see me friends die. Suppose I're a coward."

"*Zajnai* you're just smarter than the rest of us. So you're leaving?" Shadow's ears twitched. Hop wondered, *Were that disappointment?*

Hop knew if Shadow had shouted at him or called him a coward or tried to order him to stay, he'd have ignored her. But instead, she'd reasoned with him, shared her thoughts. No officer had ever done that before. More to the point, what she said made sense. If the goblins were doomed to extinction regardless of what they did, then running wouldn't help. Better for him to die trying to do something good than get slaughtered hiding in a hole.

"Ah, *drak*. I'll fight. I're mad as a *duenshee* for it, but I can *nai* run *nai* more." Then Hop smiled, despite himself. "Aside, I finded them children. I wanted a king. Guess I owe it to Billy to get him his crown."

"I never doubted you," Shadow said, grinning and showing her long, delicate fangs.

"That make one of us," Hop said in return. But the truth was, seeing Shadow smile made him happier than he'd been in a long time.

Nearly a week later, after a long, tense journey through the mountains, much of it spent dodging both Sawtooth's goblin loyalists and scouts from the Hanorians' Army of Light, Shadow led Billy, his friends, Hop, and a small army of goblins down a rock-strewn canyon, then up a cliff and into a hidden cave mouth. The cave gave way to a cramped, concealed tunnel. A few hours of scrambling and climbing brought Billy, Lexi, and Kurt back where they'd begun, to the caverns beneath Mother Mountain. Once again, they made their way through the dangerous network of underground passageways and chambers. But this time there were hundreds of goblins with them, moving purposefully through the dark.

There were other differences too.

For one thing, Lexi wasn't hurt this time. In fact, she was lighting the way with a soft white glow from her palm.

"Look how beautiful this place is," Lexi said. "All it needed was a little more light." Then she turned to Billy, smiling broadly. "Watch this."

Lexi spread her hands and shot out ten individual rays of light, one from each finger. Twirling her hands, she made the lights dance across the cavern's innumerable columns, stalactites, and stalagmites. Crystals in the rock formations refracted the light even further, creating a breathtaking display.

But Lexi's trick worried Billy. He couldn't help but think of the terrifying joy he'd seen in her face when she'd blasted the Hanorian lightship. Though her current delight carried only a faint echo of her bloodthirsty expression during the battle, seeing Lexi smile as the light danced in her hand made Billy think of Frost's story about the soulless wizardess he'd once loved.

"It's awesome," Billy managed, covering his fears. Then he realized. It *was* awesome. It was one of the most beautiful things he'd ever seen. The crystals sparkled and the light shot out of them like rainbows. Not only that, Lexi's happiness was infectious, and she looked beautiful when she smiled. "You're awesome."

Billy blushed as soon as he said it. But Lexi didn't seem to mind.

"I knew you were the Heir, you know," she said quietly as she watched the rainbows of light. "Not Kurt. I knew it was you all along."

"You did?" Billy replied, so surprised that he stopped dead in his tracks.

"It wasn't hard. You just have to pay attention. I've been watching you. Kurt acts like he's a leader and all, but you think like one, always trying to help, always worrying about everyone else. You're a good guy. You'll make a great king."

Lexi continued forward, playing with her lights, indifferent to the embarrassment and confusion her praise caused Billy.

"Not bad, runt," Kurt whispered to Billy. "Making progress."

That was another difference. Kurt was being a lot less of a jerk now. "Hey, kid," the quarterback continued, "are you sure about this whole coronation thing?"

"You were sure when it was you," Billy said, more confident than he felt. "Why shouldn't I feel the same way?"

Kurt looked troubled. "You didn't see much of what happened after the race, did you?"

Billy shook his head. "I was pretty out of it."

"It was awful. There were bodies everywhere. Hop says fifty-two goblins died. Plus the humans on that flying ship."

"They attacked us," Lexi snapped. She'd obviously been listening in. "They deserved what they got."

"And now we're the ones attacking," Kurt said. "All I'm saying is . . . I don't know if I can watch something like that again."

Billy could see the concern on Kurt's face. He also noticed a general shiftiness among their goblin companions. He knew it didn't matter how quietly the humans spoke among themselves. The goblins' ears were just too sharp. Shadow, Starcaller, Leadpipe, Frost, and even brave little Turner, they were all studying him, waiting to hear what he had to say. He knew he couldn't let them down. Not now.

"We're kinda committed here, Kurt."

"*Nai*. That are *nai* true." To Billy's surprise, Hop stepped forward, his face sad but accepting. "It're all right, Billy. Truth are, you're *nai* responsible for what happen to us. You can go home. Be safe. Forget about us and our'n."

Billy wanted to take Hop up on his offer. But there were two big problems with it. "I can't," Billy said. "I tried before."

This set off a low mutter among the goblins. Billy couldn't make out much of what they were saying, but he got the general idea. Their hero, the boy who would be their king, had tried to run from his fate? If that were true, why were they risking their lives for *him*?

Billy tried to quiet the crowd. "Wait. Wait. Let me explain."

"Let him talk," Leadpipe said, his deep bass vibrating the cavern walls. The goblins fell into an expectant hush.

It was like unscrewing the cap from a soda bottle that'd gotten shaken up in the car. Billy had been hiding the truth from himself and everyone else ever since his arrival. But now that he was being honest, everything came out in a rush. "I've always known I brought us here. I didn't mean to, but I did it. And I tried to undo it, to wish us home, a hundred times, while we were in the caves, at Frost's, over and over. It never worked. I would give anything to go home, but I can't."

Starcaller nodded sagely. "That're because you are here for a reason. Because the magic what bringed you will *nai* send you back 'til you've finished what you comed for."

"I know that now," Billy said. "I'm supposed to make things better. That Wheelwright guy, I must be related to him somehow or other. My family is Irish and African, not Polish. But in America, where I come from, everyone is a bit of everything. Which means I have as much chance of being the Heir as anyone. And I won't be able to go home until I save all of you." Then Billy's face became determined, far from his normal worried expression. "Plus, I *want* to help. After all that's happened, I can't just leave. Not with the Hanorians threatening to kill you all and General Sawtooth making things worse. I have to try."

"*Zaj*," Hop grumbled. "There're a *maja* lot of that going round."

"There is one thing, though." Billy pulled himself a little taller, set his jaw a little firmer. "If the Goblin Crown doesn't glow for me, things could get really bad. Especially if we charge in there with all these people." He glanced toward Kurt. "Maybe . . . Is there any other way? What if we sent in a small team? Like what Hop did last time. So there aren't so many people at risk."

"I'm game," Lexi piped in.

"You know you can count on me," Frost added.

"I'll go. If there're room on a small team for a big *gob*," rumbled Leadpipe.

Hop shook his head. "The reason we bringed so many *goben* are 'cause sneaky failed last time."

"But it should've worked," Billy replied. "Kurt got to the Crown and put it on. The only reason your plan fell apart is because . . ." Billy looked at Kurt apologetically. "Well, Kurt wasn't the right guy."

If Kurt was hurt by that, he didn't let on. Instead, he nodded in agreement. "If I'd put the Goblin Crown on Billy's head, we would've won. It was Billy all along."

Hop considered Billy's argument. "Sawtooth'll have more guards this time. He'll *nai* just let us slip in and grab the Crown without a fight."

"No problem," Kurt said, a little of his old cockiness returning. "All we have to do is switch up the play. They'll be expecting the quarterback sneak, like last time. Which means it's time for a Hail Mary."

Hop and the other goblins looked at Kurt in utter confusion.

"Football? No? Okay. Well, here's how it works . . ."

Football, it turned out, was a complicated human game with two eleven-man teams and an oblong pigskin ball. Hop tried to follow Kurt's explanation, which was sprinkled with strange terms like "hash marks," "face-masks," "holding," "blocking," and "quarterback ratings." Leadpipe and some of the other *kijakgoben* thought football sounded fun and resolved to put teams together as soon as they'd crowned Billy, but Hop couldn't make much sense of it. Still, Kurt's "Hail Mary" plan seemed as good as any. Unfortunately, it also felt like the kind of thing Hop might come up with himself. Which worried him, since his plans almost never went as expected.

As they made their way through the passageways leading to central Kiranok, Hop looked at the group Kurt had chosen for his Hail Mary. Billy, of course. Kurt, Lexi, Frost, and Leadpipe. A determined young female *gob* named Turner who seemed to be a friend of Billy's. Plus, Shadow and her biggest, toughest Templars, a trio of *kijakgoben* named Mallet, Breaker, and Peashoot. And Hop himself. Eleven players to fill out Kurt's team. Hop turned to Frost. The little wizard was walking by his side, serene, seemingly prepared for anything. "Ever regret it?" Hop asked quietly. "Throwing in with me? Trying to save the entire *goben* race?"

"Me? *Nai*," Frost said with a grin. "But I're half-mad. So best *nai* trust what I think."

"There are two kinds of *gob*, I say," Leadpipe interjected from just ahead of them. "The kind what lay low. And the ones what raise their heads up high. Afore we meeted you, me and Frost, we let the world do to us what it liked. But now, 'cause of you, we can say we tried to make the world a better place. And *nai* one can take that from us."

"I guess that're something," Hop said, still plagued with doubts.

"It're everything," Leadpipe said, his deep voice carrying all the conviction Hop lacked. Leadpipe's unexpected support made Hop's heart feel heavy and somehow larger at the same time, proud that he'd inspired such feelings and terrified that he could never live up to them.

The group emerged into a dusty side chamber. Hop could hear the buzz of *goben* voices up ahead, the throb of commerce, the occasional song. They'd reached Kiranok.

"We're here," Hop said somberly. "Anyone what want out, now're the time."

Shadow piped in, "God of Night, you're right. This're crazy. Count me out."

"Err—" Hop began, shocked.

Shadow cut him off, grinning. "Do *nai* be an idiot, Hoprock. I're joking. Billy are our king, and we're getting him his crown. That right, Billy?"

Billy looked every bit as doubt-plagued and uncertain as Hop. But Hop noted with admiration that, for once, the human boy kept the panic out of his voice.

"Right," Billy said. "Let's do this."

"*Ahka, ahka!* Step up and get your mushies," Turner shouted over the cacophony of the Underway.

Billy squatted beneath Turner's mushroom stand. Leadpipe had persuaded the cart's owner to go home for the day. Now Turner was impersonating a mushroom peddler while Billy hid from her customers. The young goblin had actually attracted quite a bit of business, much to Billy's distress.

"You're just supposed to be *pretending* to sell mushrooms. You don't have to work so hard at it," Billy whispered.

"If you're to do a thing, best to do it well," Turner whispered back.

Billy heard a goblin step up to the booth. "How much're the blackfans?"

"Four *jegen* a piece," Turner replied smoothly.

"A half *duen*? That are thievery."

"*Zaj*? Then go buy someplace else. Them're the best blackfans in the city."

"If I buy three, you throw in a fourth free?"

"*Yob'rikit*. That're one *duen* four."

But as Turner completed the transaction, Billy heard a long shrill whistle from farther down the Underway. It was the signal to start Kurt's Hail Mary play. Billy tensed. It all came down to this.

"Go, you *pizkreten*! Go!" Hop barked.

And go they did.

CHAPTER SIXTEEN
More or Less Where He Was Supposed to Be

Hop had heard other soldiers claim that, for them, everything slowed down during battles. They could follow the flight of arrows in the sky, see the dust dancing, and count every droplet of blood. That never happened for Hop. For him, battles were loud, fast, and confusing. That was why he spent most of his time ducking.

Hop ducked as an ice bolt hurled past his head. He wasn't sure if the blast of cold had come from Frost or from one of Sawtooth's wizards. The throne room was in chaos. Allies and enemies swirled in a mad melee, weapons and spells and bodies flying about at random. The specifics of who was shooting at him and why weren't really important, in Hop's mind. The important thing was the ducking. And the running.

Hop firmly believed that the best way to survive a battle was not to get into one. Failing that, hiding was always a good fallback. He was an excellent hider. Unfortunately, sometimes hiding wasn't an option. Sharp-eyed officers, determined enemies, or plain bad luck could ruin even the best concealment. But the worst was when people were depending on him. Hop hated that. Because then, instead of having some stupid lieutenant looking over his shoulder, Hop was subject to the merciless glare of his own conscience. He could never hide from himself.

So, while he couldn't avoid this particular fight, dashing around unpredictably and ducking at frequent intervals seemed to be his next best options. Plus, he rationalized, his spasmodic movements tended to confuse and annoy the enemy, disrupting their plans and helping his friends succeed.

Still, there was something Hop was supposed to accomplish, aside from the ducking and dodging. Best to get to it.

Hop weaved toward a pillar carved in the likeness of the ninth Goblin King, a stern-faced human wearing a broad-brimmed helmet and carrying an entrenching tool. Hop ducked under a slashing sword, dodged a flying body, and spun to avoid an arrow. Without even knowing quite how he'd managed it, he found himself more or less where he was supposed to be. And just in time too.

"Hop! Catch!" Kurt's voice cut through the din of battle.

Hop turned, reached out, and, improbably, astonishingly . . .

The Goblin Crown landed in his outstretched hands. Hop looked at it in disbelief. The plan had worked. He couldn't remember the last time he'd been part of a plan that had worked.

"Run!" Kurt shouted, snapping Hop out of his reverie.

Hop ran. He ran for his life. He ran for his people. He ran for all he was worth.

Sawtooth's world had gone mad. The Hanorian army was still a hundred miles from Kiranok, but alarms bells were already ringing. In the distance, he could hear the sounds of battle coming from the Underway near the Hall of Kings.

The boy, Sawtooth realized as he and his bodyguards quick-marched toward the fighting. *It are too soon for the Hanorians. So it're the skerbo boy. The one that're after me crown.*

As the goblin general and his soldiers rushed forward, they passed the very spot where, not so long ago, Sawtooth had first met the Dark Lady, first heard her prophecies and watched her work miracles.

"To understand the world, study the smallest grain of sand," she'd said the day he first heard her preach. "Pick up a fistful of sand, throw it into the air. Can you see the shape of every grain? Do you know how the sand formed, how it came to be in your hand, and why it dances on the wind? If you cannot, how can you grasp a soul? Or more, pretend to understand millions of individual minds, acting in conflict and harmony, in love and in hate?"

"If we can *nai* understand the world," Sawtooth had asked, "how do we live in it?"

In answer, the *duenshee* had fixed Sawtooth with her silvery gaze. Her mouth never moved, but Sawtooth heard her voice inside his head. "Be as the world. Be as the sand. Be the dance."

At the time, he'd had no idea what the Dark Lady was trying to say. Even as the days and weeks passed and he began to appreciate her prophetic vision, the meaning of that first lesson had always eluded him.

Until this moment, racing through the Underway to confront a human who was supposed to save his people, a boy he was determined to destroy.

It're the world what're insane, that're what she meaned. In a mad world, the only sensible thing are to embrace the madness.

"Faster, lads!" Sawtooth called out, unlimbering his enormous sword and charging ahead of his followers. "Time to dance."

Everything was fire. It was all Lexi could see, all she could hear. She could taste ash on her lips, feel the flames flickering across her body. Through the red haze, she could make out Sawtooth's goons rushing the Hall of Kings, trying to tackle Hop and grab the Goblin Crown. It made her angry that they thought she would let that happen.

She flung fire at them. She glared fire. She exhaled fire.

Part of her knew she should be careful, that she was in danger of losing control and burning down everyone she could see, friend and foe alike. But it felt good, to let go, to set the world alight.

Suddenly a wave of cold snuffed out Lexi's fire. Lexi spun, ready to attack whoever dared oppose her.

And she saw Frost, his oversized ears flopping as snowy winds whirled around him. She held back. Barely.

"Measure, Lexi-*jinta*. Magic misused in anger are magic regretted. You can *nai* unburn a thing. Can *nai* bring the dead back."

"We're fighting for our lives," Lexi shot back.

"*Naizaj.* But we're fighting for their lives too." Frost's

winds extinguished a fire burning not far away. Lexi saw what the fire was hiding . . . one of Sawtooth's enforcers, burnt to a crisp.

Lexi faltered. She'd done that. The hulking goblin had been charging at her, swinging a giant ax, and she'd blasted him with all she had. Too late, she realized that she could have stunned him with light, or blinded him with smoke, or even used the hot winds to rise into the air, safe from his weapons.

Except she hadn't. And now he was ash.

"Use your gift. Do as you must. But *nai* one inch more. *Nai* one life taked that you can avoid taking."

Lexi nodded, sobered. Just then, she saw Hop break free from the enemy soldiers and run out of the Hall of Kings with the Goblin Crown in his hands. Sawtooth's loyalists gave chase, hot on his heels. Lexi sent a blast wave sweeping toward Hop's pursuers, more force than fire. The blast tumbled them to the floor. She'd broken a few ankles, seared some skin. Sawtooth's enforcers wouldn't be chasing Hop anymore, but they would live.

"Better. Bit by bit." Frost followed up Lexi's blast with a rain of hail, scattering the soldiers she'd missed.

With that Frost ran after Hop, using his magic with precision to protect the one-eared goblin as he fled with the Crown. Measured, controlled. Lexi did her best to follow the little wizard's example, despite the fire in her blood fighting to be free.

Up ahead, Hop spotted Shadow and her three *kijakgoben* "wedge breakers" clearing a way through Sawtooth's men for him and the Crown. Hop fell in behind Shadow, Mallet, Breaker, and Peashoot as they battled toward the

Underway. In his wake he felt blasts of fire and ice, Lexi and Frost cutting off his pursuers.

Sprinting onto the Underway, Hop scanned for the mushroom cart where they'd hidden Billy. Instead, he saw a full company of Sawtooth's soldiers charging down the Underway, filling the entire tier from wall to railing, swarming around and past the distant cart. A trio of particularly manic-looking *goben* stepped to the fore of Sawtooth's troopers. Wizards. The sight of them sent a chill of fear running down Hop's spine. Darkness and wind swirled around the trio and ice spread from their feet. A blast of snow and ice slammed into Hop, Shadow, and her three *kijakgoben*. Hop flew backward through the air and landed with a hard thump on the cobblestones. It was all he could do to hold on to the Crown.

As Hop struggled to his feet, a sharp pain stabbed through his lower back. Hoping it was just a bruised tailbone, the former Copperplate tried to get his bearings. The charging soldiers were almost on top of him. Sawtooth's wizards were readying another spell. Shadow lay on the ground nearby, groaning and shivering. Her companions, Mallet, Breaker, and Peashoot, lay still, covered in ice. Hop gripped the Crown hard. With his protectors incapacitated or dead, his future didn't look very promising.

Then Hop heard a high-pitched shout. "Hey, jerkfaces!"

Hop turned and saw Lexi behind him, standing in the center of the Underway. The human girl glowed so brightly that Hop could barely look at her. Frost stood by her side, a dark, icy counterpoint to Lexi's incandescence.

"Eat this!" Lexi yelled.

Lexi screamed fire. An intense wave of light and heat blasted from her hands, eyes, and mouth, nearly blinding Hop. The hairs on his head and arms singed. His copper-inlaid breastplate grew uncomfortably hot.

Then Frost joined in, and ice and snow filled the Underway.

Sawtooth's wizards counterattacked with blizzards of their own. Wherever Lexi's energy hit theirs or overlapped with Frost's, melting ice mixed with super-heated air to create a thick fog. Soon it was nearly impossible to see. Even redsight couldn't penetrate the hot, clinging mist.

That suited Hop just fine. He realized he could run now. Run and not look back. Leave the Crown, forget the human children, save his own hide. But, despite himself, Hop continued forward through the gray, groping blindly toward Billy, and, more horribly, toward the enemy soldiers with their hammers, axes, and swords, not to mention Sawtooth's wizards and their blood-freezing spells.

Hope I do nai *regret this*, Hop thought, suspecting he probably would.

Still, he kept inching ahead, the Goblin Crown firmly in his grip.

Billy had somehow managed to maintain his composure while he endured the long wait for Turner's signal to emerge from hiding. He'd mostly stayed calm when the waves of soldiers tromped by. He'd even kept hidden under the cart during the first blast of blizzard winds. But hearing Lexi shout was too much. Billy poked his head out from under the mushroom cart and tried to see what was going on.

Everything was gray. A dense, warm fog filled the Underway. It reminded him of the mist on the batreme. Except there he'd been safe, if a little disoriented. Now he was certain that somewhere in the fog, his friends were fighting, possibly even dying, and he couldn't see them or do anything to help. Billy could just barely make out Turner, and she was only a foot or two away.

"Turner, what do we do?"

After a thoughtful pause, Turner said, "Wait, I guess. That are what life mostly come to, *zaj*? Waiting in the gray and hoping for the best."

This could work for us, Hop thought as he slipped through the mist. *Sure, Kurt's plan are in the smelter, but I're nice and sneaky-like in this fog, so* zajnai *I can get right up to Billy and hand him the* drakik *Crown.*

Hop tried not to think things like that, generally. He found that when he got too optimistic, life had a nasty habit of proving him wrong. Which is why he was not entirely shocked when something smacked him in the head.

It was a mace, Hop realized as he blinked back the pain. Luckily, his helmet took the brunt of the blow. Still, he felt dizzy; his brain hurt.

And the soldier wielding the mace was standing above him, taking another swing.

Gripping the Crown in his right hand, Hop brought up his left arm to block the blow. As he deflected the mace, pain shot through his forearm and his hand went numb. *A stinger,* Hop thought. From experience, he knew he'd get sensation back in his arm, eventually. Not that it mattered. With a limp arm, a bruised back, and a head-splitting concussion, he wasn't going to last long.

"Quick! The Crown're here!" the soldier boomed. More troopers charged out of the mists.

Nai *long at all.*

Then someone slammed into the soldier, knocking

him away from Hop. With a roar, the new arrival began clobbering the incoming troopers. Hop tried to identify his rescuer, but the blow to his head made it hard to focus.

"Hop? You all right?" rumbled a familiar voice.

"Leadpipe?"

"Who you think?" Leadpipe boomed.

Struggling with his blurred vision, Hop saw the *kijakgob* hammer at Sawtooth's soldiers with a huge club. He caught one square in the breastplate, and the trooper flew back a dozen feet. But for every soldier Leadpipe batted away, two more charged in. Leadpipe couldn't hold them off forever.

Just then, Hop felt a strong wind gust through the Underway, coming from the direction of Sawtooth's wizards. The wind blew away the mist, leaving him and Leadpipe dangerously exposed. They needed to get the Crown to Billy soon or they'd all be doomed.

Suddenly Leadpipe groaned. "*Ahka.* Bit of help here?"

One of Sawtooth's troopers had gotten in a lucky shot and cut Leadpipe on the left shoulder. Blood ran down his arm, and the *kijakgob* was having trouble swinging his huge club.

"*Zeesnikken eger zapergritten,*" Hop muttered. "*Wazzer!*"

Hop charged into the melee, flailing about with the Crown, kicking random shins, snapping with his teeth, doing his best to drive back Sawtooth's enforcers. Though hampered by his injuries, he managed to distract the soldiers long enough to allow Leadpipe to catch his breath. That was something, anyway.

"*Ganzi!*" Leadpipe boomed his thanks, swinging his club again with gusto.

Sawtooth's soldiers gave way a little, but more reinforcements poured in. Hop knew he and Leadpipe wouldn't be able to hold out much longer. He wasn't sure how hurt

Shadow was, but she and her bodyguards needed some healing magic, and soon. And judging by the increasingly sporadic flashes of heat and cold coming from behind him, Frost and Lexi were wearing down. Time to end this.

"Billy!" Hop shouted. "Billy, we need you!"

Emerging from hiding was one of the hardest things Billy had ever done. Hearing the battle had been terrifying, but seeing it now that the fog had dissipated was heartrending. Leadpipe and Hop were badly wounded, fighting against incredible odds. Shadow and her *kijakgoben* blockers were down, unmoving. Frost and Lexi were being pelted with snow and ice by Sawtooth's wizards. And far in the distance, Kurt dodged and ducked frantically as he tried to avoid charging waves of hostile goblins.

Billy tried to trick himself into seeing the battle like a video game, with his friends and their goblin opponents as mere bits of graphical data, the better to understand the pattern of things and plan his moves. It didn't work. The smell of blood and the moans of the wounded made it impossible for Billy to imagine the horrific landscape into any kind of abstraction. This was real. And Billy had to deal with it.

"Turner, run," Billy said. "Get out of here while you can."

But as he checked on the young goblin, he realized . . .

Turner was dead. Sweet, innocent Turner, cheerful novice of the Night Goddess, expert Sunchaser, and surprisingly enthusiastic mushroom vendor. Her body lay sprawled out only a few yards from the cart, the back of her head a crushed-in mess. Billy hadn't seen her fall, hadn't even heard it. He didn't know whether she'd been hit by a soldier's mace or a thrown rock or a hurling chunk of magical ice, but she was gone. Billy felt numb. Useless in the face of death.

"Billy!"

Hop's panicked cry cut through Billy's shock. He tore his eyes from Turner's corpse and spied Hop with the Goblin Crown in his hands. He had the Crown! Fighting back his tears, Billy shouted and waved his arms. "Hop! Over here!"

Hop looked desperately to Billy through a crowd of goblin attackers, and Billy realized there was no way Hop could get the Crown to him. The press of Sawtooth's enforcers was too thick, and despite Leadpipe's help, the one-eared goblin was in danger of being overwhelmed.

So Billy did the only thing he could think of. He climbed onto Turner's mushroom cart and yelled as loud as he could. "*Ahka! Wazzer!* Hey, you *goben*! I'm right here. I'm the one you want! *Skerbo!*"

All eyes went to Billy. Hundreds, maybe thousands of goblins looked his way, some with hope, some with amazement, some with unmitigated hate.

It gave Hop, Leadpipe, Kurt, and the rest an opening. Just for a moment, but it was enough.

"Hop!" Billy heard Kurt yell. "Fleaflicker!"

It was one of the plays they'd practiced. The goblins had a wiry strength, but their hunched posture limited their shoulder movement. It meant they couldn't throw overhand nearly as well as a human. And no one could throw as well as Kurt. Hop underhanded the Crown back toward the waiting quarterback. It sailed through the air in a high arc, right toward Kurt's outstretched hands . . .

Then a goblin soldier punched Kurt in the face, and the

quarterback went down with a thud. The Crown clattered to the ground. Billy's heart tightened in his chest and his mouth went dry. They were going to lose. It was over.

Except no one told Lexi that. With a graceful leap, she dove to the floor, grabbed the Crown, and came up throwing. "Billy, catch!"

She spun the Crown through the air, discus style, throwing it awkwardly in Billy's general direction. The Crown fluttered through the air like a dying bird, well off target. But then Lexi focused and a hot wind blasted the Crown back on course. It flew across the Underway, straight toward Billy. He reached out, stretching as far as he could to catch the Crown . . .

Only to see a big, meaty goblin hand snatch it out of the air.

"No!" Billy shouted.

But he might as well have been protesting to an empty room for all the good it did. With surprising speed, the goblin who'd caught the Crown reached out with his free hand, grabbed Billy by the neck, and hauled him off the mushroom cart.

Just like that, Billy found himself face-to-face with General Sawtooth. The goblin warlord tightened his grip on Billy's throat and shook the Crown in his face. "What're you doing with this, you *drakik skerbo*?"

The fighting stopped abruptly as all eyes went to Billy and Sawtooth. Desperate to save Billy, Lexi tried to summon her energy for a final, desperate spell, but Frost stepped up and whispered in her ear, "You'll burn 'em both. Wait. Watch. But do *nai* act in desperation unless there're *nai* other way."

Lexi let it go. As the spell drained from her, she felt like a balloon with the air let out. She dropped to one knee, completely drained.

Not far away, she could see Hop, battered and bleeding, coiled for his own mad charge. But then he noticed Frost and Lexi out of the corner of his eye. "Wait," Lexi mouthed. Hop nodded. His shoulders slumped and he exhaled heavily. He looked every bit as exhausted as Lexi felt.

With five long steps, Sawtooth carried Billy out to a bat platform and dangled him over the edge of the Underway's central chasm. Billy's feet hung in the air, with nothing between him and the dirty streets of Rockbottom but a sheer, half-mile drop. To Billy's credit, he tried to snatch the Crown from Sawtooth's hand, but the general easily moved it out of his reach.

"You're *nai* answering me!" Sawtooth snarled.

"That're 'cause you will *nai* let him talk." Lexi turned and saw Shadow struggling to her feet, glaring at her father. "Big *gob* general and you're afeared of one human boy?"

"Humans destroyed our towns," Sawtooth growled. "Humans killed our soldiers. Humans burned our farms."

There were mutters of agreement from the crowd, but Hop interjected, "*Zaj*. And afore that, we destroyed their towns and soldiers and farms. And afore that, they attacked us. And afore that we attacked them. And afore and afore and afore."

"We never attacked you at all," Lexi added. "We're not even from this world. All we've ever done is try to help. Especially Billy. He's . . . he's the best person I know. Please. Let him go."

"Bad choice of words there." Sawtooth grinned, loosening his grip on Billy's neck.

"Coward!" Shadow snarled. "I're ashamed to call you Father. That boy say he're our king. And *naizaj* he're right.

Naizaj he're supposed to save us from all the trouble we're in. But you throw him over, we'll never know. 'Cause you're too afeared to face the truth. That we need a miracle like the King coming back to unscramble all the eggs that you breaked."

Lexi could see Sawtooth hesitate, torn between his desire to eliminate Billy and his need to keep the goblinfolk of Kiranok on his side.

Lexi saw an opening and took it. "The way I see it, you've got two choices. Put on the Crown yourself and prove that you're the true Goblin King, or let Billy try it. One way or another, the truth will come out." Lexi hoped Sawtooth would take the bait. Out of ego, or a desire to prove himself to his people, or maybe even as a way to redeem himself in his daughter's eyes. She also hoped that if he did let Billy put on the Goblin Crown, it would actually glow. Because if not . . .

As if following Lexi's train of thought, Hop added, "What're you afeared of? If you put the Crown on the human boy, and it glow, he're the real thing. If *nai*, you can toss him to Rockbottom and *nai* one will shed *nai* tears."

"At least let him talk," Shadow said firmly. "Do *nai* you all want to hear him talk?" she shouted to the crowd.

A mutter of agreement went up from the assembled goblins.

Then another voice rose over the din. "I think that're an excellent idea."

Surprised, Lexi turned toward the Underway's central chasm. There, between the various bridges and gondola lines, hovered Hop's friends and their five surviving warbats. Lexi recognized the lead bat as Hop's Daffodil, and on her back stood the goblin priestess Starcaller and a war party of Templars.

"I for one are *maja* interested in what the boy have to

say," Starcaller continued from her perch on Daffodil's back, watching Sawtooth through hooded eyes. "Are *nai* you?"

Clenching Billy by the neck, Sawtooth looked up at the warbats, then down to the depths of the Underway. Sawtooth knew he was teetering on the brink, just as much as the fool human boy in his grip. He'd become the leader of the goblins because folk had been too scared to confront him. That fear was broken now; he knew it, and eventually the mob would realize it too. His only chance was to give in to Starcaller's demands while making it look like he was still in control.

"Have it your way, you old fool," Sawtooth grumbled. He lowered the *skerbo* to the platform. The boy gripped the side railing, coughing and sputtering as he caught his breath. Sawtooth glared at the curly-haired human with his best general's glare.

"They want to hear you talk, *skerbo*," he said, his voice echoing through the Underway. "So talk! Tell us how a human boy are smarter and better and *maja* kingly than me. Tell everyone how you're going to save all us stupid, weak, sad, little *goben* what can *nai* save ourselfs."

Billy tried to answer, but he could barely breathe. All that came out was a hacking rasp.

"Go on," Sawtooth said, his voice full of menace. "We're all waiting for your wisdom."

The crowd laughed at that, making Billy shrink inside. He thought of a million things he could say. How he didn't want to be here. How he just wanted to go home. But Billy knew better than to voice his self-doubts and fears. Besides, some magical force had brought him here, kept him here, so he could set things right. And that wasn't going to happen if he backed down to Sawtooth.

Billy studied the general. The goblins' warlord was muscular and battle-scarred, confident and strong; he was surrounded by dozens of armed supporters; the Goblin Crown was in his hand. If the impulse struck, he could shove Billy off the edge of the Underway into Kiranok's central chasm with barely an effort. Yet Billy sensed doubt behind Sawtooth's swagger. Deep in the general's eyes, he thought he could see a gnawing fear not that different from Billy's own.

So Billy told Sawtooth the words he himself wanted to hear. "It's not your fault."

Sawtooth recoiled in surprise. "What're *nai* me fault?" he snarled, baring his impressive fangs.

"The war. All the death. My goblin friends told me about how the Dark Lady came here and started working miracles and talking about justice. How she made you believe. And how you thought justice meant getting back all the land the humans stole. So you fought. Because that's all you really know. You're a general, and when you see a problem, you solve it like a general, with marching and soldiers and war. You meant well. Only things didn't go the way you'd planned. The Dark Lady died, and a lot of goblins died along with her."

The hint of doubt in Sawtooth's eyes grew ever so slightly. Billy wondered what it must be like to be the goblin general, to have been certain he was going to save his people, convinced he was going to win back everything that had been taken from them, only to have it all go so horribly wrong.

"Then my friends and I showed up. Humans. Just like

the people who hurt you and destroyed your dreams. The last thing you wanted was for a human to save you. And Kurt . . . the Crown didn't glow for him. So as far as you were concerned, we were just more thieves. More humans trying to take what was rightfully yours.

"Or maybe . . . maybe part of you was disappointed. Because if Kurt had been the King, you would've been off the hook. It would've been his job to fix everything you'd broken. But he wasn't. And he didn't. So you had to keep fighting. Another battle. Another war. Only that failed, too. And now you're even more frightened and desperate than ever."

"*Bosh*," Sawtooth swore quietly. "It're all *bosh* and *drak*. You're twisting it all. Like a rope. Trying to tie it into a noose for me neck."

"I don't want to hang you. I want your help."

Sawtooth looked surprised at that. "You want help from me?"

Billy nodded. It made his neck hurt from where Sawtooth had choked him. Somehow, though, he found the energy to keep going. "How could I not? I don't know anything about building an army or fighting a war. If I'm going to be king, I'm going to need help from any goblin willing to give it. Especially from you."

Sawtooth turned the Goblin Crown around and around in his hands, studying the giant ruby set in its center, his self-doubt now clear for all to see. "The Dark Lady. She touched me. She reached right into me head, and she sayed I were choosed. That I were the key to all that're to come."

Billy felt like he was finally getting through to the goblin general. "The future's still ahead of us."

"The future are ahead of you, *naizaj*. But if you are the King, then me future are dust."

"No," Billy said, trying to sound strong, in control.

"You're the commander of the Warhorde. I don't want your surrender. I want you to serve your people. And your king. Give me my crown, General Sawtooth. That's an order." Billy worried, had he gone too far? Said too much?

Sawtooth looked from the Crown to Billy and back again. Aside from the warbats slowly flapping their wings to maintain their position in the center of the chasm, the entire city was silent, standing still, watching Sawtooth . . . and waiting.

"Father," Shadow said, stepping a little closer. "Do as the boy say."

Sawtooth looked over at his daughter, his face racked with doubt and pain. Then, slowly, reluctantly, Sawtooth held out the Goblin Crown to Billy.

"Take it," Sawtooth said, so quietly that even in the crushing silence of the Underway, Billy could barely hear him.

Trying to keep his hand from shaking, Billy reached out and gripped the Crown. The moment Billy's hand came in contact with the iron circlet, its ruby Eye began to glow, strong and bright, bathing Billy in a stream of intense red light. Billy wanted to look away, but he couldn't. Something about the red light held him in place. He knew the Crown belonged to him. And in a strange way, he belonged to it.

A murmur rose up in the crowded Underway. Then it turned to a whisper, then a low rumble, and then a huge roar.

"The King!" the goblins shouted. "The King! The King!"

Next to Hop, an old *svagob* fell to her knees. Malnourished and tattered, Hop guessed she was a refugee from one of the settlements in the path of the Army of Light. But her face shone with renewed hope and tears streamed from her bright green eyes.

"The King!" she sobbed. "He're come. We're saved."

All around the Underway, goblins reacted with cautious disbelief, unrestrained joy, or a mixture of both. Hop heard someone singing "Come the King." Bells rang out. Old goblins danced, and young goblins hugged and kissed. One *gob*, a grizzled veteran with even more scars and war wounds than Hop himself, caught Hop's eye and threw him a jaunty salute.

"Good work, Copperplate," the old soldier said. "Good work, indeed."

"Wow." Kurt joined Hop, rubbing his jaw where one of Sawtooth's enforcers had punched him. "The little runt really is the King."

Awash in crimson light, Billy looked at Sawtooth, who was still holding his side of the Goblin Crown. "I'll take this now," Billy said. "Thank you."

But when his eyes met Sawtooth's across the Crown, the goblin general's martial bearing slipped. His authoritative sneer vanished, replaced by a look of panicked horror. "It're *nai* possible."

"General," Billy said. "It's all right. Please, give me the Crown."

"It're a trick," Sawtooth said in disbelief. "A filthy *skerbo* trick."

"General?" Billy watched the general's expression flicker from rage to fear to shame to confusion and back again. Billy tightened his grip on the Goblin Crown and tried to sound as kingly as he could manage. "General, you are relieved. Release the Crown."

But Billy had overplayed his hand. Sawtooth's eyes

narrowed, his lips curling in contempt. "To the Pit with you," the goblin growled. "To the Fiery Pit with you both!"

Sawtooth yanked violently on the Crown. Billy stumbled forward but somehow managed to keep his grip on the iron circlet. Unfortunately, a split second too late, Billy realized that he'd done exactly what Sawtooth wanted. Using the Crown like a handle, Sawtooth shifted his weight, spinning in a semicircle and swinging Billy into the air. Then the general let go, and Billy, the Goblin Crown still in his hands, sailed over the railing of the Underway into Kiranok's yawning central chasm, plunging toward Rockbottom's polluted creek bed a half mile below.

CHAPTER SEVENTEEN
What Do Kings Do?

S awtooth wasn't even sure why he did it. It just . . .
happened. The human boy's words had made sense.
Listening to him, just for a moment, Sawtooth
had seen a future for himself, standing at the boy's side,
leading the Warhorde, following the orders of the King.
It was a blissful vision. No more responsibility. No more
crushing guilt.

Then, as the human boy gripped the Goblin Crown
and the crowd cheered, a violent anger had come boiling
up from deep inside Sawtooth. Maybe it was the voice
of the Dark Lady, still propelling him toward his destiny.
Maybe it was pure madness

Or zajnai *it're simpler than that,* Sawtooth thought.
Zajnai *I do* nai *want saving. Redemption, happiness, peace,
forgiveness? Such things are* nai *for me. I are waded so*

maja *deep in blood that I can* nai *swim* nai *more. Let 'em see me for what I truly are. A butcher. A monster. A fool.*

Anyway, the boy are dead now. And we'll all join him soon enough.

As the warbats dove down into the chasm behind him, chasing the boy, too late to matter, Sawtooth turned to face the mob, thousands of goblins whose mood was rapidly shifting from shock to murderous rage.

"The King are dead," Sawtooth growled, drawing himself to his full height. "Long live me."

The Underway exploded with cries of shattered hope and bloodcurdling fury. "Murderer!" Lexi heard a goblin shout. "Traitor!" screamed another. "Kingslayer!"

Lexi rushed forward with the rest of the crowd, though whether it was to try to save Billy or punish Sawtooth, she couldn't really say. The press of the crowd was thick, and it took Lexi far too long to get to the bat platform. She was too late. Billy was dead. After all they'd been through, all they'd survived, Billy had been thrown to his death, and Lexi had been helpless to save him.

Lexi felt tears running down her cheeks. She hated herself for it. Crying like some useless little princess. Better to be angry. Better to get revenge. She turned away from the railing and looked for Sawtooth.

But the general was gone. Literally gone. Countless goblins, including some of Sawtooth's own enforcers, had swarmed him in an enraged frenzy. Goblin soldiers with axes, swords, and spears. Goblin wizards with icy spells and lashing winds. A goblin smith wielding his hammer. A butcher with his cleaver. Regular everyday goblins with bare hands and sharp teeth.

"Sometime," Hop said, standing at Lexi's side, "us *goben* are *nai* so different from our *vargaren*. *Vargaren* packs'll acknowledge a leader, follow him through bad times and worse. Then one day something'll snap, and the entire pack'll turn on the leader. If the leader are lucky and smart, he'll run, live the rest of his days in exile. Sawtooth weren't lucky. Or smart. Just brave and fierce and stubborn. But that're *nai* the same, are it?"

Lexi shook her head, her rage draining away and the sadness seeping back in. At the bat platform, Lexi saw dented armor, shreds of torn cape, a small bit of what might have been a finger, and a slick of blood. None of it made her feel any better. None of it took away the pain. Billy was gone, and Sawtooth's death and dismemberment wouldn't bring him back.

Off in the distance, a group of goblins paraded down the Underway with a round object stuck on the end of a spear.

"General Sawtooth woulda liked that," Hop said, eying the parading goblins. He seemed to be avoiding the subject of Billy, as if not talking about his death would keep it from being true. Hop went on, looking at the round object at the end of the spear. "*Nai* the bit where he were teared apart. But a head on a pike? That're practically traditional. Sawtooth were a big believer in traditions."

"She's not liking it very much." Lexi nodded toward Shadow, who was sitting in the middle of the street, weeping. "He was her father. No matter what else."

Watching the strong Templar cry made Lexi's own tears flow. She realized she was crying for more than just Billy. Seeing Shadow weep over her estranged father's death made Lexi think of her own mother. She and her mother had been in a constant battle for years now. Lexi couldn't remember the last conversation they'd had that didn't end in a shouting match. Still, she knew that as much as she hated her mother sometimes, if she died, Lexi would be devastated. But in a way, Lexi had already lost her mother. She was a world away. Lexi had been missing for weeks now. Was her mother crying over her missing daughter, somewhere back in the real world? Or trying to stay strong and hope for the best?

Was there any hope? Would she ever get home now that Billy was . . .

"He's gone, right?" Kurt joined them. "There's no way he . . ." Kurt trailed off, unable to finish the question.

Lexi couldn't answer. The words just wouldn't come out. "It're a long fall" was all Hop could manage before his own voice choked up. Lexi decided it was time to see Billy's fate for herself. Wiping away her tears, she stepped toward the railing. Kurt and Hop followed, but a cluster of goblins blocked the view.

"Clear the way," Leadpipe said, joining them and shoving smaller goblins out of the way. "Clear the way for the companions of the King."

Lexi, Kurt, and Hop finally reached the railing; Frost and Leadpipe joined them moments later. Bracing herself, Lexi looked down. Using the last of her energy to enhance her vision, Lexi gazed down into the depths of Kiranok, street after street, layer after layer, seeking the inevitable signs of Billy's deadly impact.

However, there was no gathering crowd of ghoulish looky-loos. No spattered corpse. Nothing. Lexi poured even more energy into the vision spell, tapping reserves she didn't know she had, weaving enchantments to let her see even farther, to peer into the shadows just like a goblin. Redsight, they called it. Back and forth she scanned. Up and down. Telescoping her vision, looking for heat signatures with redsight, all without luck.

Then Lexi spotted a red glow. Close. She'd been looking right past it. A pulsing red light just a layer or two below her. And she wasn't the only one who saw it.

"Billy?" Hop asked.

"Oh my God," Lexi whispered, overcome with emotion. "He's . . ."

"Alive," Billy gasped.

Somehow, despite all the odds, Billy was alive.

He remembered falling—the rush of air, the plummeting feeling in his gut. Then came the painful moment of impact, far sooner than he'd been expecting. He'd slammed into one of the cables that pulled the gondolas back and forth between the two sides of the Underway. Billy grabbed for the cable, but he missed and fell again. This time he collided with another bat platform a level below. He rolled off the platform, tumbled into the street, and finally crashed into a vendor's cart loaded with children's toys.

That explained the pile of stuffed toy bats, rats, and *vargaren* lying around him.

"*Ahka*, you drop this?"

Billy blinked back the pain and looked up at a small goblin girl with her hair braided into dozens of tiny, beaded pigtails. She was missing half her teeth, and Billy could see her adult fangs just starting to grow in.

She was holding the Goblin Crown.

Billy must've dropped it when he hit the bat platform. He sat up, wincing, setting off a miniature avalanche of stuffed animals, rubber balls, and tiny musical instruments. "Yeah, I think I did."

"Do that mean you are the King?"

A crowd of goblins gathered around Billy and the little girl goblin, but no one appeared eager to approach him. Still, it was only a matter of time.

"What's your name, miss?" he asked the little goblin.

"I're called 'Peeppeep,'" she answered. "'Cause I're never quiet."

"Well, Peeppeep, to tell you the truth . . . I don't know if I'm the King or not. Why don't you hand me the Crown and let's see?"

Using both hands, Peeppeep held out the Goblin Crown. Billy gently took it from the little goblin, feeling its heft and metallic chill. Once again, the bright red glow beamed from its ruby Eye, throwing crimson light on Billy and the surrounding goblins. All around him, goblins fell to their knees and bowed their heads. All but Peeppeep.

"That light are pretty," the little goblin said. "But scary too."

"Yeah," Billy replied, struggling to his feet. He hurt everywhere, but kings don't sit groaning in piles of broken children's toys, no matter how much they ache. "It is a little scary."

Then Billy heard a familiar voice shouting, "Long live King Billy!"

It was Hop. Billy looked up. Hop, Frost, Leadpipe, Kurt, and Lexi were crowded on the bat platform above his head. Soon the entire Underway had taken up Hop's cry. "Long live King Billy!" echoed through the chasm.

Trying to keep his hands from shaking, Billy slowly placed the Goblin Crown on his head. It was too big and immediately fell over his eyes. Sighing, Billy pushed it back until it was balancing on his forehead. Clearly, he had a lot to learn about wearing a crown.

The crowd didn't seem to notice. They just kept cheering his name. "Long live King Billy! Long live King Billy! Long live King Billy!" Billy could hear the hope in their voices, as if the mere fact that he was wearing the Goblin Crown had instantly reversed all their setbacks and disappointments and defeats. He knew it wouldn't be that easy, that putting on the Crown was just the beginning. Still, he couldn't help but grin. Kurt's crazy Hail Mary play had actually worked.

William Tyler Smith Junior, known to his family, friends, and enemies alike as Billy, was the King of the Goblins. Billy, the perpetual new kid at school. Awkward, under-achieving, surprisingly freckled, ear-blushing, never-fit-in Billy, had finally found his true calling, and now the fate of an entire embattled culture depended on him.

"So other than glow, what do kings do?" Peeppeep asked as the cheering continued unabated.

"I don't know," he answered honestly. "I guess I better figure that out."

And quick, he thought as the crowd thundered his name.

After the cheering died away, one of Starcaller's priests, a scary-looking old *kijakgob* named Mendbreak, tended to Billy's many injuries. Despite his intimidating appearance, Mendbreak was surprisingly gentle. In addition to various bumps and bruises, Billy had a broken rib, torn ligaments in his shoulder, and had somehow damaged his liver. Though Mendbreak never said it aloud, he gave Billy the impression that without magical intervention, he might have died. After a few healing spells, Mendbreak sent him off with a potion to help him sleep and a warning to be more careful in the future.

Other healers patched up Kurt and Hop and tended to Shadow and Breaker, who were suffering from severe frostbite. Sadly, no amount of magic could revive the two other *kijakgoben* Templars. Sawtooth's wizards had frozen Mallet and Peashoot solid. Three of Sawtooth's enforcers had died as well, along with one innocent bystander, an elderly butcher hit by a stray crossbow bolt.

Then there was Turner. Billy insisted on seeing her body again as soon as Mendbreak finished his treatment. Hop led him to a quiet room off the Underway where the dead lay on slabs, preserved with spells until their funeral services. Even seeing Turner lying there, Billy couldn't believe she was really gone.

"What do goblins do for funerals?" Billy asked Hop, feeling hollow inside.

"Say a few words, sing some songs. Then the dead are chopped up and used as fertilizer or feed to the *vargaren*. So nothing are wasted. In the old days, the relatives would eat a bit themselfs, but that do *nai* happen much *nai* more. She were a good friend?"

"I barely knew her. But she could have been." Billy looked at Turner's formerly expressive face, now rigid and unnaturally pale. "A few years ago, I never even thought about people dying. Then my dad got sick, and I couldn't think about anything else. I mean, my dad is going to die. Soon, probably. It makes me wonder. What's the use? Fighting so hard to do the right thing, to make a difference? When everyone ends up the same in the end."

"The priestesses and priests of the Night Goddess say after we die, the Goddess will judge us by our actions. That She will reward the good with a seat in the stars and punish the unjust by hurling their souls into the sun to burn forever."

"Do you believe that?"

Hop considered Billy's question for a moment, then answered, "Us *goben*, we have two kinds of sight. Dayvision and redsight. So we know there are always at least two ways of looking at anything. On first sight, *zajnai* the religious types have it right. Which mean we best do good . . . or else. On second sight, *naizaj* this're all we get. And in that case, we owe it to ourselfs and everyone around us to make this world a paradise, make this life a seat in the stars. Your friend Turner, she tryed to do that, *zaj*? To treat people right. Make 'em happy."

"I think she did." Billy surveyed the room, the seven dead goblins on their slabs. "All this . . . because I asked to be King."

"You never wanted the Crown. You haved it shoved on you. By me. By the Goddess, if She exist. You're King 'cause we need you. So blame me for what happened here. Goddess know, I do. And aside . . ." Hop continued in a quiet, reflective voice, "You can *nai* live in fear of death. I walked that road, and it're a lonely path. These past weeks, I suppose I learned something, despite meself. I learned you have to face life and all that come with it. Responsibility, to yourself and others. Duty. Hard work. Laughter. Love. Sadness. That're the harder road, true, but *zajnai* it're the better one."

"I'm going to earn this," Billy said, determined. "I'm going to make it all worth it." He looked down at Turner, peaceful in repose, the crushing wound to the back of her head hidden by the position of her body. "I promise."

Billy had a dream that night, a strange mix of wish fulfillment and nightmare, fueled by his still-aching bruises, his troubled mind, and the sleep-draught Mend-break had given him.

Billy stood on the glacier atop Sunchase Peak, Torrent at his side. He turned and looked behind him, at the trail he'd taken up the mountain. A long line of men stood along the path. And his father stood right up front.

William Senior looked strong and healthy, better than any day since his diagnosis, his dark brown face smiling gently. "Billy. Some people want to meet you," he said quietly, gesturing down the trail.

He walked past his father. The next man in line was his grandfather, who'd died when Billy was only seven. He gave Billy a warm hug, smelling of the tobacco that had destroyed his lungs and ended his life. "Make us proud."

The next man had a weathered, heavily freckled face. Billy guessed this was his great-grandfather. Billy had never met him, but he'd heard the stories. His birth in a distant land, the war that left him orphaned at a young age, a life spent working on cargo ships crisscrossing the seas, his brief marriage to Billy's African American great-grandmother. How in the end, he'd disappeared back to sea, abandoning her and her newborn son. He smelled of engine oil and saltwater. He didn't hug Billy or speak, he just studied his great-grandson with eyes the color of stormy seas.

Then came Billy's great-great grandfather. Blond hair, ruddy skin, dressed in the uniform of a British soldier from the First World War. Billy recognized him instantly, but not from family pictures or stories. He knew him because he'd hidden behind his statue in the goblin's Hall of Kings.

"You . . . you've been here," Billy said. "In Kiranok. Like me."

"Bloody confusing, in't it? All this goblin business? I'm Ian Smith. Your great-great something-or-other."

"How'd you manage it? You were their king, right? You saved them?"

"Tried, I did. Missing in action, I suspect the reports read, when I didn't come back."

"You didn't come back? But you were a real soldier. A grown-up."

"Precisely. Doomed from the start, most likely. Chin up. You'll do better."

Then he was gone. The rest of the line was a blur of faces, hundreds of men, several more vaguely familiar from the statues in the Hall of Kings. Only a few tried to talk to Billy, and he couldn't understand any of them. One spoke what he suspected was German. The others addressed Billy in a gentle language full of "sh" and "va" sounds. Polish?

The last person in line was a teenager barely older than Billy. He wore rough-spun medieval-looking clothing and carried a wooden carpenter's toolbox. The Goblin Crown sat on his head, slightly askew. He gave Billy a sheepish grin and shrugged apologetically.

"Piast?" Billy guessed. "Piast the Wheelwright."

"*Tak*," the young man answered. *"Jak Cię zwą?"*

He's asking my name, Billy guessed. "Billy. Billy Smith."

Piast took off the Goblin Crown and handed it to Billy. "*Z Bogiem, Królu* Billy." It sounded like Piast was wishing him luck. Billy got the feeling he was going to need it.

The goblins put Lexi up in a sprawling home on an upper level of the city, complete with a soft bed, a well-stocked kitchen, and a view of the Underway. They gave Billy and Kurt rooms somewhere nearby, but Lexi was too exhausted to pay them a visit. She staggered into the bedroom, collapsed on the bed, and fell asleep before she could even fully take in her surroundings. When she awoke, Gooddark, the kindly goblin woman who'd been sent to take care of her, informed her that she'd slept for a full day and night. "Nice and restful, just what you need."

It hadn't felt restful to Lexi. She'd dreamed of falling ash and burning hair. When Gooddark presented her with fried sausages for breakfast, looking for all the world like burnt fingers, one whiff of the browned meat sent Lexi rushing to the nearest chamber pot so she could vomit up what little she had left in her stomach.

Gooddark made comforting noises, apologized, cleaned her up, then fed her clear broth and plenty of water. After a while, Lexi started feeling a bit more . . . human. But she never wanted to see a sausage again.

Gooddark told Lexi that Billy's official coronation banquet was only a few hours away and that Lexi would be a guest of honor. Lexi knew Billy would be disappointed if she didn't show, so she let Gooddark help her get ready. The goblin woman styled her hair into an elaborate, swept-up construct studded with rubies and gold. She put a ring on each of Lexi's fingers, intricate pieces made of gold and silver, rubies and sapphires, a fortune in jewels. Then she dressed Lexi in a silk gown, freshly made to her exact measurements and dyed a deep red. Gooddark showed Lexi the final effect in a floor-length mirror. The red of dress perfectly complemented her skin tone and dark eyes. The gold rings gleamed, catching the light, and the rubies sparkled in her black hair. Lexi had to admit, she'd never looked more beautiful.

To Lexi, it felt like a lie. Gooddark had made her look like a storybook enchantress, but Lexi knew the truth. She was a walking bomb waiting to explode.

"A touch dramatic for me taste." In the mirror, Lexi saw Starcaller approach, examining Lexi in her dress. "But I suppose that're what folks expect at an event like this. Drama."

Lexi turned to face the old goblin priestess. "Why do you think they picked red? Red for blood? Or red for fire?"

"Do *nai* read so much into it. It're the same color as the tunic you weared. Most like the seamstresses thinked it your favorite."

The dress was indeed the same shade as her first-day-of-school sweater. Lexi had always liked red. Only now the color had so much more meaning. To Lexi, it reminded her of the inner fire that fueled her temper and her newfound magic, a part of herself that made her feel powerful and good . . . and scared her to death.

"I was thinking. Would it be too late to change it for something else? Something, I don't know, pink or green or blue?"

"You can wear whatever you like, Little Spark, but the fire in your blood will still burn bright. That're the real Lexi, looking back at you in that mirror. Best learn to love what you see."

Lexi looked at her reflection. "A monster?"

"*Nai.* A woman with power and the ability to use it. A force in the world. Do *nai* fear who you are, Lexi. Embrace it and harness it and you can become great. But suppress your power or deny it, and it'll explode out when you are least ready. And *nai* good will come of that."

"I killed people, I think. Some of Sawtooth's men. Those humans on the lightship."

"And you feel terrible about it. It make your stomach churn and your hands tremble to think about it."

"Yeah. It does."

"Good. You have power and you were forced to use

it to defend your friends. That make you like a soldier. It mean you'll do things that're *nai* pretty. Using power responsible-like, that're your task. Do what you must, but do *nai* grow to like it."

"So I have to go to the party, but I don't have to enjoy it?" Lexi asked, managing a grin.

"*Zaj.*" Starcaller returned her grin. "That're responsibility, all right. But do *nai* dismiss the gratitude of those you helped. Take in the gratitude along with the guilt. Balancing them two things, that're your responsibility as well. Feel proud because of what you accomplished. Feel guilty from what you haved to do. But never let your pride make you forget your guilt, and never succumb to guilt and despair so long as you remain a force for good in this world."

"You make it sound easy."

"It're *nai* the easy way. But it're the only way that work, I can tell you that." Starcaller patted Lexi on the shoulder, comforting her, then walked toward the door. "Wear the red. It're who you are."

Lexi studied herself in the mirror. The truth was, she looked good in red.

The official coronation was a small affair in the Hall of Kings, administered by Starcaller and attended by just Billy, his friends, and a few local officials.

Starcaller placed the Goblin Crown on Billy's head, said a few words, and that was that. Once again, Billy noted how heavy and uncomfortable the Crown was. What was the old saying? "Uneasy lies the head that wears a crown"? His head was feeling pretty uneasy. Despite the fact that someone had lined the iron circlet with suede to make it fit better, it still kept slipping down his forehead. He could tell wearing the Crown was going to be a learning experience in more ways than one.

As Billy processed out of the Hall of Kings, he took one last look around the room, at the carved stone faces he'd seen in his dream, Piast with his toolbox, Ian in his brimmed helmet, and all the rest, seeing for the first time the vaguest of family resemblances, one to the next.

"So now what?" he whispered to them. The statues of his ancestors remained stone silent. Billy knew if he was going to make a difference here, he was going to have to figure it out for himself.

The private ceremony gave way to a very public coronation banquet. On the streets of the Underway, goblin cooks laid out huge tables heavy with every imaginable variety of meat, fish, fruits, and vegetables. There were mouth-watering stews, giant piles of roasted mushrooms, cut melons with cream, and steamed greens topped with fried grasshoppers. The entire population of Kiranok turned out for the feast. There were stages for musicians, dance floors, jugglers, even free bat rides for the little ones.

Billy and his friends sat at a huge semicircular table on Broadbridge, a massive arching structure that crossed Kiranok's central chasm near the Hall of Kings. Billy wore new clothes for the occasion, highlighted by gold arm rings and a gem-studded tunic. Kurt wore a similar outfit. It was all a little much as far as Billy was concerned, but Hop and Shadow had insisted. It was important that he look sufficiently regal.

Billy was doing his best to manage it, but as far as he was concerned, no one at the head table looked as good as Lexi. He'd heard the phrase "breathtakingly beautiful" before, but he'd never thought much about it. Now, though, whenever he looked at Lexi in her red dress and sparkling jewels, he had a hard time breathing. So in order to keep his composure, he tried not to look at her too often. It wasn't kingly to stare. Or blush. Or both at the same time.

Instead, he tried to focus on the steady stream of goblins coming to pay their respects. In groups of ten or twelve, the goblins would step in front of Billy, execute courtly bows, and move on. Occasionally they'd mutter a blessing. He'd respond with his best royal nod, which usually made the goblins smile as they filed away.

As Copperplates moved one batch of goblins out and the next in, he caught a glimpse of Hop off in a corner, whispering to Shadow. The two of them had spent most of the day huddled together, talking quietly. Billy was pretty sure Hop had a crush on Shadow, but their conversation seemed more conspiratorial than flirtatious. Billy suspected he figured prominently in whatever schemes they were hatching.

"Hey, Your Highness," Lexi interrupted his thoughts. "Stop brooding. We won. At least pretend to enjoy it."

"Yeah. Cheer up, squirt," Kurt added. "You don't look half bad wearing that thing."

"We're not done," Billy pointed out. "We're still a long way from home. The goblins are still in danger."

"Getting home, helping the goblins, we'll figure it out," Lexi said confidently. "So smile a little. Nobody wants a grumpy king. Grumpy kings are scary."

Despite her encouragement, though, Billy could tell Lexi was working hard to keep her own spirits up. He could see something in her eyes, something haunted. She'd done so much for him, suffered so much. But as he studied her, Lexi still managed a smile, one that lit up Billy's whole world as bright as her light spells. Billy smiled back despite himself.

"There. That's better," Lexi said, reacting to his grin.

"I know it's selfish, but I'm glad you guys ended up here with me," Billy admitted. "I couldn't have managed all this alone."

"Good thing you spilled your lunch all over me then." Kurt chuckled. "Been an adventure, actually. So I guess I'm glad too."

"You know, when we first ran into you, I thought you were kind of a jerk," Lexi admitted to Kurt. "But there's a lot more to you than that, isn't there?"

"I have levels," Kurt joked. "Unexpected depths." He looked at Lexi and Billy. "We all do."

Billy laughed, finally relaxing a little. The food, the music, and the general good mood made the banquet fly by. Goblin dancers spun and contorted. Goblin musicians played upbeat whirls and jigs. Goblin chefs brought Billy and his friends one amazing creation after another.

Eventually the party began to wind down, and Billy's doubts and concerns reasserted themselves. He noticed that though the goblins were still eating enthusiastically, laughing, singing, and dancing, it felt as if they were trying too hard. Then he spotted Hop, still deep in conversation with Shadow, now joined by Frost and Leadpipe. The faces of the four goblins were serious, concerned, in stark contrast to the forced frivolity of the other partygoers.

"Excuse me," Billy said to Lexi and Kurt. "Be right back. King stuff."

Billy got up and headed the goblins' way. He was supposed to be in charge now. Time to start acting like it.

Sometimes, Hop observed to himself, things could go so

completely wrong that they'd come out the other side and end up right.

In the past few months, all Hop had done was fail. He'd failed to escape the war, failed to lie low in Kiranok, failed to make Kurt king, failed to hide out in the Flyer Corps, and then failed to get his bat-riders free of the war. Along the way he'd failed to avoid attachments, failed to duck responsibility, and failed to pass off authority to other people.

As a result of his failures, here Hop was, the right hand *gob* to the new King, wearing silk and gold, sipping *zobjepa*, and talking to the most beautiful *svagob* he'd ever met. Frost and Leadpipe were at his side, and his other friends, Lexi, Billy, and Kurt, Daffodil's crew, the other bat-riders, they were all here, enjoying the banquet. He should be happy. He almost *was* happy. The trick, Hop reflected, was to ignore the actual substance of the conversation he was having with Shadow, Frost, and Leadpipe. Pretend they were talking about the weather or the latest mask-play at the Amphitheater. He'd almost managed it when Billy . . . King Billy . . . sliced through the crowd and interrupted Hop's fantasy.

Billy studied the four goblins. "So what's going on? You four look worried."

Hop sniffed his *zobjepa*. The mushroom wine smelled of honey, peppers, and freshly plowed fields, of simple things done well, and of the quiet, peaceful times that he feared he would never see again. "It're *nai* important. Go on back to smiling for the crowd, and we can talk tomorrow."

"I'm kind of a dork, you know?" Billy replied. "I mess up a lot, and I'm not good at big speeches or snappy comebacks or any of that. But I'm good at watching people. And I've noticed, before you tell a lie, you always rub your fangs against your lips. Just like now."

Hop felt the tip of his left canine pressing against his lower lip. He was going to have to work on that.

"We should tell him," Leadpipe said softly. "He are the King."

Hop looked from Billy to his fellow goblins and back. Shadow nodded discretely. That sealed it.

"It're the humans," Hop confessed. "Their army are at the mouth of Jezpor Valley. That mean they'll get here in a week. *Zajnai* less."

"There're thousands of 'em," Frost added grimly. "Tens of thousands. They mean to end us. Destroy Kiranok and wipe us out to the last *gob*."

Hop watched Billy's reaction. To his surprise, the young King didn't flinch. He just nodded thoughtfully.

"So what do we do about it?" Billy asked.

Hop reflected on the various strategies he and Shadow had been discussing. In the end, it had come down to weighing bad options against worse ones. Plus, there wasn't a single thing they could do right at that moment to make things better. Except . . .

"There're a *goben* song," Hop said with a thoughtful expression. "It're called 'Tomorrow Come Tomorrow.' It say that bad things are always coming, but you have to hold on to the good. That are what help you through. So tomorrow we can worry and plan. But this night? Tonight you make folk feel good. You wave and smile and give 'em pretty speeches. 'Cause dark times are coming. And when they do, folk'll say 'Remember the night we crowned King Billy? Remember how brave he looked? How proud we all felt? As long as King Billy are leading us, we can survive. We can win.' You give 'em hope, Billy."

Billy shook his head. "It doesn't seem like much."

"It're everything," Shadow said. "A king do many

things, but giving folk hope, nothing are more important than that."

Hop looked at Shadow in admiration. Her violet eyes were bright against her dark skin, like amethysts on a swath of black silk.

Hop nodded in agreement. "With hope, anything are possible."

But Billy remained unconvinced. "Maybe that's true. But there's one problem." The human boy looked around at the crowd. "They know. All the goblins here. They know that something terrible is coming, and that we're doing this to distract them."

Hop snuck a glance at the crowd as well. More importantly, he listened. As the feasting had given way to drinking, there'd been less and less laughter, and what there was sounded either hollow and muted or overly loud and insincere.

"You're right," Hop said sadly. "They know."

Billy shook his head. "Giving them hope is one thing. But what we're doing right now, it's a lie. Worse. We're not just lying to them; we're making them lie to each other. Forcing them to pretend to be happy. It's wrong. I won't start my reign on a lie." Billy thought about the problem for a moment, then came to a decision. "That song you were talking about. 'Tomorrow Come Tomorrow.' I want the band to play it. All the bands. All at once. On my signal."

Hop considered Billy's command, then looked over at Frost, Leadpipe, and Shadow. From their expressions, they agreed with their new king. And the more Hop thought about it, the more he did too.

"We'll need a thousand heartbeats to get ready," he said to Billy. "Then a nod'll do."

Billy watched as Hop, Leadpipe, Frost, and Shadow rushed off to carry out his command. Hop took a slight detour to talk to a small group of goblins along the way. A pretty young female with cornrows, a wiry goblin boy with big, staring eyes, a quiet, intense older goblin, and a few others. They were Hop's warbat crew—Flutter, Snails, Bead, and the rest. After a quick discussion, the fliers scattered through the Underway to assist Hop. Billy started counting his heartbeats.

At one thousand, he looked up and spotted Hop, who was standing on a nearby bat-taxi platform. Billy nodded.

Hop waved a piece of cloth in the air, once, twice, three times. On the third wave, musicians all over the chamber struck up a haunting tune. On the nearest stage, a huge *kijakgob* with a deep bass voice and a tiny soprano *jintagob* began to sing, their melodies blending in an inhuman harmony.

Sweet are the mushroom wine
And warm are the fire
Safe in your arms me love
Feeling all warm and fine . . .
And I wish I could stay
All the rest of my days . . .
But I only have tonight.

The song had an instant effect. The entire population of Kiranok went silent. There was no talking, no laughing; the dancing and drinking stopped. There was only the song:

Outside the wind are blowing
Outside the soldier calling
Outside the vargar *cry*
Outside the winter die
But I can nai *hear 'em . . .*

Nai *tonight*. Nai *tonight*.
Tomorrow come tomorrow.
But nai *tonight,* nai *tonight.*

In the morning I will go
By the dawn I'll grab me spear
And kiss our derijinten *good-bye*
And try nai *to look back*
To all I leave behind

At the chorus, the other goblins began to sing along.
Hop, Shadow, Frost, and Leadpipe joined in. Soon the
entire chamber was singing as one:

But nai *tonight. Nai* tonight.
Tomorrow come tomorrow.
But nai *tonight,* nai *tonight.*

Tonight nai *care for kings*
Or war or wrongs or rights
Tonight I'll drink me wine
By the fire in the night
With you me love, with you
You're all I see tonight.

Tonight. Tonight. Tonight.
Tomorrow come tomorrow.
But nai *tonight,* nai *tonight.*

It are the memories that matter
The hope that bear us on
When the dawn break me heart

It're you that lead me home
Our sweet children laughing
The hearth fire crackling
In the heat and the mud
In the pain and blood
Those things I'll remember
Ever fight to regain

And when tomorrow come
Promise me nai *to cry*
Promise me nai *to mourn*
And I'll promise you nai *to die*

Nai *tonight.* Nai *tonight.*
Tomorrow come tomorrow.
But nai *tonight,* nai *tonight.*

To his surprise, Billy felt his eyes grow damp. He wasn't alone. Leadpipe was openly weeping, huge tears rolling down his massive face. Frost waved his hand, and tiny snowflakes flickered away from his cheeks. Shadow wiped her face discretely. Even Hop, sarcastic, pragmatic, cynical Hop, had a watery sheen in his yellow eyes.

A determination dawned then, filling Billy's heart and driving away the lingering doubts and fears. From his seat at the head table, he looked out over Kiranok, with its countless tiers, its hundreds of bridges, and its goblin throngs. Lit by torches and glowing fungus, sparkling from the crystalline deposits in its stonework, festooned with garlands for the coronation, the city never looked more beautiful. Seeing it like this made Billy feel fiercely protective. After all, it was *his* city now. And he would do anything to keep it safe. Somehow he would save Kiranok and everyone in it. Somehow he'd make sure the song of the goblins would go on and on.

So Billy Smith, the Goblin King, stood up on his seat and raised his glass in a toast. Because that's what kings do.

As loud as he could, Billy said, "Goblins. Friends. I will not lie to you. The humans are coming. They will be here soon. But not tonight."

A cheer went up at that. Somehow they'd heard him all over the Underway. Billy noticed Lexi and Frost both concentrating. A gentle wind blew and his mouth felt warm. His voice filled the city. Billy continued, not sure where he was finding the words he was saying, words that expressed a confidence he almost never felt. Wherever they came from though, he was glad he'd found them.

"Tonight we are united. Tonight we are happy. Look around. At your friends and neighbors. Your family. They're what will get you through the times to come. Remember this night. Remember hope. Remember love. And remember this: we will survive."

Another cheer, though Billy thought he could hear a hint of fear and doubt this time. And who could blame them?

"We will," Billy said, quieter now, trusting Frost's and Lexi's magic to carry his voice. "I promise you that. We will save Kiranok and make sure that goblins do not disappear from this world. But to do that, I'll need your help. The help of every single one of you. Will you help me?"

"*Zaj!*" came the reply, like thunder, a hundred thousand goblin voices shouting as one. "*Zaj! Zaj! Zaj!*"

"Then there's nothing we can't do," Billy said with quiet confidence, looking to Shadow as he echoed her words. Thanks to Frost's and Lexi's magic, he didn't have to shout anymore. It didn't seem to be the kind of thing you *should* shout. You didn't have to shout things that you really believed. And Billy believed.

"For Kiranok!" Hop added, raising his glass of mushroom wine. "And for King Billy!"

"For King Billy!" the city thundered. "King Billy! King Billy! King Billy!"

And Billy's name echoed through the vast stone halls of Kiranok for a very long time indeed.

EPILOGUE
A Happy Pause

A nd happily they lived until they lived *nai* more."
That was how all good *goben* stories ended.
Hop wished he could say that about his own tale.
But he knew his story was far from done. Billy's story too.
The next chapter would come all too soon.

Still, if this wasn't a happy ending, at least it felt like a
happy pause. Billy had told Hop's folk the truth, prepared
them for what was coming, and, despite the boy's self-
doubts, just having him in Kiranok wearing the Goblin
Crown was worth more than he knew. Even Hop had
been surprised at how much he'd been moved by seeing
the Wheelwright's Heir start his reign.

So tomorrow there'd be time to worry about their
story's conclusion. Tomorrow Hop, Billy, Shadow, Frost,
Leadpipe, and all their friends would plan and plot, make

the hard decisions and painful sacrifices. Tomorrow would come, like the first day of harvest after a long, lazy summer, like waking from a dream. But not tonight.

Tonight was perfect. Tonight Billy was the King of the Goblins, and songs filled the air. Tonight was for celebration and family and friends. Tonight was for hope.

Frost looked over at Hop as the cheers for Billy echoed through the city. "*Ahka*, Hop. Call me crazy," the tiny wizard said playfully, "but are that pride in your face? Can even cynical, doubting Hop recognize a job doed right? Are you actually . . . happy?"

Hop considered Frost's words, looking from the *jintagob* to his hulking brother to dark, beautiful Shadow to the thousands and thousands of goblins toasting and cheering for Billy, Lexi, and Kurt.

Then the one-eared goblin smiled.

"And happily he lived," Hop said, then drank deep from his mushroom wine and added, "until he lived *nai* more."

The story of Billy and Hop and their
friends will continue in . . .

THE FALLEN STAR

The Second Book of

BILLY SMITH AND
THE GOBLINS

APPENDIX A
Gobayabber for Beginners

Through the magic of the omniscient narrator (that's me), the goblin language (or *Gobayabber*, as goblins call it) in *The Goblin Crown* has been translated into more or less recognizable English. However, efforts have been made to maintain an authentic goblin accent. This means that it has been necessary to use a few untranslated bits of *Gobayabber*.

Goblin verbs are regular and undeclined. To approximate *Gobayabber* grammar, the author (still me) has used the third person plural case for all verbs in spoken *Gobayabber*, regardless of the gender or number of the subject. Also, when an English verb is irregular, the narrator has made it regular. So for example, while an English speaker would decline the verb "to swim" as follows: *swim, swam, have swum, will swim*, a goblin would decline it as *splurshur*, *splursht, artsplursht, nursplursh.* This has been translated into English as *swim, swimmed, have swimmed, will swim.* Likewise, *to see* is declined *see, seed, have seed, will see.* Technically, the verb *to be* should probably have been rendered *be, beed, have beed,* but it sounded super-awkward so the narrator stuck with *are, were,* and *have been.* And let's not even get into *should, could,* and *would.* Translating *Gobayabber* are hard, *zaj*?

Following is an index of the *Gobayabber* terms found in *The Goblin Crown*:

Ahka "Look here." An expression of alarm or excitement or interest.

Bokrum A giant mountain sheep. Domesticated *bokrumen* are used by goblins as riding animals and to pull plows and carts.

Bosh A lie. Falsehood. Excrement. An expletive. The plural, *boshen,* is also used.

Chom "Good," "well done." Literally "tasty." Instead of applauding, Goblins chant "*Chom-Chom! Chom-Chom!*"

Derijinta "Little one." A term of endearment used for goblin children.

Drak The unusable bits left over once ore is smelted to metal. Junk. A mild expletive. Can also be used as an adjective, *drakik,* meaning "junky" or "worthless."

Drakbonch Someone with a head full of junk. An idiot.

Drogob An adult male goblin. "He-goblin."

Duen Silver, both the metal and the color. Also the nickname for a silver coin used by the goblins as currency. Officially a Kiranok Regent (a *vikrek Kiranoki*), sometimes also called a "snowcap" from the image of the Mother Mountain on its face, a *duen* is enough to buy a decent meal or child's toy or piece of simple clothing. A *duen* is worth eight *jegen*. Fifty *duenen* equal a gold *krogn*.

Duenshee Literally "silver stranger." A tall thin, magically powerful humanoid. *Duensheen* are dangerous, unpredictable, and, from a goblin perspective, quite insane, hence the goblin saying "mad as a *duenshee*." Humans call the *duensheen* "elves."

Enik, menik, mynta, mogh, katcha "One, two, three, four, five." The first five numbers in Gobayabber. Also the goblin words for "thumb, index finger, middle finger, ring finger, little finger."

Ganzi "Thanks." Literally "I balance." See *nurganzit*.

Genzirjad "Come Cold Day." The Autumn Equinox. The first day of fall, when the Sunchase is run. *Genzirjad* is sometimes called "Balance Day"—*Ganzirjad*—since the two words are similar.

Glinkspangen "Copperplates," the Goblin nickname for the Kiranok City Guards, after their copper-embossed breastplates. Sometimes shortened to *Glink*.

Gob A goblin. Plural *goben*. Goben also use the word *gob* colloquially the way humans use "guy," "fellow," or "man."

Gobayabber The goblin language.

Graznak An "empty jar"—a wizard who has lost his or her soul to magic. A *graznak* is like a zombie powered by magic, constantly casting spells to survive.

Hanoryabber Hanorian. The language of the humans from the empire bordering Goblin lands.

Jeg A large milled steel bead used as currency. A *jeg* is enough money to buy an apple, a handful of mushrooms, or a hot tea. Goblins use *jegen*, half *jegen*, quarter *jegen*, and eighth *jegen*. See also *krogn* and *duen*.

Jintagob An unusually small Goblin. Plural = *jintagoben*. Humans sometimes call *jintagoben* "kobolds" or "gnomes."

Kijakgob An unusually large Goblin. Plural = *kijakgoben*. Humans sometimes call *kijakgoben* "trolls" or "ogres."

Kijakhof A giant rabbit-like herbivore. *Kijakhofen* may be found both in the wild and as domesticated livestock on goblin farms. Some breeds of *kijakhofen* are also raised as house pets.

Kiranok "City of Stone." The largest goblin city in the world, located under Mother Mountain. The full name of the city is actually "*Kijakkiranokzargroztorme-megeshkarbeniknirtghulkt*," which means "Great City of Stone under the Soaring Mountain Mother Blessed by the Divine Night."

Krogn A gold coin. A *krogn* is worth fifty silver *duenen* or four hundred steel *jegen*. A krogn is enough to buy a fine steel sword or a riding *bokrum*. Most goblins never see a *krogn* in their entire lives.

Maja "Very," "a lot," "much," "more." Goblins sometimes repeat this word for emphasis, so *majamaja* means "a large amount" and *majamajamaja* means "a very large amount." Also used as an emphatic prefix. So *majanai* means "very much no" and *majazaj* means "absolutely yes"

Nai "No," "not," "none." Often used as an interjection at the end of a sentence.

Naizaj "Maybe," "could be." Literally "no-yes." Sometimes used as an interjection at the end of a sentence, but more often as an uncertain response to a question. For example, if asked, "Are you eating that?" a goblin might respond, "*Naizaj*," which in this case would mean "Maybe yes, maybe no." Goblins use *zajnai* and *naizaj* interchangeably.

Nurganzit The future form of the verb *ganzir*, meaning "to balance." Goblin for "Thank you," *nurganzit* is both an expression of gratitude and a promise for future reciprocation. "I will balance your gift with a gift in the future." Informally sometimes shortened to *ganzi*.

Pizkret A goblin insult. Literally "wayside," which implies something you'd throw away along the road. Trash or night soil. Also a rude or stinky person. A jerk. Sometimes used among very close friends as a term of camaraderie.

Prenir y'biben An impolite way of saying "be quiet" or "leave me alone." The goblin equivalent of "shut up" or "bug off." Literally: "Clean my socks." Can be further shortened to *y'biben*.

Skerbo A human. Literally "Tiny Ear." Derogatory.

Svagob An adult female goblin. "She-goblin"

Vargar A large carnivore native to the Ironspine Mountains and the surrounding woodlands. *Vargaren* resembled huge wolves with lion-like manes and one or two prominent rhinoceros-like horns growing from their snouts. Goblins use domesticated *vargaren* as pets, hunting animals, and mounts.

Veshakorz "Very quick." An idiomatic expression that translates literally as "Death's whisper" or more roughly as "fast as death."

Vikrek Kiranoki A "Kiranok Regent," a common silver coin. Better known as a snowcap or a *duen*. See *duen*.

Wazzer An expression of excitement. Sometimes used as a way to draw attention to oneself. Roughly equivalent to "Wow!" or "Yo!" or "Hey!"

Yabber To talk. Language. A conversation.

Yob'rikit "Excellent!" "Wonderful!" An exclamation of excitement. A clipped version of the goblin expression *Yob ir ikit*, which means, roughly, "Smells like breakfast!" Goblins really like breakfast.

Zaj "Yes." Often used as an interjection at the end of a sentence.

Zajnai "Maybe." See *naizaj.*

Zeesnikken eger zapergritten A fatalistic goblin aphorism that translates literally as "Bee stings on top of mosquito bites." It has roughly the same meaning as the human expressions "If it's not one thing, it's another" and "Out of the frying pan, into the fire."

Zigpar Roughly translated, "hindquarters." Colloquially a stupid or rude person. An insult. Derogatory.

Zobjepa A mildly alcoholic beverage brewed from honey and mushroom juice and flavored with red pepper. Also known as "mushroom wine."

APPENDIX B
Goblin Names

Goblin names are complicated affairs. Every goblin has a single "true name" made of two components. The first few syllables are the individual goblin's personal name. The last few are a family suffix. So Hop's full true name is Korgorog. Korg is his personal name, while the name suffix "-orog" is the equivalent of a human family name (except that it's passed down from a mother to her children rather than from the father). So all of Hop's immediate relatives on his mother's side of his family have true names ending in "-orog."

But goblins almost never call each other by their true names except in the most formal or intimate of circumstances. In fact, using a goblin's true name inappropriately is considered a terrible insult. Instead, all goblins go by nicknames. Until their first birthday, all goblin babies are called "Baby." Goblins say this avoids unnecessary confusion. Once he or she turns one, each goblin is given both a true name, by the father, and his or her first nickname, a "child name," which is bestowed by the mother and is usually something endearing or cute. Hop's child name was "Mushy," short for "Mushroom."

Eventually, when goblins get older, they take on a new nickname, their calling-name. A respected elder usually bestows the calling-name, though occasionally it's self-chosen. Receiving a calling-name is a hugely important rite of passage for a goblin. A goblin is not considered an adult until he or she is given a calling-name.

To further confuse matters, the full calling-name of a goblin is often (but not always) shortened or modified further. So Atarikit Bluefrost becomes "Frost," Sergeant Zigertok Ratflyer is better known as "Flyrat," and Korgorog Hoprock is usually just "Hop." But Bohorikit Leadpipe is called "Leadpipe." Except when he's not.

To top it all off, it's not unheard of for goblins to change their calling-names when starting a new job, moving to a new village, hiding from the law, or just hoping to improve their luck. For example, during his second stint in the Warhorde, Hop goes by the calling-name "Borrowedcap" or "Cap" for short.

Following is a list, organized by calling-names, of the goblins in *The Goblin Crown*:

Acorn: Zororashtag Grindacorn, a restaurant owner from Kiranok.

Bead: Vishingorex Beadsplitter, chief archer of the war-bat Daffodil.

Breaker: A *kijakgoben* Templar.

Cap: See *Hop*.

Cotton: A young laundress at Tower Gulkreg.

Cuttingword: Late wife of General Sawtooth. Affectionately known as "Cutty."

Flutter: Ghiyolar Flutteringmoth, a female flashgob assigned to the war-bat Daffodil.

Flyrat: Sergeant Zigertok Ratflyer, a veteran aeronaut of the Warhorde.

Frost: Atarikit Bluefrost, a diminutive wizard from Kiranok.

Gooddark: A kindly, older *svagob* from Kiranok.

Hop: Korgorog Hoprock, a city guard ("Copperplate") originally from the Bowlus Plateau but lately of Kiranok. Sometimes also known as "Borrowedcap" or "Cap."

Kettle: Hammerkettle. An orphaned apprentice blacksmith from Kiranok, nephew of Zorarashtag Grindacorn.

Leadpipe: Bohorikit Leadpipe, a giant goblin. Brother of Frost. Also known as "Lead."

Mallet: A giant Templar.

Mendbreak: A *kijakgob* priest and expert in healing magic.

Moonfall: A skilled goblin wizardess a few years older than Frost.

Peashoot: A female *kijakgoben* Templar.

Peeppeep: A small goblin girl. Peeppeep is a typical goblin child name.

Roofscraper: One of Sawtooth's *kijakgoben* bodyguards.

Rumblejaw: Another of Sawtooth's *kijakgoben* bodyguards.

Sawtooth: General Skargorek Sawtooth, supreme commander of the Warhorde. Usually called "Sawtooth" but sometimes called "The Tooth," especially by his men.

Shadow: Ishkinogi Slipshadows, a temple guard of the Night Goddess and daughter of General Sawtooth.

Snails: A spotter assigned to the war-bat Daffodil.

Starcaller: Ulgarkiren Starcaller, the Grand High Priestess of the Night Goddess and Matriarch of the goblin religion.

Turner: Yesigerath Silkturn, a novice of the Night Goddess.

APPENDIX C
The Hanorian Empire

F or countless generations, goblins have been locked in a perpetual struggle with the human-dominated Hanorian Empire over territory and resources. The Hanorian Empire is situated to the east of the goblin territories, controlling most of the land between the Ironspike Mountains and the sea. The Empire's lifeblood is the River Venstell, a wide, slow-moving, muddy river which drains the Hanorian heartland, a vast area of rolling hills, scattered forests, and endless stretches of fertile farmland.

The Hanorian Empire's capital, Gran Hanor, is a beautiful metropolis straddling the Venstell not far from its delta. Intercut by canals, bedecked with the houses of the powerful scions of the Empire, and packed with life, energy, and commerce, Gran Hanor has been called the Heart of the Empire, the Azure City, and the River's End. Residents call it the Big Fish, from its piscine shape and its tendency to swallow people whole. Or possibly because of its smell.

The Imperial Palace, located on an island in the middle of the Venstell, is one of the most breathtaking sights in the entire Empire, with its soaring Thirteen Towers (there are actually more than thirty), the gleaming Golden Dome (repainted every three years) and the famous Bridge of Heads (now only rarely displaying actual severed heads). Over fifty emperors have reigned from the sparkling Crystal Hall at the palace's heart (plus the occasional empress, usurper, regent, crown prince, grand vizier, and even a half dozen or so "Chief Commissioners of the Peoples' Assembly").

The Hanorian Empire is divided into baronies, duchies, counties, bishoprics, shires, and one "Farmers' Collective." Its inhabitants are mostly human, and though economically, culturally, and ethnically diverse, are united by language (Hanorian) and religion (the Faith, the worship of the Sun God).

Following is a list of Hanorians who appear in the pages of *The Goblin Crown*:

Alyseer Darrig: Teenage daughter of Donegan and Sarlia. A refugee living in the Court of the Orbs.

Azam: An athletic refugee from the Court of the Orbs. An accomplished fire-spinner.

Donegan Darrig: Leader of the Fastness's refugee Celestials.

Jesserel: A young female refugee. Prone to tears.

Sarlia Darrig: Celestial refugee. Sunworker. Wife of Donegan and mother of Alyseer.

ACKNOWLEDGMENTS

This is my first novel, which means I had absolutely no idea what I was doing. The fact that *The Goblin Crown* exists at all is due to many people who helped along the way, including the outstanding folks at Turner Publishing, most notably Stephanie Beard and Jon O'Neal, my hard-working representatives, Paula Munier, Jeff Field, and Hrishi Desai, and talented artist Tom Fowler, who created a spectacular cover. I'd also like to thank Ignacy Ż., along with John S., Blanche R., Evelyn S., and Beata S., for their help with Piast's Polish dialogue, and Michael M. for his input on Gobayabber. But I'd most especially like to thank my many beta readers: my aunt Barbara D., Paul W., Brian T., Phillip R., Kathryn and John P., Jim P., Bryan M., Lynn M., Blaine K., Deric H., Sam and Craig F., Paul F., Danny B., and John and

Lisa A. An extra big thanks to my young beta readers: Nicole and Michael A., Doug and Drew C., Isabella F., Alexandra P., and most notably Zach and Caleb R. and their amazing mother and dedicated schoolteacher, Carolyn R., who shared an early version of this book with her gifted students, among them Kenny, Justin, and Nick, and sent me their detailed and extremely helpful reviews. *The Goblin Crown* improved vastly from everyone's feedback. And finally, my eternal gratitude to my wife Celeste for her patience, love, insight, and unwavering support.

ABOUT THE AUTHOR

ROBERT HEWITT WOLFE is an accomplished television writer and producer. He got his big break writing the episode "A Fistful of Datas" for *Star Trek: The Next Generation*. Since then, he's worked on over three hundred episodes of television for shows like *Star Trek: Deep Space Nine*, *The 4400*, *Alphas*, and *Elementary*. He developed the syndicated hit *Andromeda* and helped adapt Jim Butcher's acclaimed *Dresden Files* novels for television.

Robert is an army brat who mostly grew up in San Francisco. He attended UCLA, where he earned a BA in Film & Television and an MFA in Screenwriting. He lives in Los Angeles with his wife Celeste and their fluffy dog Baxter. In his spare time, he likes hiking, traveling, and playing tabletop role-playing games and video games. Robert can be found on Twitter, dispensing dubious wisdom about writing, television, and geek culture as @writergeekrhw.